THE WORLD STARTS ANEW

THE STAR AND THE SHAMROCK - BOOK 4

JEAN GRAINGER

CHAPTER 1

Ballycreggan, 1955

Erich Bannon sat on the velvet-covered seat in the dining room of the house he'd considered his home since he was seven years old. He looked through the open door, hoping for inspiration, the pen poised, the fresh clean sheet of writing paper waiting expectantly. Dappled light shone through the coloured glass of the front door, illuminating the tiles on the floor in the hallway.

Dear Abigail, he began.

He would just be honest, write it quickly and get it posted. Dragging these things out didn't help.

Thank you for your letter and the picture. You look so happy and tanned now, but I suppose getting out of the Irish rain is good for anyone's skin. Everyone knows Irish people don't tan, they rust!

I can't imagine you out in the orange groves every day, and feeding chickens and growing tomatoes. It really suits you, though, and I'm glad you're happy. Your hair has gone so blonde in the sun, and you look beautiful.

He paused again. This was going to be the hard bit. He exhaled.

Thanks as well for the kind invitation to come and join you, even for a visit. But I feel like I have to be honest and say I won't be going to Israel. I understand the pull of the Promised Land, and I absolutely understand why you and so many others want to establish a home, a place of safety for our people. But, Abigail, it's not for me.

My home is here, and I know you will be disappointed (at least I hope you will be a little!), but my life was turned upside down when I was seven and had to leave Berlin. Mutti put Liesl and me on that train in 1939 never knowing if we would ever see her again. And then we moved to Liverpool, got bombed out of there and finally landed up here in Ballycreggan. We found a home here with Daniel and Elizabeth, and then Mutti reappeared after the war. We've all endured so many years of fear and turmoil, and I don't feel like I want to be separated from my family ever again.

As well as that, Daniel, Willi and I have really grown the business and are so busy now. We have building jobs going on all over the place, and they need me.

I am so fond of you and loved our time together, but our lives have gone in different directions and I think it's only fair to both of us to end things.

I will always be there for you as a friend if you ever need me, and I do hope we see each other again. But for now, I think it is best to go our separate ways.

The last words looked harsh, but Abigail was such a lovely girl that it wasn't right to string her along pretending that Israel held the same attraction for him as it did for her.

Something had told him even before she left for Tel Aviv that there was a chance she wouldn't come back. She was so enthusiastic about it all: the Law of Return, the whole notion of the homeland for all Jews, the Promised Land. And while he understood it coming from those who survived the Nazis, people who'd lost so much more than bricks and mortar, he was surprised she felt it as strongly. Abigail was from Dublin. Her whole family remained untouched by the war, and yet she felt this longing, this magnetic pull of Israel.

But then he was obviously the exception rather than the rule. He watched as one by one his friends left Ballycreggan, and the farm that had been set up as a sanctuary for the Kindertransport children, to join kibbutzim in Israel.

When Simon went, it was a blow. But, unlike with Abigail, Erich could kind of see why it drew his best friend in. Simon had grown up at the farm, and while the rabbi and the others did everything they could to make it feel like home, it *was* an institution. Simon had some cousins in Israel who were getting on well; they'd set up a fruit business in Haifa. They'd written, begging Simon to join them.

He and Erich had been best friends since they were in short pants, and while Erich was happy for his friend if it was what he wanted, the idea of leaving Ballycreggan, of farming oranges in the humid heat, was something that baffled Erich.

Ruth and Levi were next, then Ben and Viola, and now Abigail.

He was sad it had ended this way. At one time he thought he loved Abigail, and he could hardly believe his luck last year when she agreed to go out with him. She'd always been nice to him whenever he visited Liesl at university in Dublin, but he was sure she just saw him as Liesl's little brother. But the weekend of the going-away party for the Kindertransport children of Ballycreggan, she'd kissed him and told him she liked him too, and the past year had been a romantic whirlwind of trips to Dublin to see her and holidays in Ballycreggan for her. They'd walked hand in hand on the beach, went to the pictures and just enjoyed being young and courting.

He finished off his letter.

Take good care of yourself, Abigail.

Love, Erich

Before he changed his mind, he quickly licked the envelope and folded the sheet of paper, and he decided he'd post it there and then. Abigail looked radiant in the photo she'd sent, so while he was sure this letter might make her a bit sad, she wouldn't be heartbroken. He was under no illusion that some handsome young Jewish man wouldn't be waiting in the wings to take his place in her life.

As he walked towards the front door, he caught sight of his reflection in the mirror of the oak hallstand. He was twenty-three but worried that he looked younger. Abigail always said how handsome he was, and he smiled at the memory. He genuinely wished her all the best.

He knew he looked like his father, though in truth Erich's memo-

3

ries of him were hazy. He'd been a little boy when Peter Bannon was picked up by the Brownshirts on the streets of Berlin, never to be heard from again. But seeing his mother's startled look sometimes when he walked into a room, he knew she thought she was seeing a ghost.

He wondered what his father would have made of all of this Israel business. He was a Gentile but never objected to *Mutti* raising him and Liesl in her Jewish faith, so they never really considered themselves as anything but Jews. Erich gave a rueful snort. Neither did the Nazis. As far as they were concerned, his family were Jews. Would his father understand everyone's obsession with that hot, sandy place so far away?

He'd discussed it with Daniel, but his adopted father was pragmatic in that as in everything. While Erich felt sad at the mass exodus for Israel of the people he held dear, Daniel understood it and wished them all well. Daniel had no interest in moving there himself – he was blissfully happy with Elizabeth in Ballycreggan – but he thought the others should go. He even said that he and Elizabeth would like to visit the Promised Land someday.

Erich ran his hand through his dark hair. He'd have to tell Liesl; Abigail was her friend after all. He'd call to her and Jamie on the way back from the postbox.

He let himself out of the house and walked onto the main street of Ballycreggan. He'd arrived in the town as a boy, and he'd done all of his schooling there, in the Ballycreggan national school, alongside the local children and Jewish refugees from the farm. It all felt like a lifetime ago and, in lots of ways, like the only life he'd ever had. He belonged there; there was no doubt in his mind. Liesl had gone to university in Dublin and had even gone back to Germany for a while, but he had no interest in further studies. Getting out of school was a godsend; he was not cut out for sitting at a desk all day learning pointless things, adding letters to other letters in algebra, or being able to list the rivers of Africa. It had all seemed so pointless. He loved working with his hands, and Daniel and Willi were great teachers. By now, there were very few building jobs he wasn't competent at. He could do wiring, plumbing, blockwork and carpentry, and he loved that every day was different.

Bridie waved as he passed on the other side of the road. She was sweeping the step outside her pink sweetshop, the very first place Elizabeth took them when they first arrived, almost fifteen years ago now. Elizabeth's house and school in Liverpool had been flattened by a bomb, so they'd had no choice but to move to Ballycreggan and take up residence in Elizabeth's late parents' house. It had seemed at the time like just another confusing upheaval, but now he silently thanked that Luftwaffe pilot. If the bombing hadn't happened, they would never have come to Ballycreggan.

He remembered still Bridie's shop from that first day, the smell of molten sugar and the jars stretching as far as the eye could see – clove rock, bullseyes, acid drops, chocolate-covered lollipops… It was magical then, and to be honest, it was still magical now. He loved the smell of the toffee apples that Bridie made in her kitchen, and he loved how she weighed a quarter pound of whatever sweets you wanted but then threw in two more – for luck, she'd always say with a mischievous wink.

He bumped into Mrs O'Hanlon, the priest's sour housekeeper, as she came out of the greengrocer's. She dropped her bag of vegetables.

'I'm so sorry, Mrs O'Hanlon! I wasn't paying attention. Are you all right?' Erich picked up a turnip and several potatoes and returned them to her shopping basket.

The housekeeper made no secret of the fact that she disliked all foreigners and was deeply suspicious of Jews generally, but she had to admit to liking the children from the farm. She had no choice since Father O'Toole and the rabbi were such good friends. The priest would tolerate no anti-Semitism from anyone.

'I'm fine, Erich, but please retrieve Father O'Toole's dinner from the street if you wouldn't mind.' Her imperious tone suggested Erich was ten years old, not a grown man.

'Of course.' He gathered the remaining vegetables and apologised again.

'So are you not going off to the Middle East then?' she asked.

Erich fought the urge to ask her why on earth she would think that. 'No, Mrs O'Hanlon, I'm not.'

''Tis a wonder you wouldn't. I mean, isn't your friend, the blondie one from Dublin, gone over there now? And sure there's hardly a soul above in the farm nowadays, only the old rabbi rattling about with your poor mother and Mrs Braun. God knows what they're at up there. I mean, I said to Father O'Toole, "Would the rabbi not be better off down here in the village?" That place up there was all well and good during the war, and thank the Lord and his Blessed Mother the sanctuary could be located there for the poor wee mites, but they're grown up and gone now, and I just don't know what is going on.'

Erich tried not to smart from the suggestion that he would obviously go to Israel now. Was he the only person who thought he belonged in Ballycreggan?

Mrs O'Hanlon continued. 'Sure, during the war you had to come here, and 'twas grand, don't get me wrong, but I'm sure everyone would be happier now back in their own places?'

'Well, Mrs O'Hanlon, returning to their own places isn't really an option for most European Jews since their property is either in German hands or flattened, and their families murdered in the death camps.' Erich knew his reaction was a bit harsh, but he was stung by her suggestion.

She seemed to draw herself up, her thin body in a puddle-coloured coat straightening in indignation. 'Yes, well…'tisn't we who did that, so…' she retorted, her cheeks flushed pink.

Erich wasn't sure what point she was trying to make but knew that taking this conversation any further was pointless. Mrs O'Hanlon was the nosiest woman in Ballycreggan, and both Daniel and Elizabeth had made a pastime of not giving her information no matter how hard she dug for it.

'Och, I don't know, Mrs O'Hanlon. You're probably right,' he conceded, just to get away from her, and she visibly relaxed. 'Now I must get on. My sister is waiting for me.' He smiled politely and made to leave, but the housekeeper gripped his arm.

'And how is Liesl? I saw her in the library last week.'

Erich remained nonchalant. 'Aye, she's mad for the books, Mrs O'Hanlon. She's the brains of the family, I'm afraid.' He winked and gently eased himself out of her grip.

'And how's your friend, the girl from Dublin, the one who went out foreign? Amanda, is it?'

Erich struggled to remain impassive. 'Abigail. She's grand, Mrs O'Hanlon, thanks. Now I really best get going.' He gave a last tug of his arm, releasing himself from the claw-like clasp.

He threw the letter in the postbox outside the Catholic church and strolled back down the other side of the street. After a cold winter, there was a touch of spring in the air, and the huge horse chestnut tree in the middle of the village green was beginning to bud. The sky was blue for once.

He felt a bit of guilt at the contents of his letter but mostly relief. He'd known for months there was no future for him and Abigail, so finally telling the truth was a weight off his shoulders.

Jamie's bar was still closed, but he went around the back and knocked. His sister and brother-in-law lived up over the pub. Liesl taught in the school, and Elizabeth was now the principal.

He looked up as his sister's wet head popped out of the window.

'Well, 'tis yourself.' Liesl greeted him in the usual Ballycreggan way, a phrase that confused them at first when they heard it as children but now was a catchphrase between them. 'The key is under the flower-pot. Come on up. I'm just out of the bath, but I'll only be a minute. Stick the kettle on. Oh, did you bring any soda bread?'

'No, I didn't. Liesl, you'd want to watch yourself – you eat like a farm labourer.' He grinned and retrieved the key. He was forever teasing her about her healthy appetite, which, while robust, had not made her gain a pound.

He let himself in the back door of the village's only pub and was immediately met with the faint smell of beer and cigarette smoke from the night before. Jamie opened the windows during the day and kept the place immaculately clean, but the not-unpleasant odour remained.

The bar was owned by Daniel. He'd bought it from Johnny O'Hara, who'd kept it badly for years and was now living with his daughter. Daniel offered it to Jamie to run, and so far he was making a marvellous job of it. He'd cleared the rubbish built up over the years of Johnny's neglect and made it into a lovely bright and clean place. The pub that had once been a grim little shebeen was now the village hub, the headquarters for the local Women's Institute, the meeting place for most local clubs and committees and the spot where all local functions and parties were held.

Jamie was a great businessman, and he worked closely with Masie McGovern, who owned the village tearoom. Masie did the catering for any events, supplying sandwiches and cakes and that way Jamie made sure he tread on nobody's toes. He was universally loved in the village, and Erich couldn't have wished for a better brother-in-law.

He put the kettle on as Liesl came into the kitchen, drying her long dark hair with a towel. Erich knew people thought his sister was beautiful, and he supposed she was, but she had eyes for nobody but Jamie Gallagher, with his huge physique and copper curls.

'I wrote to Abigail, breaking it off,' he told her.

'I hope you were kind?' Liesl raised an eyebrow. She knew his feelings on the subject, as he'd confided in her weeks ago.

'Of course I was. But you were right – there's no point in carrying on if it's never going to turn into anything. I don't want to go there, she doesn't want to come back, so that's all there is to it really.' Erich changed the subject. 'Where's Jamie?'

'Gone to Belfast to pick Derry up from the train,' Liesl said with a sigh. 'He's coming to stay for a week.'

'I thought you liked him better than the other members of your beloved's family,' Erich said with a chuckle.

'I do, and that wouldn't be hard. It's just...oh, I don't know, I don't really feel like having visitors at the moment.'

Erich looked at her more closely. She looked pale. 'Are you all right, Liesl?' he asked.

Ever since the horrific incident four years ago when Kurt Richter, an old family friend – or so they thought – came back into their lives and tried to kill Liesl, the family worried for her. She had jumped from a third-floor window to escape him and had injured herself badly – so badly she was wheelchair-bound for months afterwards.

'I'm fine.' She smiled.

'What?'

'OK, look, we're not telling anyone yet, but I'll burst if I don't tell you. You must keep it to yourself, all right?' Liesl's eyes danced with excitement.

'What?' he asked again.

'I'm pregnant.'

Erich was speechless, so he just hugged his sister. Recovering from the surprise, he said, 'That's brilliant news! Congratulations, Liesl! I'm so happy for you and for Jamie. You must be so excited.'

CHAPTER 2

'If you can get to the timber yard to pick up the eight-by-fours before they close, you can make a start on Casey's job, and I'll follow on with Willi when we finish off the job in the convent.' Daniel pored over the order book, allocating jobs for the day. They had five different projects on the go at once.

Erich, Daniel and Willi were gathered in what was once the large open area behind Jamie's pub, which had been transformed from a graveyard for old farm machinery and briars into a neatly organised builders' yard. Daniel had an engineer's eye, and things out of place irritated him. Erich had been trained the same way, so every chisel and screwdriver were where they should be. When Willi Braun joined the business, there was a little tension, as though Willi was rapidly becoming a skilled craftsman, he was a bit careless with tools and had an annoying habit of not returning things to their proper place. Daniel and Erich complained so much about it, he had become accustomed to their ways and now the place ran smoothly.

'Right,' Erich said, gathering the tools he would need.

Willi put the kettle on. His limp was barely noticeable now due to the success of his prosthetic. It was a heavy contraption made of wood and leather, but Willi never complained. He'd lost a leg on the Eastern

10

Front fighting with the Wehrmacht, and he always joked it was the best thing that ever happened to him as it got him out of the damned war and home to Berlin where he discovered Ariella, hidden in his mother's attic. What was an ignominious beginning transformed into his personal love story, and after a gruelling few months hiding Ariella and his mother from the Nazis in the dying stages of the war, they were free. They'd all three made it to Ballycreggan, where Ariella was reunited with her children and now lived, in his words, happily ever after. At thirty-eight, he still had his boyish good looks and was permanently cheerful.

'Erich,' Daniel called, 'that's the wrong box of drill bits for that drill.'

'What?' Erich looked down at the tools in his hand – Daniel was right. He was clearly distracted.

'Tell me to mind my own business if you want, but an absent-minded builder often winds up missing fingers. You've been miles away.' Daniel sat down at the lunch table he'd built for their breaks and gestured Erich should join him. The two were as close as any father and son, and Erich trusted him implicitly.

Willi arrived and placed three mugs of coffee and a box of home-made cakes on the table. 'Out with it, Erich. What's going on?' Willi smiled and Erich reciprocated.

He might as well tell them. They'd find out sooner or later anyway. 'Abigail is staying in Israel. So I wrote to her and broke off the relationship. There's no point, you know?'

'She's staying there for good?' Willi asked.

'It sounds that way.' Erich shrugged. 'She said at first it was just for a visit, just to see it. She went with a group from her synagogue in Dublin – mostly young like her – and they met up with a group from New York, some family members of someone she knows. They saw how they are trying to cultivate the land, to use it to grow crops, and she said there is such a sense of purpose there, a feeling of coming home. I don't begrudge it to her, but it's not for me.'

'Fair enough.' Willi shrugged.

'Are you upset about it?' Daniel asked.

Erich thought for a moment. 'I'm fine, but I don't know... First everyone from the farm, then Simon and now Abigail... It feels like everyone wants to go to Israel, like they have this calling or something, and I just don't understand it. I feel like I'm missing something or that I'm betraying who I am, but I just don't feel it, you know? Israel might as well be the moon as far as I'm concerned.'

Daniel patted his shoulder. 'I understand. But you're all adults now and everyone must make their own decisions.'

'Well, Erich, that's your choice.' Willi was pragmatic. 'And though it's sad for you and Abigail, I admire you for doing what you want. You could go over there and be miserable, but if she really was the one for you, then nothing would stop you being with her. So something deep down is telling you she isn't the one, no matter how much you like her, because if she was, wild horses wouldn't stop you being on a ship to Haifa.'

'I suppose,' Erich agreed. 'I think it's not just Abigail though, it's everyone leaving. Abraham and Dieter are in Vienna, Benjamin went to Prague, and his whole family – well, what's left of it – are going to Israel now too from there. Viola, Anika and Ben, all gone to Jerusalem, the Missenbergs went to New York, Karl Kolitz went to London, Levi, Ruth...the list goes on. They were all my friends. I even miss Levi's grumpy face. And I know I have you all, but you're all fine, you know, living your lives happily. Liesl and Jamie are doing so well, and I feel like I'm just plodding along. I'm twenty-three years old, I live with my parents, I work with you two, I went to America once, and that's been it.'

Daniel smiled. 'But you said you don't want to leave Ballycreggan?'

'I don't. I just... I don't know. I've no idea what I want to do.' He sipped his coffee, feeling better for having told them. 'I got a letter from Bud, inviting me over to Biloxi, he suggested I make a big trip of it, see some of America. It's great timing and I'd like to go, I've always wanted to see New York and I feel like I could use a holiday, but we're so busy.'

They didn't know yet about Liesl's baby, but if he was going to take a trip, he'd want to be back before his niece or nephew made an appearance.

'You should go. Bud would love to see you, and as you say, you could use something to look forward to. We all need a holiday, Erich.' Daniel grinned. He was constantly berated by the family for never taking a day off.

'But what about all the work we have on here? I can't just take off for ages and leave you two to manage on your own.'

Daniel shrugged. 'We can manage. I was thinking we might take on two apprentices – one electrician, one carpenter – and maybe a block layer as well. We have enough work now. People are recovering after the war and wanting to have all the new things fitted – hot and cold running water in every house, nobody is happy with an outside toilet any more, electric upgrades, not to mention how many enquiries we've had to install televisions. I was amazed that even Elizabeth said she wanted one. She saw the BBC broadcast in a shop in Belfast and is fascinated. I could live without it myself, but…'

'If Elizabeth wants one, then Elizabeth shall have one. You've never refused her anything yet.' Willi winked at Erich as he made a gesture with his thumb pressing into the palm of his other hand.

'I don't pretend anything to the contrary, my friend,' Daniel confirmed with a smile. 'I'm under my wife's thumb and very happy to be there.'

'So we're expanding?' Erich asked.

'We have to, or else all three of us will burn out.' Daniel nodded. 'We have too much work for just us, so now would be a good time for you to take a break. Once they are trained up, and hopefully it works out, we might look at taking a holiday ourselves.'

Erich laughed. 'I'll believe that when I see it.'

'No, I mean it. Elizabeth and Ariella want to take a trip, but as you say, we can't go now. If we set it up, get some staff, then down the line it could happen. So how about we find some apprentices, you go off to America for a while, and by the time you get back, we'll have seen how well they are working out. Then maybe next summer we could take off for a trip of our own.'

'And you're not just doing this to cheer me up, are you?' Erich asked doubtfully.

'Erich, I'm an Austrian engineer, a species not generally given to rash emotional outbursts.'

Willi and Erich laughed. The family always teased Daniel about how rational he was about everything – only logic made sense to him.

'So no. It's a good business move, I think, and I want to do it. I'm not getting any younger, and to be honest with you, I'd like to spend a bit more time at home. I'm not thinking of retiring yet, but Elizabeth and I have all we need, and you and Liesl are grown up now and fending for yourselves more or less, so we'd like to be able to take a bit of time off. If we employ more staff, then I won't need to be here all the time.' He paused. 'I promise it's just for a visit, but Ruth and Levi have invited us to Jerusalem to see them, and we're thinking we might go sometime.'

Erich shook his head. 'It better be just for a visit. I'm sick of losing everyone to that country.'

'It will be, I can assure you, but we'd like to travel a bit, maybe visit England. I know Elizabeth would like to visit Rudi's family there, and I'd like to meet my old college friend in Bristol, Stephen Holland. If it wasn't for his sponsorship, I would never have got out of Austria, and I never got to thank him. So we'd like to do that and just see a bit of the world, you know?'

'I do, and I think you should definitely do it.' Although Erich knew that when Liesl told them the good news, their plans might change, because if a baby was on the horizon, neither Daniel nor Elizabeth would consider missing it.

CHAPTER 3

*L*iesl and Jamie walked hand in hand from the bar to Ariella and Willi's house. His parents were visiting from Kerry and they thought they would take the opportunity to tell everyone about the baby.

'You look like you're facing the gallows.' Jamie smiled ruefully.

'I know, and that's what it feels like too, to be honest, Jamie,' Liesl replied dully. She'd been ill all morning, and the last thing in the world she felt like doing was having an encounter with her mother-in-law.

'It's a dose, pet, but look, let's just get it over with. She's a royal pain in the neck, I know. She had another go at me last night about us getting married in a registry office. I told her she'd have to just get over it. Besides, neither the Jews nor the Catholics would marry us without the other one converting, so what does she think we should have done?'

Liesl could hear the frustration in her husband's voice. He was embarrassed at his mother's overt horror at anyone who wasn't a Catholic. But at the end of the day, she was still his mother, so it was a constant juggling act for him between her and his wife. Liesl knew Jamie would take her side every time, but these visits every few months were very trying. Peggy Gallagher had made some effort in the early days, but her true nature was just beneath the surface at all times.

As they entered Ariella and Willi's lovely Victorian cottage with its exquisite gardens, Liesl heard her mother.

'Erich, darling, can you bring this to the table, please?'

The Gallaghers were staying with Elizabeth and Daniel, and everyone was gathered at Ariella's house for lunch already. As well as Jamie's and Liesl's families, Rabbi Frank and Frau Braun were also invited.

'Ah, Jamie and Liesl! *Liebchen*, you're just in time.' Ariella embraced them. 'Come sit – the food is ready.'

There were hugs all around, and soon they were seated at the table. The aromas, normally mouthwatering, caused a wave of nausea to rise up from Liesl's stomach. Jamie caught her eye and she quickly shook her head; she would get through this and get home to bed.

Ariella had cooked a delicious kosher meal of chicken soup with matzo balls, brisket, roasted chicken and melt-in-the-mouth potato latkes. There was no dairy at all, as to mix dairy and meat was not allowed. Liesl knew by Peggy's face that she viewed it all with deep suspicion.

'Oh, Mrs Brown!' Peggy insisted on saying the name like the colour, not 'Braun' as it was pronounced by everyone else. 'I've never had potatoes without butter.'

'Oh, we eat butter and cheese as well, Mrs Gallagher,' Ariella explained with a smile. 'Just not with meat. So for example, a bagel with cream cheese would be a good breakfast, but for lunch or dinner we would always serve meat.'

'Well, it's really very tasty. These potato cakes are lovely.' Jamie's father was one of the quietest men Liesl had ever met, allowing his wife to do all of the talking for the both of them, but it was nice to see him try.

'Thanks, Donie. I love cooking.' Ariella topped up the wine while Peggy looked on longingly.

Liesl had explained to her mother and Ariella found it odd at first, the Irish way of calling a married woman Mrs such-and-such but referring to her husband by his first name, but it was one of the many quirky things about life in Ireland she had come to accept.

Liesl knew Peggy was partial to the sherry, though she would never admit it. It was all sipped in secret, but Jamie and his brothers had laughed about their mother's secret booze stash for years.

'Would you like a glass?' Ariella offered, seeing Peggy's look.

'I don't really drink…' She sounded convincing.

'Era, have a glass, Mam. It's nice, according to my missus.' Jamie nudged Liesl, who was drinking water.

Though Jamie was a member of the Pioneer Total Abstinence Association, having made a promise not to drink alcohol at his confirmation when he was aged twelve, Liesl did enjoy an occasional drink before she was pregnant. It was something he teased her about, making out that she was a regular drinker just to wind her up.

'Well, I don't know… I have never really had wine…' Peggy held her glass out.

'Try a little. You don't have to drink it if you don't like it,' Daniel said kindly, and she smiled.

Peggy had a soft spot for the tall, handsome Austrian, and she hung on his every word when he spoke. Her dislike of Jews did not stretch to Daniel apparently.

'Well, if you think I should, Daniel.' She tittered like a schoolgirl, and Elizabeth and Liesl shared a secret smile.

'How about anyone else?' Daniel offered the bottle around. Liesl placed her hand over her wine glass, and he raised an eyebrow.

'No, thanks, Daniel. I'm fine with water,' Liesl said with a smile, swallowing to try to diminish the nausea.

Willi raised his glass in a toast. 'Well, we're delighted you are all here, and thank you so much to Ariella for cooking this lovely meal for us all. We'll have to go for a long walk tomorrow to make up for all of this, but it's worth it.'

'Hear, hear!' Rabbi Frank raised his glass. 'To the cook.'

'To the cook,' they all chorused with a grin.

'Well, Elizabeth made dessert and Frau Braun made the latkes, so it was a joint effort,' Ariella explained.

'Well, aren't we the lucky men to have such fine chefs among us.' Willi gave his wife a one-armed squeeze.

'Living on my stale bread and watery soup in an attic for four years would have either made you a terrible cook or an extraordinary one. I'm glad it did the latter,' Frau Braun joked.

They were all still getting used to the softness that had come into her personality over the years. Willi's mother still was capable of a sharp tongue and she didn't suffer fools gladly, but the move to Ireland and a peaceful life had been good for her. Decades of an abusive marriage to the dreadful Hubert Braun had made her hard, but she was gradually softening. It was inconceivable that the Frau Braun who had arrived in 1945 could ever make a joke.

'If I'd not had your bread and soup, I would never have survived at all,' Ariella said sincerely. 'You shared whatever you had, and I suspect you went hungry yourself so you could feed me, so nothing ever would taste as good, even now.'

Frau Braun shrugged, but Rabbi Frank spoke. 'Did you know, Mr and Mrs Gallagher, that Ariella had to go into hiding, and that Frau Braun here, whose husband was a high-ranking Nazi official, took her in and hid her in her attic, keeping her safe for the duration of the war? Liesl and Erich got to be reunited with their *mutti* again, and we all got to meet Willi and Frau Braun, all because of her incredible bravery. I want to nominate her to Yad Vashem, the authority commissioned by the Knesset in Israel to commemorate the lost Jews of Europe, as Righteous Among the Nations. It is an honour bestowed upon non-Jews who took extraordinary risks to help their Jewish friends and neighbours in the face of indifference and downright hatred. She has converted to Judaism now, but at the time she wasn't a Jew. I think she is worthy of recognition, but she is refusing to allow me to tell them.'

Katerin Braun exhaled impatiently. 'I don't want all that fuss and nonsense. I did what I did and we're all here to tell the tale, so let's just leave it at that, shall we?' Her German accent hadn't become less pronounced, and though she had gained a few pounds since arriving in Ireland, she was still small and wiry, and she looked to be any age between fifty and ninety. She and the rabbi spent their time keeping in contact with the Kindertransport children who came to Bally-creggan during the war years and helping them locate lost family members. The torrent of information about deported and murdered Jews in the post-war years had slowed to a trickle, but still now and again they managed to make a connection and people were reunited. The rabbi had considered relocating to Israel as well when peace was finally declared but in the end decided that Northern Ireland was his home.

'You see what I have to deal with, eh?' The rabbi raised his hands in frustration. 'She is so stubborn.'

'She is, Rabbi,' Ariella agreed. 'And tenacious and brave. And we both know she has a will of steel, so she's not for changing, and we wouldn't have her any other way.' She reached over and placed her hand on her mother-in-law's.

Katerin Braun rolled her eyes dismissively. 'All this old talk. Let's eat.'

The conversation around the table was relaxed and easy, and Erich and Jamie's father were deep in chat now that Donie was out from the domineering clutches of Peggy, who was on her third glass of wine, topping herself up surreptitiously. Daniel was telling a story about the building of the Schönbrunn Palace in Vienna, and Peggy was hanging on his every word. All around the table, there was a happy hum of convivial conversation. Though normally Liesl would love it, she now longed for it to end. She and Jamie were going to make the announcement about the baby and leave. She caught his eye, indicating he should get on with it. She could then make her excuses soon after and go home to bed.

Everyone looked up as Jamie stood and tapped his glass with a teaspoon. The table fell quiet, and for once the big Kerryman looked a bit unsure.

'Will you?' He looked down at Liesl.

She shook her head sweetly. 'It's all yours.'

'So, um…we're so happy you're all here, and thanks again to Ariella for the lovely food and to Elizabeth for that apple pie – amazing. But we are also happy to have you all together because Liesl and I…well, we wanted to tell you that Liesl is expecting a baby for December.' He blushed as a grin split his face.

Jamie hadn't changed a bit in the five years that they'd known him, and it felt like he'd always been part of the family. His copper curls were as unruly as ever, and a combination of lifting barrels of beer and being the best full back the Ballycreggan football team ever had made sure he maintained his muscular physique. Liesl knew her family had worried for her, and it cheered everyone so much to see her so happy, especially considering how things could have gone so badly after the Kurt Richter episode.

The injuries she sustained meant she still got tired and had to rest, but there was a time after the fall that they thought she might never walk again. Richter had a lot to answer for. Part of her wished he hadn't died in the fire he set while trying to kill himself and her so that he could have faced justice for his crimes, but it wasn't to be. It was over and done with and best left in the past.

The table erupted into cheers and claps of delight. A baby in the family was wonderful news. Even Frau Braun looked overjoyed. Hugs were exchanged, and Daniel raised his glass in another toast. 'This is wonderful news, really marvellous. We are turning into a bunch of old timers here, so we need a baby to keep us all young. Congratulations, Liesl and Jamie! We are delighted, and this baby will be welcomed to our large and complicated family with open arms.'

Everyone chuckled. He wasn't wrong; it was tricky for outsiders to get to grips with who was who.

To everyone's surprise, Donie Gallagher got to his feet. His wife, still enjoying the wine, looked startled, as she normally did the talking in their family. She was about to interrupt him, but he gently placed his hand on her arm. 'I'm not much of a one for speeches, but I just want to add our congratulations to Jamie and Liesl. We are very happy that our first grandchild is on the way, and we will help in whatever way we can.'

'Thanks, Dad.' Jamie smiled.

'Oh, you'll have to come home to Kerry for the christening!' Peggy announced, her words slurring slightly, her tongue loosened by the wine. 'Father Brendan will be delighted to do the honours. You should all come! We can have a big do.'

Peggy Gallagher loved all of her sons, but undoubtedly the one who became a priest was the one of whom she was the most proud. It was a rare occasion that she didn't manage to shoehorn the information that Father Brendan was a member of the clergy into even the most casual of conversations. Liesl found her brother-in-law positively creepy, so they hardly ever saw him. Brendan was appalled that his brother had married a Jew, a fact that bothered neither Jamie nor Liesl one bit.

'Mam,' Jamie said gently, 'this baby won't be christened because the baby will be Jewish. That's how it works. If a mother is a Jew, then the baby is too.'

'Ah, Jamie, don't be ridiculous. Sure her father wasn't even a Jew, so she can't be a full Jew herself anyway.'

'Mam!' Jamie was horrified. 'Stop this now...'

'No, Jamie.' Peggy Gallagher got to her feet, swaying a little now, and pointed her finger at her son. 'This is Ireland, not Israel or any other mad place. This child's father is Irish, the child will be born in Ireland, and the religion of Ireland is Catholic.' She hiccupped loudly. 'So we can't have that. I mean...' The short, stout red-haired woman looked around the table for an ally, and finding none, carried on regardless. 'Look, you know I found it hard to accept that you were marrying outside of your faith, but we are fond of Liesl, and of all of you. But this baby will be a Gallagher, not a...' She waved her hand in the direction of Ariella and Elizabeth. She'd clearly forgotten their surnames. 'Anyway, it is only logical that he or she would be baptised into the one true faith –'

'Stop it now.' Jamie's voice cut through hers in a tone nobody had ever heard from him before. 'You are upsetting my wife and my family, and if you can't keep a civil tongue in your head in the light of the hospitality you've been shown, I'd rather you just left. And just so

21

we're clear, our child will be Jewish, one hundred percent, and won't be baptised by Brendan or anyone else.'

'Jamie! I'm shocked at you! Please address your brother as Father Brendan.' Peggy hiccupped and plonked back onto her seat once more. The wine had made her florid complexion even more livid.

Jamie cast a glance at his father, and everyone else was silent.

'I think we might get a bit of air.' Donie Gallagher rose and pulled on his wife's arm as he tried to get her to rise from her chair. He was tall and thin while she was short and squat, and he stood no chance of physically lifting her.

'I do not need air,' Peggy announced. 'I need to sort this out for once and for all.' She took her wine glass and, to everyone's horror, downed an almost-full glass in one gulp.

Elizabeth jumped in. 'Well, how about we clear the table, and maybe we can all sit outside. It's a lovely day, and it's a shame not to admire the garden that Ariella has created.'

'Using forced labour, I might add,' Willi added with a chuckle to lighten the mood.

All around them the family cleared plates and moved chairs as Liesl and Jamie sat and watched his father try to cajole his now very drunk mother out of the chair.

'No, Donie. I won't have it – I won't!' Her voice was querulous and loud. 'Sure that child will go to limbo if it's not baptised, and then what will we do? We can't allow this. I mean, it's all right for them' – she waved her hand in the direction of the family clearing plates – 'but for a Gallagher… What would we tell people? What would we tell Father Brendan?'

Liesl took Jamie's hand. 'Leave it,' she advised him. 'There's no point in creating a bigger scene. Let your father manage her.'

By now Peggy was at least on her feet, albeit unsteady, and Donie led her outside.

Jamie turned to his in-laws, embarrassed. 'I'm so sorry about that. I don't know what to say. And after you being so hospitable and everything…'

Ariella hugged her son-in-law. 'Don't worry, Jamie. She's just had a little too much wine and she isn't used to it. Please, forget it.'

'But it's unforgivable. I thought she'd come to terms with our situation.' He was furious that his mother would be so rude and hurtful to these kind people.

'Jamie,' Rabbi Frank said, 'I know emotions run high, but we must remember, we all are happy that this new life is joining us. We Jews have suffered persecution for so long, but please, Jamie, do not feel bad. It is the way of things. Your mother has her beliefs, but you are your own man. And you and Liesl are starting your own family, a cause for much joy, no? So let us not dwell on the negative. Most people see two young people who love each other and are happy and living good and virtuous lives. You will be wonderful parents, and this baby is lucky. So please, do not dwell on the bad. Focus on the good.'

'He's right, you know.' Frau Braun sidled up to Liesl, murmuring quietly. 'Forget about her. She will visit once every two years, and you'll just have to put up with her. Maybe lock up the drinks cabinet though, next time.' She gave Liesl one of her rare smiles, and it succeeded in lifting Liesl's mood.

'You all right?' Erich moved to stand beside his sister as Frau Braun left. Jamie was busy stacking the extra chairs brought from Elizabeth and Daniel's house for the occasion.

'I suppose so.' Liesl sighed. 'Is she out there still?'

They both moved to the window of Ariella's pretty drawing room. There in the corner of the garden, vomiting into a large shrub, was Jamie's mother. His father gave her his handkerchief to wipe her mouth.

'It was that chicken – that's what's making me sick,' Peggy complained loudly as Donie tried to clean her up.

'Nothing to do with the gallon of wine she threw down her neck,' Erich said with a grin.

'I think I'll get Daniel to drive her home. She and Donie are staying with us. She'll need to sleep that off, and I hope she gets a terrible hangover,' Elizabeth murmured, uncharacteristically cross. She was so protective of Liesl and Erich, she was like a mother lioness if anyone hurt them.

'I think that's likely,' Erich said, then chuckled to Liesl, who was still feeling queasy, having eaten almost nothing. 'Anyway, don't mind her. Are you all right?'

'Fine.' Liesl sighed. 'I just feel bad for poor Jamie. He loves us all and he's mortified that his mother could behave like that. I did tell him he should prepare her, as I thought she might say something or look sour, but I don't think anyone expected that performance.'

'No, probably not,' Erich agreed. 'But you know it won't affect how anyone feels about Jamie. She's just a mad old bat.' He gave her a one-armed hug. Though he was younger and had relied on Liesl all of his life, he towered over her now.

'True.' Liesl shrugged. 'At least we'll be spared the weird Father Brendan.' She yawned. 'I'm actually exhausted myself.'

'You look terrible.' He winked. 'Will I walk you home? Or do you want to wait for Jamie?'

'No, he's got to go in and get the function room ready for the cricket club supper dance this evening. But I'll be fine to walk home if you want to stay?'

'No, I'm ready to go anyway. That's enough excitement for one day.' He chuckled again.

They said their goodbyes, and Liesl spent a few minutes with her husband, who was, as she suspected, embarrassed and upset by his mother's performance. He insisted on doing the washing up, helped ably by Willi, while Daniel drove the rabbi and the Gallaghers home.

CHAPTER 4

'Well, that was eventful.' Elizabeth smiled as she poured cups of tea for Ariella, Frau Braun and herself in the kitchen once all the clearing away was done.

Frau Braun sat quietly, lost in thought. The performance of the Irish woman had brought up a lot of memories she would rather forget. Living in Germany all through the years building up to the war, she'd been terrified the truth about Willi's Jewish birth mother would come out. Hubert's indiscretion with the Jewish maid in their house had hurt her deeply, but ironically, that action had given her a son, and she'd adored him from the moment he was placed in her arms as a newborn. Peggy Gallagher was a trial, no doubt about it, but was Frau Braun as bad back in those days? Possibly. And she had to be honest about her attitude to the Jews; there was no point in white-washing history just because she'd seen the error of her ways and later converted. She had agreed with Hitler, at the start anyway. The Jews did appear to have everything – they had the best houses, they controlled business and banking – and ordinary Germans felt hard done by. All Hitler did was tap into a seam of resentment that was already there. Peggy resented the Jews too, or at least disliked or mistrusted them. It felt wrong to be too judgemental.

'She's a product of her society.' Ariella stirred milk into her tea. 'I suppose she just can't contemplate anything different. I don't care. I've seen enough hatred in my lifetime to not be fazed by Peggy Gallagher, but I do feel for Jamie.'

'And Liesl and Erich too – they are horrified,' Elizabeth agreed. 'We forget that they know what happened but they didn't really see it. I mean, coming to England and then here, and discovering to our astonishment a whole Jewish community here before us meant that, for them, their faith was something everyone accepted. I think they are not as accustomed to anti-Semitism as you are.'

'That's true.' Ariella nodded. 'I thank God every day they never saw what I saw. Seeing the people who survived on the cinema screen is one thing, but seeing them in real life, or witnessing the open hatred in the streets… They were spared that, so it makes Peggy's outburst more shocking to them.'

'I was as bad,' Frau Braun admitted. 'I would have been horrified if Willi had brought home a Jewish girl, and that's the truth. I'd have done anything to stop it, and not because I was afraid his true identity would come out, but because I didn't like Jews.'

'People change, though, Frau Braun,' Ariella said quietly. 'And what you did by protecting me proves that.'

'They do, and I did,' Frau Braun remarked. 'But that doesn't mean everything gets erased. I heard her, and I saw myself. This place – it's not like the rest of the world, you know. The people here had an opportunity to see Jews as just ordinary people and they became friends, but sometimes I think Liesl and Erich have an overly rosy view of the world. Erich especially. Peggy Gallagher is more the norm than the exception. I know because I was just like her.'

Both Ariella and Elizabeth knew this wasn't meant as criticism of their beloved children – in fact, Katerin Braun was very fond of them – but she said what she thought without sugarcoating it, and she was probably right.

'Well, after the business with Kurt Richter, Liesl is under no illusions,' Ariella added. 'But yes, Erich hasn't been exposed to the hatred in the same way. He seems in good form these days. I was worried the thing with Abigail was upsetting him, but he seems fine about that, though everyone leaving for Israel is taking its toll on him.'

'He's thinking of visiting Bud,' Elizabeth told them. 'He confided in Daniel that he was feeling a bit left out, and so a trip to America might be just what he needs.'

'And what if he decides he wants to stay in America?' Frau Braun demanded. 'They are all leaving, if not for Israel, then America or England, or even back to Europe, though God knows why anyone would want to go there nowadays. And then where would you be with him all the way over there?' Frau Bran knew it wasn't her place to be so outraged, but she loved that boy, though it would be hard to admit it.

She never imagined for a moment how pulling Ariella off the street that day and hiding her in the attic would turn out. She couldn't allow her thoughts to dwell on it at the time as the risks were unconscionable, but she just had to do it. They survived against all the odds, and life since had been kind. She had managed to save one life, but not only that, her beloved son fell in love with Ariella and had included his mother in this new adventure, populated by good, kind people. Life was strange.

'He's twenty-three, Frau Braun, a grown man. He can go if he wants to,' Ariella said sadly. 'Though I'd hate for him to leave. I can't bear the thought actually, but he has his own life to live.'

'Well, the new baby will be something nice for us all to look forward to.' Elizabeth tried to be optimistic. It was clear that she too hated the idea of Erich leaving.

'Are we ready to be grandmas?' Ariella chuckled.

'Well, you certainly don't look it,' Elizabeth remarked.

Ariella Braun looked the picture of youth and vitality. Though now approaching her forty-sixth birthday, her red hair was as vibrant as ever and her green eyes had lost none of their sparkle. She was tiny and slim, but anyone who underestimated her strength, physically or emotionally, was mistaken. She'd endured so much as a hidden Jew in Berlin –that nothing daunted her now.

'Neither do you.' Ariella returned the compliment, but both

women knew it wasn't true. Elizabeth's once-dark hair was now streaked with grey, and she was almost a decade older than Ariella.

Frau Braun observed Elizabeth. She had a handsome face, strong and kind, but she looked her age. She'd abandoned the idea of ever having children, having miscarried her only child the day she was told that her first husband, Rudi Klein, was killed on the last day of the Great War. They had often discussed how the letter she'd received in 1939 from Ariella, her cousin Peter's wife, a woman she'd never heard of let alone met, begging her to take then ten-year-old Liesl and seven-year-old Erich came as a shock, but she never hesitated. And it was the best decision of her life. The war had been immeasurably cruel on so many families in every possible way, but Elizabeth always remarked, like Frau Braun, how she had gained an entire family from it. She could never have envisioned as a lonely widow in Liverpool that the greatest conflict the world had ever seen could have granted her two children, an adoring husband and an extended family that was the joy of her life. In that respect, the women had a lot in common.

'We both know that's not the case, but thank you for pretending.' Elizabeth laughed with her friend.

Frau Braun knew that the feelings Elizabeth had had initially at the resurfacing of the long-missing Ariella were complex. She had been delighted for Liesl and Erich, of course – genuinely, it was all she wanted for them, as the poor darlings had lost so much – but she hated the thought of returning them to their real mother. But from the moment Ariella arrived in Ballycreggan, she'd been clear. She and Elizabeth were both the mothers of the children and they shared them, and for that Elizabeth would be eternally grateful. She knew the gratitude was reciprocated, as Ariella hiding and surviving was only possible because her children were safe. The fact that the women became closer than sisters in the process was an added bonus.

Ariella, though she was a devoted mother, had a different attitude to most women around Ballycreggan who wanted to be stuck in their children's business morning, noon and night. She said she believed in planned obsolescence of parents. Making her children independent was important to her, and so she allowed them, inasmuch as she could, to make their own decisions. The only notable exception was when Liesl brought Kurt Richter to Ireland, thinking Ariella would be delighted to see her old friends' son. What Liesl didn't know was that Ariella knew Kurt was bad news, and it almost killed Ariella to see Liesl with him.

Ariella changed the subject. 'Now, how on earth are we all going to manage another three days of Mrs Peggy Gallagher?'

'Well,' Elizabeth mused, 'I'd imagine she'll be so embarrassed, if she even remembers it at all, that she'll keep a low profile. I wouldn't be one bit surprised if something urgent didn't crop up in County Kerry demanding their immediate return.'

'She'll probably be mortified in the morning,' Frau Braun added.

Ariella nodded. 'That's true. Poor Jamie, though. I felt so bad for him. I know he goes to Mass every Sunday – Father O'Toole is really fond of him – but he is fine with Liesl being Jewish and bringing the baby up as Jewish too.'

'Peggy won't let the fact that they married in a registry office go either, though,' Elizabeth said with a sigh. 'She should be happy her son is keeping his faith if it means that much to her, not harassing them. The men of the various cloths can accept it, so why can't she?'

Elizabeth was agnostic and had never attended any of the three places of worship in the village apart from ceremonial occasions. She kept her own counsel on the subject, but if pressed, she said she thought religion caused more problems than it solved. Despite her stance, though, she was held in high regard by the rabbi, the priest and the vicar.

'Isn't it funny how those three clergymen are such good friends?' Ariella added. 'I suppose they have all seen enough of life to know that for every rule, there are fifty exceptions. I doubt there's a place in the world except Ballycreggan where you'd see a Catholic priest, a Jewish rabbi and a Protestant vicar having coffee together three times a week. I think the friendship they forged over the years, and the way this parish has had to pull together through the war years and after, means that doctrine and dogma always come after people. It's a very special place here, and we're so lucky to call it home.'

'He's not well.' Frau Braun heard herself blurt it out. She had to – it was too much to bear alone.

Ariella and Elizabeth turned to her.

'Who? Father O'Toole?' Ariella asked, her brow furrowed. 'I saw him yesterday and he looked fine to me.'

'No. The rabbi.'

'But he was just here. What do you mean, not well?' Elizabeth asked.

Frau Braun swallowed. Should she betray him? Was it for his own good, or should she keep out of it?

'Frau Braun, please, tell us,' Ariella urged.

'He'll murder me for telling you, but I think you should know. I wasn't snooping, but a letter arrived from Belfast and I assumed it was some paperwork to do with the community there. He goes there once a month, as you know – they have no rabbi since Solomon Feinstein passed away. Someone is coming from London, I believe, but Rabbi Frank is caring for them in the meantime. And we get so much correspondence from the searches we are still conducting, and I open all of his post.' She felt guilty about interfering, but the weight of what she knew was bearing on her.

'This was a letter from the hospital, saying that the tests had showed some further areas that needed investigating and so he needed to go back for more treatment.'

'Treatment for what?' Ariella asked. 'I never knew he went for any medical appointments.'

'Neither did I. The stubborn, stupid man never said a word.' Frau Braun shook her head and tutted. 'I confronted him then, made him tell me, and it seems he's got a tumour in his bowel.'

Elizabeth fought back the tears. 'Oh no. This is terrible news.'

Frau Braun nodded.

'What can we do?' Elizabeth asked. 'He still lives up at the farm, and I know you're there too, but perhaps you should both move into the village? Be a bit more comfortable?'

Frau Braun looked resigned. 'You know what he's like. That farm is – I don't know... It's like he wants to keep it open in case any of them want to come home.' She struggled to control the tears that were threatening.

The rest of the world was moving on, trying to put the war years behind them, but for Rabbi Frank, those six years, and the subsequent years when the Jewish children floundered in uncertainty, became his life's purpose. As each child left, either as adults to fend for themselves, or as children to family members, or en masse to Israel to a kibbutz to be raised among strangers, united only in faith, he made them promise to stay in touch. He in return promised them that he would always be there for them, that they always had a home in Bally-creggan while he was alive and that Daniel and Elizabeth would be there after he was gone. Leaving the farm would not be something he would do easily.

'As well as all of that, the synagogue is there,' she went on, 'so that's going to be the hardest for him to leave. It was such a makeshift place at first – you'd remember it, Elizabeth. He talks about it often, those early days. Now it looks so lovely. He keeps it beautifully, the spice boxes polished, the menorah, the shofar, the pile of siddurim ready on the shelf for anyone to take to pray. So many Shabbats, Chanukahs, bar mitzvahs, weddings – they all happened there. It's hard for him to leave it, as it's like a shrine to the past or something. So it's not just about leaving the farm. It's about closing the door on all he built, the memories of the days when it was full of children and adults praying and living and, more importantly, surviving together.'

'Well, we can always relocate the synagogue to the village,' Elizabeth said. 'I'm sure we could find somewhere suitable. That place is too big for the small community now anyway.'

Frau Braun shrugged. 'You know what he's like, a stubborn, pig-headed old fool.' She knew her words were harsh, but she was so worried.

'But if he's not well, he'll need care and some comfort...' Ariella said, her voice betraying her sadness at the news.

'I'll get Daniel to talk to him.' Elizabeth glanced at Frau Braun. 'Don't worry, he won't let on he heard it from you.'

Frau Braun was relieved. The rabbi might listen to Daniel. 'He's infuriating, but you're right – he can't stay up there. We get along fine there at this time of year, but it's cold in the wintertime, and the rooms are too big for just the two of us.'

'You could both move in here?' Ariella offered.

Frau Braun thought about it. She'd decided when she arrived that she wanted to work at the farm, and she did her best caring for the children for several years, feeling more tenderness and kindness for the little ones than even she thought she was capable of. 'Perhaps.' She paused, wondering if she would sound deluded if she told them what she had in mind.

'Or have you another idea?' Ariella asked.

'Well,' she began uncertainly, suddenly feeling foolish, 'I was thinking that I got some money from the sale of my house in Berlin, and I have an inheritance from my father, and my salary from the post office was saved, so I might have enough to buy a small house in the village. Nothing fancy like this, or yours' – she waved her hand around Ariella's sumptuously decorated living room, then nodded at Elizabeth to indicate her house was as grand – 'but something small. And I thought...' She paused again, afraid to voice her idea.

'That you and the rabbi could live there?' Elizabeth finished for her kindly.

'Well, he could be my lodger. I had lodgers in Berlin, so I'm used to it, and it would mean I could keep an eye on him. We'd be more comfortable, warmer and that...' Her voice trailed off.

Neither Elizabeth nor Ariella needed to voice it; she could see the reservation on their faces. The idea of the very proper rabbi living with a woman he wasn't related to might be too much for him, even if under the most platonic of arrangements. The farm was one thing. He'd lived there for nearly seventeen years, and Frau Braun worked there and was entitled to accommodation, as were all the volunteers, so the fact that they were the last remaining two made it acceptable.

But moving into a house together would start the tongues wagging without a doubt. That was if the rabbi would even consider it.

'Well, you won't know until you ask,' Elizabeth said.

'I don't know. He might...' Frau Braun wished the ground would open and swallow her. She thought she must sound like a stupid old woman with ridiculous notions.

She hadn't admitted to anyone how she really felt. She could barely allow herself to even think it. Despite her constant grumbling about how impossible the rabbi was, how stubborn, how pedantic, how set in his ways, she was fond of him, loved him even, and she knew he would be lost without her.

'Look, would you like Daniel to speak to him about it?' Elizabeth offered. 'He's going to have to talk to him about his health anyway, and he could offer it as a suggestion, see how he took it? If it went well, then maybe you two could discuss the details?'

Though Daniel was raised a Christian, he was in fact Jewish, something that only became apparent when the Nazis arrived to his door in Vienna in 1939 demanding he register as a Jew. His parents had wanted their son to live a life without prejudice, so they turned their back on their faith and reinvented themselves. Daniel's life took several twists and turns, but he ended up at the farm in Ballycreggan and subsequently embraced Judaism. The rabbi taught him and oversaw his education on the faith of his ancestors, and as a result, the men were close friends.

'Maybe that would be best, see what he thinks?' Frau Braun grasped at the idea. Every fibre of her being wanted to withdraw the suggestion, as she felt it made her look so pathetic and needy, but something stopped her. Maybe Daniel could raise it without it seeming like the plea of a desperate, lonely widow?

'I'll speak to him this evening, and we'll take it from there.' Elizabeth patted her hand. 'Don't worry. We'll figure it all out together – we always do.'

CHAPTER 5

*R*abbi Frank was troubled. He opened the letter from Karl and allowed the enclosed folded-up twenty-pound notes to fall on the desk. There must have been a hundred pounds there. That boy would be the death of him.

Dear Rabbi,

How's tricks in Ballycreggan? All good, I hope. I enclose a few bob to go towards heating and what have you – I remember how cold that place was! And I know you said you don't need it, but please, if you ever want more, just shout. I've got plenty.

Life here with me is fine. Well, I got in a bit of bother recently, you know yourself, but some friends of mine were able to sort it so I managed to avoid some time at His Majesty's pleasure! Prison doesn't suit me, as you know, and thanks for coming to visit me last time. I know I said I'd do my best to stay out of trouble, and I am, but you know how it is.

Anyway, I'll sign off, but you know where I am if you ever need anything. I'll write next month as usual.

All the best,

Karl (Charlie)

Charlie Kolitz, as he was now known since taking the English version of his name, had always been a troublesome child. He arrived at the farm as a precocious boy and was most unhappy to find himself in Northern Ireland. His cousins had, after the Great War, emigrated from Poland to London and, according to Charlie anyway, had been doing very well for themselves. He insisted often and at volume to anyone who would listen that he was supposed to be with them there, and not on a farm in Ballycreggan.

Despite his protestations and rejection of the life he lived on the farm, the rabbi cared for him every bit as much as the others. Charlie was incorrigible but had a razor-sharp sense of humour and was kind under it all.

He left the farm the moment he could, when he was sixteen, and joined the family business in London. Unfortunately, the family business turned out to be of the criminal kind, and very soon the rabbi had to visit Charlie in prison. He made the journey, hoping he could help the lad, get him to see how there were those who cared for him in Ballycreggan or that there was a whole new life waiting in Israel, but the rabbi came home empty-handed. Charlie saw his incarceration as nothing more than an inconvenience, and though he seemed determined to continue his life on the wrong side of the law, he apologised to the rabbi for being such a difficult charge and thanked him profusely for his care.

Despite his many misdemeanours, he was actually a lovable character, and the rabbi hated how his life had turned out. He wished he could get through to him. A few months after Karl was released from prison he'd read a newspaper article linking him to a racketeering gang. The journalist suggested that his crimes should carry a hefty sentence but predicted that Charlie Kolitz would probably get off lightly. The journalist was right, and Charlie got away with it. The rabbi dreaded to think how a judge could have been prevailed upon to hand down such a verdict. It would indicate that Charlie was moving up the ladder in the organization. Charlie's elderly uncles were the top men in a huge-scale criminal enterprise, the families involved all Jewish. They were feared and respected in the East End of London and had a kind of Robin Hood–type reputation. They took care of their own, but they were ruthless. Charlie was next in line for the throne.

Despite his nefarious life, Charlie was better than many for keeping in touch, and he wrote every month. His letters were full of concern for the old rabbi and for his friends back in Ballycreggan. You'd never think he'd spent his years there doing his best to get away. His time on the farm seemed to have taken on a kind of nostalgic glow in the eyes of the now-hardened Charlie. It was strange.

The rabbi used to return the money he would send each month, but now he didn't because it hurt the lad so much. Instead, he used it to help trace families displaced during the war. He figured some good might as well come from ill-gotten gains. He tried relentlessly to make him change his ways, choose a more righteous path, turn away from criminality, but it was a futile struggle. Charlie was happy with his life and would not change it for anyone.

The rabbi was lost in thought when Daniel appeared at the door; clearly he had something on his mind.

'Ah, Daniel, what can I do for you?' He smiled.

'It's more what we can do for you,' Daniel said, taking a seat.

'That sounds ominous.' The rabbi began writing something on a pad.

'Look, Rabbi, this is ridiculous. There's no point in pretending you're not getting older. You are going to need care, and we want to do it. Staying up here, in a place designed for fifty people, you and Frau Braun rattling about, is just not practical.' Daniel wasn't going to be bullied into submission.

'Oy veh! You decide what is practical, yes?' The rabbi waved his hand in a gesture of dismissal. 'I am happy here, Frau Braun is happy here, we have all we need and important work to do. So I'll thank you to leave me to get on with it. Daniel, I'm sure you have walls to build somewhere?'

Despite mastering the English language, the rabbi's accent was still very much German. His family had been rabbis at the same synagogue since the 1700s in Berlin, and the fact that it was razed during his watch was something that weighed heavily on him. He was lucky to escape with his life, and that too, the survivor's guilt, was something he struggled with. His way of dealing with it was to work himself to the bone for the children who came under his care. Even now, when most of them were adults, he was tireless in his efforts to keep them connected, to keep them safe. He corresponded weekly with each and every one, regardless of how often they replied, because he wanted them all to know there was a home for them with him if things didn't work out in whatever life path they chose. Even the route Charlie had taken. He wrote references and used his many connections all over the world to help the children who had been placed in his care, and it was truly a vocation. He never gave up the idea of reuniting them with survivors either. People even now were coming forward, and family ties were being reconnected. He would never give up.

'I know about the cancer,' Daniel said quietly.

Rabbi Frank stopped writing and looked up from his desk. 'You know so much, eh?' He shook his head and muttered in Yiddish about interfering women.

Daniel must have understood because immediately he responded,

'Don't blame Frau Braun, she cares about you – we all do. You've spent your life helping others, so now let us help you.'

'I don't need your help.' Rabbi Frank sighed and removed his glasses, placing them on the desk that was strewn with correspondence.

He hadn't changed physically much over the years he knew, but looking closely in the mirror that morning he could see that his skin had taken on a yellowish pallor and he'd lost weight, not that he had any to lose.

He was small and wiry but had the strength of an ox, or at least he used to. His long beard was white, always had been, but his salt-and-pepper hair was now as white as his beard and growing increasingly thinner. He could feel the scrutiny of Daniel's gaze.

'I'll manage this on my own until I can't, and then I will go to the hospital and I will die. Simple as that.'

'And what about us?' Daniel asked in frustration. 'We're just supposed to let you decline here until you can no longer cope? Where in the Talmud does it say to make a martyr of yourself, eh?'

'I'm not being a martyr. I just want to be left alone.' He sounded tired.

'Well, I'll tell Ariella, Elizabeth, Willi, Liesl and Erich that, shall I? And Frau Braun. And Father O'Toole and Reverend Parkes and everyone in the village, the people who care about you, who see you as their family. I'll just tell them that you don't want any more to do with them, that the last seventeen years meant nothing to you and you just want to let the cancer take you and that's that.'

The rabbi looked taken aback at the passion in his voice; Daniel was normally the epitome of calm.

'No, that's not what I'm saying…' he tried to explain but Daniel interrupted.

'Frau Braun wants to buy a house in the village – she has the money – and she wants to offer you a room there as her lodger. She wants to care for you. You could move the office there, and myself and Erich and Willi would fix up whatever you need. It would make life more comfortable for you and easier on us not to have to come all the way out here every time we wanted to check on you.' Daniel ran his hand through his grey hair, still thick and slightly longer than most men wore it. 'She was afraid to offer it in case you thought she was making an improper suggestion, but it's what she wants. I think she's had enough of the draughts and the constant battling the elements here on the farm. She's not getting any younger either and needs a bit more comfort, but she won't leave you alone up here.' Daniel's voice betrayed his frustration with what he saw as bloody-minded stubbornness.

'She thinks she knows what's best for me? Like I'm some kind of child that needs caring for?'

'No. She's not treating you like a child, she's trying to show you that she cares, we all do.' Daniel exhaled.

· · ·

'AND I CAN'T GO to live with a woman I'm not married to. It wouldn't be right.'

He went back to his papers, wishing his friend would just let it go.

'Marry her then.'

The silence hung between the two men, neither wanting to be the first to speak. Daniel's sentence was like an unexploded bomb sitting between them, and it was as if both were afraid to make one false move.

David Frank didn't know whether to laugh, or to be cross, or to dismiss the idea, but the silence went on.

Eventually he heard himself just be honest.

'A lot of good I would be as a husband at this stage of my life, eh? Nearly dead already, ancient, falling apart. No, she would not need that stupidity in her life now. She's had a long, hard life and needs peace.' He shook his head sadly.

'Perhaps she needs love? Maybe you both do?' Daniel said quietly. 'She hasn't said so, not directly, and certainly not to me, but Elizabeth thinks she has feelings for you, not just as her rabbi or someone she's worked with for so long. She thinks that Katerin loves you, Rabbi, and if I've come to learn something about my wife over the years, it's that she's very rarely wrong.'

Rabbi Frank focused on his writing, trying to process this extraordinary information. Could it be true? Surely not. It was ridiculous.

'Nonsense.' The rabbi dismissed the thought and went back to his writing. 'And I'm surprised at you, a grown man, talking like this, like we are in the first flush of youth. Frau Braun and I have both been through a lot, seen too much, to go all starry-eyed and foolish now. Frau Braun is a *klip*, and she should mind her own business. I don't have time for this, so please, let me get back to my work.'

Daniel refused to budge. Folding his arms across his chest he spoke,

'Rabbi, we both know that the last thing in the world Frau Braun could be called is a gossipy woman, so that's not fair. She's decent and kind and only told us about your illness because she cares, so do not take this out on her.'

'Yes, yes, everyone knows what is best for the old rabbi...' He shooed Daniel out of his office.

CHAPTER 6

*E*rich had promised Elizabeth he would pick up a few things for her in the large grocery shop in Newtownards; it was no bother since he was out there pricing a job anyway. It was dark and cold and the town was deserted, everyone rushing home to their fires and a warm meal. As he stood in line waiting to pay for his purchases, someone bumped into him. He turned to see a hefty middle-aged man very much the worse for wear, with a strong smell of whiskey emanating from him.

'Shorry…shorry…' the man muttered, swaying slightly.

'It's fine.' Erich moved forward in the queue.

He left the shop and put the shopping bag on the back seat of his mint-green MG TF 1500 Midget with chrome spoked wheels, his pride and joy. As he pulled out into traffic, he spotted a very pretty girl locking up a small shop. She turned and smiled at him as he stopped and gestured that she should walk in front of his car. Then, in a split second, from behind and to the side, a car overtook him and hit her with a sickening crunch.

The other car screeched to a halt, and Erich recognised the driver as the man who'd bumped into him in the shop.

The girl lay on the ground. Erich jumped from his car and ran to her. Nobody else was around. The other man staggered out of his car and abandoned it, moving quickly in the other direction, not even checking to see if she was all right. Erich realised he could do nothing about that now; the girl had to be his priority.

To his relief, she was conscious, but her arm was at an odd angle. She groaned as he took off his jacket and gently raised her head. She was about his age, blonde, with a dark-brown beauty spot just below her mouth. He thought there was something odd about her face, and then he realised she had two different-coloured eyes. One was blue, the other green. It altogether made for a very striking girl. Erich thought she looked like a film star.

'You're all right. You're going to be fine.' He hoped his voice sounded soothing.

'I'm fine, but my arm...' She winced as she tried to sit up.

'Hold on.' He pulled his jumper off and fashioned it into a sling, then helped her into a sitting position. 'That's right... If you can just get your arm in there... That's it.'

Erich made a decision. She seemed capable of moving, and he could have her at the hospital quicker than waiting for an ambulance. 'Can you stand? If you can, I'll take you to the hospital.'

She nodded, her face twisted in pain.

He put his arm around her, avoiding her broken arm, and helped her to her feet. She walked slowly to his car, and he helped her in. She sat in the passenger seat, her head resting on the door, clearly in pain.

'The hospital isn't far, so if you can keep it still while I drive, we'll get you sorted out in no time,' he said.

She turned and gave him a half-smile. 'Thanks.' She exhaled and winced.

There was a bottle of poitín in a bag on the floor, a present from an old farmer they'd done a job for a few weeks ago. It was an illegal spirit distilled from potatoes and Erich thought it was disgusting, but it might help.

'Have a slug of this. It's vile I'd say, but it will take the edge off the pain.' He offered her the bottle and she took a drink, grimacing and coughing as she swallowed the strong spirit.

'And another drop?' he suggested.

She made a face but complied.

'OK, let's go.' He turned the key and the engine roared to life. He drove as fast as he dared while trying to avoid the potholes.

'My name is Erich Bannon, by the way.'

She smiled through the pain. 'Róisín McAreavey.'

'I don't speak Irish, but that means "little rose", doesn't it?' Erich asked, making conversation. 'I only know that because my friend said everything in Irish with "een" on the end is small.' He hoped to take her mind off the winding roads.

'It does.' She nodded slightly. 'Some people spell it the English way, but I spell it the Irish way. The pronunciation is the same – "ro-sheen".'

'It's a lovely name. Would you rather not talk? If it's too bother-some, just say so, but it might take your mind off the arm until we get there?'

'It's fine. Now that the sling is on, it's bearable, and that disgusting drink is making me a wee bit woozy.' She winced as he took a sharp right turn.

'Not long now,' he said. 'I'll take you to the Ards Hospital. They'll get you fixed up good as new. I went there last year when I got a knock to the head playing football, and I was fine afterwards.'

'So are you from around here? Your accent has a touch of some-thing else in there too?'

He kept his eyes on the road; the last thing they needed was an accident. 'Well spotted. I lived in Germany until I was seven, then I lived in England for a year, and then I came to Ballycreggan, out the coast, you know? I'm Jewish.' He had learned over the years to avoid speculation and preconceived ideas about his German nationality and to just say it right away. People were often either apologetic, embar-rassed or uncomfortable, but it was better than them thinking he was a Nazi.

Róisín didn't seem to have any preconceived ideas, which was refreshing. 'Oh, did you grow up on the farm there?' she asked. 'I heard about it.'

'No, but I knew everyone that did. My sister and I were taken in by my father's cousin – she's the school principal in Ballycreggan – and she looked after us. It's a long story.' He smiled.

'Well, it's good that you got out, isn't it? So many others didn't, God love them.'

It was such a novelty to hear someone who responded to his remarks honestly and with genuine emotion. She spoke with the hard edge to her accent of Belfast, an hour away, but he thought she sounded lovely.

'We were very lucky. Our mother was very brave, our adopted mother was kind and loving, and we were surrounded by good people. So speaking of accents, you're not from here either by the sound of it?' Erich continued to navigate the narrow streets of Newtownards, making his way to the hospital.

'Aye, well, I'm from the Falls Road in Belfast originally.' She gasped as he went over a pothole and the car jolted.

'Sorry, I couldn't avoid that one.' He glanced at her. She really was very pretty.

'Not your fault. Thanks for the spin.'

Hearing she was from the famous Falls Road meant she was a Catholic. He'd learned that Northern Ireland was a deeply divided place, and one learned to exercise caution with strangers so as not to say the wrong thing. He had been here long enough to understand the nuances of a deeply divided place. Ballycreggan was unusual, and the arrival of a whole load of Jewish refugees had altered the community irrevocably, but the rest of the province remained very sectarian.

He stayed out of such conversations inasmuch as possible, as regardless of who you spoke to, it was a lose-lose situation. The Protestants in the North were loyal to the British Crown, unwaveringly so, and their republican Catholic neighbours saw themselves as rightful Irish citizens of an occupied land. It was complicated. Ireland had been a colony of Britain since the arrival of the Anglo-Normans in 1169, but the successful War of Independence in 1921, in the South mainly, secured a free state and later a republic for twenty-six of Ireland's thirty-two counties. The now Irish Republic was overwhelmingly Catholic and felt no allegiance – only animosity as far as Erich could see – to Britain. The North was a different story, though. The six counties in the North that formed most of the province of Ulster were predominately Protestant and would not countenance joining the papists in the South, in 1921 or at any other time, so they fought to remain part of the United Kingdom. The decision to divide the island was a bitter one and played out in a civil war between 1921 and 1923. But that bloody and bitter conflict changed nothing, and so the North remained part of the UK.

'And do you still live in Belfast?' he asked.

'No. My daddy is dead, and my mammy wanted me and my brothers out of there, as it was getting too rough, so she got a wee house off the council in Raggettstown. We moved there a few weeks ago.'

'Oh, Raggettstown is not far from me, only ten minutes by car.' He turned into the road leading to the hospital. 'Do you like it?'

'So we're neighbours.' She managed a smile. 'Raggettstown is all right, but it's been hard, you know? It's mostly Protestants there, and they're a bit wary of us. My brothers are into the whole "us and them" thing, but to be honest with you, I can't be bothered with it.'

'I know exactly what you mean,' Erich agreed, finding himself really warming to this girl.

'And what about you? What do you do?' she asked.

'I'm a builder. We have a family business in Ballycreggan.'

'Och, aye, I've heard of you, I think.'

'Well, we're the only building contractors for about fifty miles, so it's likely.' He grinned.

He luckily found a space right outside the hospital and pulled in, rushing around to open the door and help her out of the passenger side. A cold gust of wind made him shudder; he was chilled now that Róisín was wearing his jumper as a sling. He led her across to the front door, and as they entered, the pervasive smell of disinfectant assailed his nostrils.

'I'll wait for you if you like, or would you rather I contacted your mother or…?' Erich was unsure what was best now that they had arrived.

'Are you sure? I don't want to ruin your whole evening?' she questioned as they waited at a glass-panelled hatch to tell the receptionist they were there.

'No, it's fine. I was only going home after work anyway. But I could telephone someone in Raggettstown, or if your mother has a phone?'

Róisín laughed. 'Indeed, and she does not. A phone! She's as likely to wear a diamond tiara peelin' the spuds!'

A nurse approached them. 'And what have we here?' she asked, one eyebrow raised sceptically.

'She was knocked down by a car and hurt her arm,' Erich explained.

The nurse, who had iron-coloured hair and looked to be in her sixties, eyed Erich up and down disparagingly, her look saying she wouldn't be at all surprised if he had something to do with it.

'Erich just saw the accident and brought me here. He's been very good,' Róisín added.

'Very well, come with me.' She led Róisín away and dismissed Erich with a curt nod.

'I'll wait,' he said as they retreated.

'There's no need,' the nurse called without turning around. But Róisín turned her head and made a face, and he grinned. He would wait.

CHAPTER 7

*D*aniel was dismantling an old wireless as Father O'Toole entered the yard.

'God bless the work,' the priest said by way of greeting.

Daniel stood, stretching the muscles of his back, and smiled. 'Hello, Father, what can I do for you?'

He liked the parish priest very much. Patrick O'Toole had served the church for many years and saw how dogma and doctrine didn't serve people as well as humanity and compassion did. He was a burly man but walked with a noticeable limp due to having had displaced hips as a child. He had a shock of white hair that circled his head, but the top of his head was shiny and bald. He had rosy cheeks and an infectious chuckle.

'Well, Daniel, I've come to beg a favour actually,' the priest confessed.

'Ask away.' Daniel wiped his hands on a rag. 'Coffee?' he asked as he filled the kettle.

'I don't want to keep you from your work. I saw the job you did in the convent, and honestly, it's a credit to yourself, Willi and Erich. It's beautiful, and it will make life so much easier for the sisters. They are thrilled with it, so they are.'

Daniel smiled. The commission had come from the Mother Superior. She'd seen a job they'd done on a private house that turned out to be the nun's sister's place, and so they got a huge commission to modernise the kitchens and dining hall of the convent.

'And we put on some kilos in the process.' Daniel patted his flat stomach. 'Sister Agatha is a wonderful cook.'

'She's that, certainly,' Father O'Toole agreed.

'Anyway, I was going to have a break, so if you want a coffee?' Daniel shook the coffee cannister. Though rationing was over, proper coffee was still hard to get and expensive.

'I'm a tea man, but if you have that, I'd have a cup?' the priest said as he walked around admiring the various jobs in different stages of progress around the workshop.

'Of course.' Daniel set about making the drinks.

'So the reason I'm passing by is to ask you to consider taking on two young lads. I heard you are after a pair of apprentices, and there's a woman recently moved from Belfast, a cousin of mine actually, with two fine sons looking for work. They're seventeen and nineteen, and she's anxious to get them into something. To be truthful with you, their eldest brother, Fiach, is in jail – he got mixed up in something he shouldn't, IRA, criminality, I'm not sure of the details but you get the picture – and this woman, a widow, got the others away for fear they'd go down the same road.' He accepted the cup of tea gratefully. 'I don't know the boys, but the mother is a decent woman. Normally I wouldn't ask, but she's up against it, trying to make ends meet, and she could do with having the pair gainfully employed.'

'Have they any experience?' Daniel asked.

'I think they've done a bit of labouring, but no, I'd say not. But she assures me they are good lads and very willing. Quick to learn too. Even if you gave them a try for a few weeks, sure if they're not for you, then you can give them their cards. I wouldn't expect any more than that from you.'

Daniel shrugged. 'Well, I have been looking, but there are very few young lads around, to be honest with you – they've all gone to England working. There's plenty of money to be made there building up after the war and they're out from under the watchful eye of Mammy and Daddy so they jump at it. So if you give these lads a recommendation and they want to have a try, then sure, why not?'

The priest gave a broad beam. 'Well, that would be just smashing, Daniel. I'd really appreciate it and so would their mother.'

'Well I haven't time to train anyone up just right now but tell them to be here in two weeks time, 8 a.m. sharp and in working clothes, and we'll see how they go.' Daniel drained his coffee. 'Now I'd best get back. I promised Elizabeth I wouldn't be late this evening.'

'Well, I'm sure the prospect of the lovely Mrs Lieber and a delicious meal are enough to get you home quickly anyway, but I won't get in the way any longer.' The priest waved and placed his cup on the sink. 'Thanks again, Daniel. I won't forget you for this.'

* * *

TWO DAYS LATER, as Erich was locking up – Willi and Daniel were going directly home from the job they were on – he saw her, sitting on the wall opposite the yard.

'Well, 'tis yourself.' He smiled. 'How's the arm?'

He'd driven her to the corner of her road the night after the accident; it was almost eleven by the time she was discharged with a sling and a bandage. He hadn't seen her since, though she had sent him a card thanking him for looking after her and saying she hoped they could see each other again.

'Much better, thanks. It was dislocated, not broken, so I just had a bit of bruising. But I'm on the mend.'

'Glad to hear it.' Erich thought he would seize his chance. 'Would you like to go for a cup of tea or a drink? My brother-in-law has the pub here, and it's very respectable, I promise.'

She smiled and his heart lurched. Those strange eyes, her perfect figure, her lustrous blonde hair – she was gorgeous.

'Could we go for a drive maybe? I didn't get to admire your car properly the last time.' She giggled.

'Of course.' He led her to his car and opened the door for her.

As they drove out of Ballycreggan, they chatted easily. She was relaxed and interesting. They talked about work. She didn't really enjoy her job but it was a means to an end, and he told her all about the various projects they had on.

'Listen, Erich, I...' She seemed hesitant.

'What?' he asked.

'Well, it's nothing. Just that my brothers, Colm and Neil, are going to be starting with your company, and I kind of... Well, I never said I knew you or anything, and they are really protective, like stupidly so. So if you could not let on that you know me, that would be better?'

Erich shrugged. 'Daniel mentioned that he was taking on two cousins of Father O'Toole – is that them?'

'Yes, he's my mammy's cousin. So is that all right? Not to say anything?' She looked less sure of herself than she had up to this.

'Sure. There's nothing to tell anyway.' Erich smiled. 'I barely know you.'

'I'd like it if we could get to know each other, though.' She kept her eyes firmly on the road ahead.

Erich wasn't used to girls being this forthcoming. It was refreshing. 'I would too,' he said, turning around a bend and pulling into a picnic area overlooking the sea. It was deserted.

'Don't worry, I'm not going to ravish you or anything.' He chuckled. 'I just thought we might go for a walk along the cliff? I've a spare coat in the back if you want it.'

'Great, I'd love it.' She jumped out of the car, and he handed her his jacket. It was big on her but she looked so lovely as the wind blew her hair.

They walked out onto the well-worn path that snaked around the headland, and to his astonishment, he felt her hand slip into his. He looked down at her and squeezed her hand gently.

On and on they walked, laughing and joking. She told him that her eldest brother was in prison and that it had nearly broken her mother's heart. He was involved with the IRA and headed up one of their many criminal enterprises. She talked about her father, who'd been accidentally shot by a British patrol when she was only twelve, and explained that was the reason her family hated the British. He told her all about his father and the Nazis, and they realised they shared more than they could ever have guessed. As they returned to the car, before he turned the key, she leaned over and kissed him on the cheek.

'Thank you. I had a lovely time.' She smiled.

'So did I,' Erich said, rubbing one finger down her cheek.

They moved together and soon were kissing. She responded to him with an enthusiasm he'd never experienced with any girl before, and eventually he withdrew, chuckling.

'I'd better get you home, Miss McAreavey, before Father O'Toole sets the police on me for corrupting his innocent wee cousin.'

She grinned as he started the engine. 'Can we do this again?' she asked.

'Oh, I would think so.' Erich winked and drove back in the direction of Raggettstown.

* * *

TEN DAYS LATER, Colm and Neil McAreavey were standing outside the yard as Daniel and Erich walked down the street in Ballycreggan. Both lads seemed ideal, athletic and strong, and both looked up and greeted Daniel with a smile. They had dark hair and pale skin, and Erich thought they looked nothing like their sister.

In the week and a half since Róisín had turned up at the yard, they'd seen each other twice and both dates had gone wonderfully. She was hilarious, she could make him weep with mirth, and they were on the same wavelength as regards people's obsession with religion or politics. They had no interest in either and were happy to live in their own little bubble. He'd not told anyone of their relationship, and he knew she hadn't either.

'Good morning, Mr Lieber, and thanks for the start,' the taller – and Erich guessed older of the two – said, stamping his cigarette out with his boot and kicking it to the gutter.

'Good morning. Daniel will do. And this is my son, Erich – you'll be answerable to him mainly. So let's get inside and see what's what, shall we?' Daniel opened the small cut-out door in the large yard doors. Willi had very helpfully put the large door on a roller so they could open it completely when necessary to accept deliveries or take out finished pieces. There had been great excitement in the village last month as they rolled out a full spiral staircase of spalted beech, an exquisite piece of craftmanship by Willi.

The yard was as they left it every evening, a perfect example of tidy efficiency. On one wall were screwdrivers, arranged by size and heads, then saws, chisels and spanners, each assigned its own peg. Beneath that was a bench on which were bolted several vices and levels, and beneath the bench were compartments for bigger tools. There were a series of different level surfaces with levers and pulleys overhead used for manoeuvring larger pieces. To the left were two lathes, one for woodworking, another for metal. Against the wall was a table with four chairs and a gas ring with a kettle. The workshop smelled of sawdust, linseed and leather, and the taller of the two boys sniffed appreciatively.

'Right. The first thing is that taking things and not replacing them where they belong is a hanging offence.' Daniel smiled but he was only half joking. 'The second capital crime is making me weak coffee.' He spooned a generous amount of coffee into his mug and added water from the kettle.

'Right you are, Mr Lieber,' the older boy said.

'Daniel will do.' He reiterated.

'So which is which?' Erich asked, hanging his jacket on the hook for that purpose beside the lunch table.

'I'm Colm,' the older one said. 'And this here is my wee brother Neil.'

Erich thought they looked like good craic, perhaps up for a bit of fun, and he felt a cheer he hadn't felt for a while. They were younger than him of course, but it would be nice to have lads someway close to his own age around the place.

'Morning, all,' Willi said cheerfully as he arrived, then stuck his hand out to greet the newcomers. 'Willi Braun.'

'Good morning. I'm Colm McAreavey and this is my brother Neil.'

'Nice to meet you, Colm and Neil.' Willi smiled and then turned to Daniel, who was running his finger down a list he had written.

'All right,' Daniel said. 'We have a lot on, and so I think I'll go to the Phoenix in Newtownards and finish off the panelling there. Paddy says his customers can't enjoy their pint with the hammering, so I'll hopefully get finished before the thirsty early-morning drinkers arrive.'

The Phoenix was an early morning house, popular with men coming off night shift in the factory there.

Daniel turned to Willi, who was pulling on his overalls. 'So if you can go and price the job up at the doctor's office? Mrs Crossley says they need the waiting room redone but the doctor wasn't sure – you might need to do some negotiations there.' He winked and Willi groaned. Mrs Crossley had notions above her station. They'd redone her drawing room last year, and she nearly broke their hearts with the demands.

'And that leaves the new milking parlour up at Davy Powell's. So maybe if you take the boys up there with you, Erich, we might as well get started with the foundations today.' Daniel ticked off the jobs on the list. 'The site is marked out already, so it's all ready to go. You take the truck because you'll need the picks and shovels, and I'll take the car.' He drained his cup and took the keys of his old Ford off the nail. 'Righto, men, let's get to work.'

Erich drove the truck up the hill out of the village, and as they cleared the brow of the hill, the sea shone azure below them. Neil sat beside him, and Colm took the other window seat. The emerald-green of the fields and the black rocky outcrops, jutting into the sometimes-aqua, often-grey sea created a breathtaking combination of colour, and Erich loved it. The RAF station at Ballyhalbert, which had been an airfield and a hive of activity during the war, was now idle. The entire place was off limits to the public, which always struck Erich as sad.

'That place' – he pointed at the airfield – 'used to be so busy, trucks coming and going day and night when I was a kid. It was so exciting, and we used to name the different planes as they took off and landed.'

Colm observed the area before him but didn't seem as impressed as Erich thought he might be.

'The RAF know how to put on a show right enough,' Colm said.

But Erich heard the note of derision there. To be expected, he supposed. The republican element of Northern Ireland could never see anything laudable in what they called the forces of occupation.

'You were lucky the Jerries didn't decide to blow you all to kingdom come on account of your RAF neighbours, Erich.'

'I suppose we were. There was a bombing raid one night... Well, there were several bombs dropped over the years, but one night in 1941, I think it was, we got a right hammering.' Erich was anxious to stay on their good side. He really liked Róisín, and if he and her brothers got along, then maybe one day she could tell them about him and they wouldn't mind.

CHAPTER 8

*D*ear Bud –

    Erich normally had no bother talking by letter with his American friend. He didn't want to seem rude, but he did need to clear something up before he visited.

Thanks so much for the open invitation. I've been working with Daniel for six years now, and I think I'm entitled to a holiday! The last time I took time off was to come to your wedding. Can you believe that? It's been great, though. We've really built the business up and now it's a proper company.

Now, I just want to say thank you for the offer of an introduction to your cousin Marigold, and while she sounds delightful, I actually have my eye on a girl here. You know that Abigail and I called it a day? She wants to stay in Israel and I don't want to go there, so there was no point in keeping it going. But anyway, I met a girl – well, she got knocked down right in front of me, actually, and I took her to the hospital. Anyway, her name is Róisín, pronounced 'ro-sheen' – yes, it's one of those Irish names – and I think she's smashing.

We've gone to the pictures a few times and for picnics, and she seems to like me too. It's early days and I don't want to rush things, and we're keeping it all a bit hush hush at the moment because her family don't know and her brothers work for us, so it's a bit complicated. The usual rubbish. She's a

Catholic and I'm a Jew – when will people get over this? I had booked to go and visit you before I met her, so I'm still coming if you'll have me, but I'm kind of off the dating market. I'm sure Marigold will find someone much better anyway.

In other news, Liesl is sick a lot nowadays. She looks wretched. Apparently it's normal at the start of pregnancy, but she looks like something the cat dragged in – though of course I didn't say that in case you're recoiling in horror!

She and Jamie are getting their place ready for the new baby, who will be joining us in December, so I can't imagine the size of her bump by the time I get back!

I sail to New York and I can't wait to see it all, so I'm going to spend a few days there before catching the train to Biloxi.

I'll wire you with the exact details as soon as I know. I can't wait to see you and Gabriella and of course meet little Tommy. Imagine you and Liesl, both parents! I can hardly mind myself!

See you soon, Bud.

Erich

HE SEALED the envelope and strolled up the street to the post office. He was in much better form these days, as life was really looking up. He still missed his friends who had gone to Israel, of course, but Colm and Neil were good substitutes. They were great fun, and he enjoyed going fishing after work or having a kickaround on their lunchbreak with them. He wished he could tell them about him and Róisín, but she insisted they wouldn't approve. He thought she was wrong – they liked him and they all got along – but she made him promise not to say a word.

He agreed because he loved spending time with her. She was a cracker. She was so lively and full of fun. She was a year younger than him, but she had all sorts of plans to travel the world, to learn all sorts of things; she even wanted to learn to fly a plane.

She was wonderful. Most girls would hate the idea that he was going off to America on his holidays, but she was all questions and excited about it. He'd even asked her if she'd like to come, but she'd laughed and said her mother and brothers would need to be sedated if they thought she was going into the next county, let alone to America. But she promised him they would go together one day. Her older brother Fiach had been to New York a few years ago and told them all tales of the Big Apple. It was one of the few times she'd mentioned Fiach positively. Erich got the impression that she was afraid of him if anything.

Colm and Neil on the other hand were constantly saving their wages to go and visit Fiach. They'd been twice already since Daniel had taken them on and were due to go again next week.

Róisín was excited for him about the trip and kept asking questions about Bud and Gabriella and the baby and the sorts of things Bud had in his house. Erich explained that he had yet to visit Bud's current house, but that Bud's parents' place, where Erich had stayed when he visited for the wedding, was modest enough. Bud's family were well-to-do, he thought, but they were not ostentatious people. But Róisín would never be convinced that everything American wasn't bigger and better than anything in Ireland.

Her all-time idol was Grace Kelly. She had pictures of her and knew every bit of trivia you could imagine. Erich told her as he kissed her in the car after seeing Spencer Tracy in *Bad Day at Black Rock*, that she reminded him of the actress Anne Francis, and she was delighted, though she said jokingly that he was only saying that to get her to go further than kissing.

She wasn't like other girls; she seemed to enjoy the kissing as much as he did, and if his hands wandered a little, she didn't appear to mind. He loved how other lads admired her – she really was beautiful – but most of all, he loved how she made him laugh.

He popped the letter in the post and whistled as he stuck his hands in his pockets and strode down the street. Jamie came out of the pub and started sweeping the path outside.

'Good morning, Erich. What has you up at this crack of' – Jamie checked his watch – 'eleven o'clock?' It was a running joke that Erich liked to sleep late on his days off.

'I've been up since ten, I'll have you know.' Erich grinned. 'I was just posting a letter to Bud, telling him I've booked my passage.'

'Good for you.' Jamie finished sweeping and started moving barrels out to the footpath to be collected by the brewery and replaced with full ones.

'Want a hand?' Erich asked.

'Never say no.' Jamie passed him an empty beer keg.

'How's my grumpy sister?' Erich asked with a wink.

'I heard that,' Liesl's voice sang out from behind the bar. 'I've just taken some scones out of the oven and I was about to offer you one with a cup of tea, but with that kind of attitude, young Mr Bannon, I think I'll be keeping my scones to myself.'

'Well, you look like you've been going hard at the scones yourself, so maybe I'd be doing you a charity by taking a few off your hands.' Erich winked at Jamie, who stayed out of it.

Jamie was used to the playful banter between his wife and her brother. They were the closest siblings he had ever seen, and Erich, while he loved to tease her, deferred to Liesl in everything. The entire family knew that the best way to get Erich to do anything was to have it come from Liesl. She'd promised her mother as a terrified ten-year-old on the platform of the railway station in Berlin that she would take care of her little brother, and that was a promise that she would keep till her dying breath.

She came out from behind the bar and gave Erich a playful thump on the arm. She barely had any bump at all; in fact, if you didn't know she was expecting, you would never have guessed. She still had a slight limp as a result of the fall, but other than that she looked as she always did – tall, elegant, dark-featured – except there was a paleness to her cheeks and she seemed tired. She was nauseous all the time seemingly. She had brown eyes and hair so dark it looked almost black. At twenty-six, she had grown in poise and grace and was in the eyes of everyone a beautiful, capable young woman.

'So,' Erich said as he followed her up to the flat over the bar, 'are you delighted to be almost on holidays at last?'

She busied herself with the kettle. The aroma of baking permeated the air. The little flat was fine for her and Jamie – it had a bedroom, a kitchen, a bathroom and a little sitting room – but they would need more space once the baby came.

'Oh, I am. The first three months, I was so tired, just bone-weary, and dealing with the lively boys and girls of Ballycreggan does nothing for my energy levels. So it will be lovely to sleep until I wake, no alarm.'

'But it's better now? The tiredness, I mean? That's normal, though, isn't it?' Erich split a currant scone in two and slathered each side with butter and home-made blackberry jam.

She smiled.

He was trying not to be, but he was anxious that everything would be all right with her and the baby.

'Ah, yes. Doctor Crossley says he thinks women should be confined to bed for the first twelve weeks.' She chuckled. 'Could you imagine? The whole place knowing your business before you hardly knew it yourself then?' She turned and called down to the bar, 'Jamie! Do you want a cup of tea?'

'No thanks, love,' he called back. 'I've to get the bar stocked out the back for the dance tonight. I hear there's a right rowdy crowd coming.'

Erich laughed. 'Oh, desperate hellraisers altogether, the cricket crowd.'

'So how's the romance going?' Liesl asked, sitting opposite her brother.

'What romance?' Erich answered innocently.

'Ah, Erich, would you come off it? I know you're seeing someone, so tell me, who is she?' Liesl rested her elbows on the table.

Erich rolled his eyes in exasperation. 'No chance of a private life around here, that's for sure.'

'No. So spill the beans.' Liesl grinned. 'Oh, it's not Daisy Butler, is it?' She made a face. Daisy Butler had had a thing for Erich since she used to put notes in his lunchbox at school.

'It is not Daisy Butler – would you have sense?' He exhaled. 'Look, if I tell you, you must keep it to yourself, all right?'

'All right,' Liesl agreed.

'It's Róisín, Colm and Neil's sister.'

'The two apprentices Daniel took on? How do you know her?' Liesl seemed genuinely taken aback.

Erich quickly told her the story.

'So how come we haven't met her yet?'

'Ah, no reason really, but her family might not take too kindly to her choice, it seems. Her mother and brothers are protective, and we just can't be doing with all the questions. I really like her, though, Liesl. She's so full of life and fun. And she's gorgeous too,' Erich added with a wink.

'I don't doubt it. But, Erich,' she said, her brow furrowed, 'is it because they are protective or because you're Jewish?'

He shrugged and sighed. 'I don't know, nor do I care, to be honest. She wants to travel, so maybe we'll get out of here, live somewhere people aren't obsessed with where you worship or who your family are. I'm sick of it, and so is Róisín. We often talk about it, and we think the same on this.'

'You'd leave here for a girl?' Liesl asked. She knew what Bally-creggan meant to him.

'Maybe.' He sipped his tea. 'I don't know. It's early days, but I wouldn't rule it out. Probably not Israel, but America maybe – who knows?'

Liesl, he knew, would hate for him to leave, but she would always have his best interests at heart.

'Well, don't do anything rash, but I can see you really like this Róisín. As Bridie says, 'What's for you won't go by you.'' Liesl did a wickedly good impression of the Ballycreggan sweetshop owner who had a high-pitched, squeaky voice.

'Well, taking romance advice from the Ballycreggan spinster is probably the level I'm at, all right.' Erich laughed ruefully. Rumour had it that Bridie never had much of an eye for the lads, but she did have a friend, a woman from Portrush, who came to stay three times every year on her holidays. Liesl wondered if there was more to that relationship, but nobody ever asked.

'So tell me more about this Róisín,' Liesl probed.

'Well, she's lovely and great craic, you know? We have a laugh.'

'Is she very religious?' Liesl poured a second cup of tea.

'Not really, I don't think. The family are very republican, hate the British and all of that, but she's not like that.' He shrugged. 'That's why we go to places far away, and she doesn't come here nor do I go to Raggettstown – it's just easier.'

'Erich, look, I know it's not my business, but how long will that last? I know it's hard. Look at Jamie and me. His mother would drive you to distraction, as we all know. But in the end, people will have to accept you or they won't. But skulking around seems like a bad idea. Wouldn't it be better to know for sure? It sounds to me like they might have more reasons than being protective – maybe they won't accept a Jew.'

Erich shot her a look. It was a subject they rarely discussed. She was very interested in the treatment of their people, the events of the war, the State of Israel and the reparations to the Jews, but he just wasn't. He knew his family thought he was a bit head in the sand about it all, but whenever the conversation came around to the war, or the ramifications of it, he either changed the subject or went quiet.

'Maybe not, but maybe she's just telling me the truth, that they are protective,' he replied, on the defensive.

'Well, Catholics are sometimes not that...' – Liesl sought the correct word – 'that understanding of the Jewish situation, and they might have some prejudice, that's all.'

'So again with the Jewish pity.' Erich sighed exasperatedly. 'The persecution, the way we were treated – not just under Hitler, but forever, it seems. Nobody likes us. They blamed us for the plague, Catholic mothers won't want their good girls getting mixed up with a Jew... I'm sick of it, Liesl, sick to the back teeth of the whole thing. It means nothing to me. I was born to my parents, and because my mother happened to be Jewish, here I am stuck in the middle of this conflict that seems to have been going on for centuries, and I never chose any of it.'

He ran his hand through his dark silky hair. 'Honestly, sometimes

I've a good mind to renounce my Jewishness, become whatever – Irish, British, an American, I don't care – anything but this thing, a weight that we are stuck lugging around like a big ball and chain forever.'

Liesl placed her hand on his. 'You don't really mean that, do you?'

'I do, maybe, I don't know.' He sighed. 'Look, when I was a kid, you know, being part of something, that mentality, that siege feeling, that we all need to stick together...I don't know, it was safe or something. But for me – and I'm only thinking this out for myself now – I don't think I need that any more.'

'And what about your faith? Does that mean anything?' Liesl asked gently.

Erich shrugged. 'It's all tied up together, isn't it? Family, community, education, faith. If I reject one aspect, it's like I'm rejecting it all. I don't want to walk away. In fact, staying here, when everyone else left' – he smiled – 'almost everyone, I mean, was an act of me choosing this life, this place, these people. But I just wish it wasn't so much about being Jewish. I just want to be a person, you know? Not a Jewish person, not a survivor, not a Kindertransport child, not the son of a man killed by Nazis – not any of it. I just want to be me, and I feel the weight of it all crushing me down sometimes, the expectation. That's why I like Róisín so much. She asked me about it once, I told her, and we left it at that.'

'But it sounds like she's under just as much weight, with all the Irish republican stuff?'

Erich helped himself to a second scone. 'Yes, she is, but it's her family that are involved with politics, not her.'

'And the oldest brother, Daniel said something about him being in prison in England, is he there for something political? Is he IRA? What's his name?' Liesl asked.

'It's pronounced "fee-ack" but spelled F-I-A-C-H. But you know the way those Irish spellings are. Róisín is the same. It's all a bit mad. She says they do it to confuse the British.' He chuckled at the memory of that conversation, when she'd told him all of her cousins' names, one more complicated-sounding than the next and none of them bearing any relationship in pronunciation to how they were spelled.

'Yes, he was IRA. I'm not sure what he did exactly, but he seems to have connections to some kind of criminal gang here that had links in England. I don't know the details. She didn't say and I don't ask. I do know he pleaded guilty, so they know that he did what he was accused of doing. She's wary of him, but Colm and Neil talk about him like he's some kind of hero, so I don't know.'

'Be careful there, little brother,' Liesl warned.

'There's nothing to be careful of,' Erich retorted, defensive again. 'Róisín is a lovely girl. She's working in a shop in Newtownards, and we talk about good things, nice things, you know? She's funny and interesting and couldn't care less what religion I am, nor could I care what she is. We just like each other.'

'Hey, no need to get all prickly. I want you to be happy, but I just want you to have both eyes open, all right?'

Erich smiled. 'All right. So changing the subject, I posted a letter to Bud.'

'I can't believe you'll have been to America twice and I've never gone.' Liesl placed her hand protectively on her bump. 'And I suppose I'll hardly go now.'

'Maybe when the baby is big enough, you and Jamie could take him or her over there? I know Bud would love to see you – he asks about you all the time. And Gabriella is really nice, and now they'll have little Tommy, so your baby would have a playmate.'

'I'd love it, but I don't know if Jamie could leave the bar for that long. It sounds like a fabulous idea – we could maybe go during the summer holidays from school.'

'Tell you what. If you two want to plan to go next summer, I'll look after the bar for Jamie.'

'You're on.' Liesl smiled.

They chatted amicably for a while, then Erich stood up to leave. He wanted to get some work done at the workshop that afternoon and then back in time to dress up and go to Raggettstown to collect Róisín. He'd gone to Belfast on a shopping spree for his holidays but was going to wear his favourite outfit tonight. It was an electric-blue sports coat in corduroy that had a scarlet lining, with a light-blue linen shirt and navy trousers that tapered slightly and had a cuff at the ankle. The girl in the shop said he looked like a dreamboat, though that could have been for the commission, but he was fairly confident that it was a good look. Róisín loved everything modern, and like him had no patience for tradition and harking back to how things were long ago.

'Right, I've to go to the workshop and fix a door lock that's seized before I go home to spruce myself up for my date, so enjoy your early night and cup of cocoa, grandma.' He chuckled as he kissed the top of Liesl's head.

The conversation with Liesl had made him think, though he wouldn't admit it to her. Was there more to it? If Róisín's family wouldn't support her being involved with a Jew, then where did that leave them? Liesl was right; they couldn't hide forever. Maybe he'd suggest they go to the dance instead of to the pictures in Belfast tonight, bring it all out into the open. They'd have to do it sometime, otherwise what was the point?

CHAPTER 9

$\mathcal{E}$rich strolled across the street to the yard and let himself in. The doorlock that needed fixing was a complicated one and was from the Powells' back door. Mrs Powell had spotted them working on the foundations for the new milking parlour and lured Erich in to look at the lock that had been seized shut for years and years. He wasn't too hopeful but said he'd take it apart and see what could be done.

He changed into overalls and set to work. He'd enjoyed things like this ever since he was a kid and Daniel would let him take things apart just to see how they worked.

The workshop was unusually cluttered; the new furniture for Dr. Crossley's waiting room had arrived and was being stored there until all the decorating was complete. It was comprised of a large velvet sofa in dusty pink – entirely unsuitable in everyone but Mrs Crossley's eyes – and two matching chairs.

He tinkered with the lock for over an hour, and to his immense satisfaction, it now clicked open and closed easily.

Colm and Neil would be happy to hear he got it working. Mrs Powell made the best apple pie, and if they were in her good books, an ample supply could be secured. He ate well – Elizabeth and his *mutti* were both wonderful cooks – but the McAreavey boys always looked hungry. He'd never been into the house, as he dropped and collected Róisín two streets away, but she described a tiny terraced house with no garden, just a yard. Daniel had started bringing enough sandwiches for everyone from home, and Colm and Neil tucked in gratefully every day. They were good workers, quick to learn and enthusiastic. They were great company too, always joking and laughing, and though Neil had been exceptionally quiet at the start, he was beginning to come out of himself a bit more now, and so the workdays flew by. Erich felt awful lying to them, especially when they teased him about girls, saying how they must be all falling for a rich, good-looking fella like him, but he'd promised Róisín he'd keep their relationship a secret.

The brothers had been in Liverpool the previous weekend. They took the boat to Stranraer from Larne, then had a long journey by train to Liverpool, where they visited their brother. They'd told Erich how their mother longed to go too, but it was too expensive. They had decided as a family that it was best for Colm and Neil to go, as they could rough it, sleep on the boat, and see how Fiach was getting on. He was in Walton Gaol in Liverpool so they had a long bus ride on the other side.

The way the boys spoke about their older brother and the way Róisín did were very different. Róisín confided to Erich one evening as they walked to his car after a night at the pictures that since her father died, Fiach had become the man of the family. His word was law and he ruled the family with an iron fist, even from within jail.

The whole family was an odd set-up, but Erich chose not to think about it. Róisín was the best thing that had ever happened to him and that was all he cared about. But now Liesl's words were ringing in his ears. Was she hiding him away because he was a Jew? And if she was, was there any point to continuing their relationship? He knew Róisín wasn't, but if her family were prejudiced against him, could she turn her back on them? Should she? But then the boys couldn't be prejudiced; they worked for three Jews and seemed happy. They never gave the slightest impression they were in any way against Jewish people. If fact, if anything would incense them, it would be her going out with a Protestant or an Englishman. That's where their real hatred lay.

Erich and Róisín rarely discussed it, which in itself was strange. They talked openly about other things, things neither of them ever confided to anyone else.

He'd told her about the time that Daniel was accused in the wrong of being a German spy and faced the death penalty. It pained him to recall those dark days and he rarely discussed them with anyone, but he and Róisín were able to confide in each other. He told her how it was through Elizabeth's tenacity alone that Daniel was released. She uncovered the true spy and found evidence to secure her conviction, thus resulting in Daniel's release, but it had been a close call.

Elizabeth described many years later her feelings at seeing the man she loved in a cell, worn and thin and under the authority of a harsh regime; it had almost broken her heart.

Róisín talked about her father, about how nobody said it – they all made out like it was a random shooting – but her father was in the IRA and wasn't shot by mistake. She told him how her father was violent at home too sometimes, how he beat her mother and how Fiach didn't step in to stop it even when he was old enough. She'd cried in his arms when she said she was glad he was dead and glad Fiach was in jail, and how she wished she'd never have to set eyes on him again.

He thought about the dance tonight. The idea of holding Róisín in his arms as the band played slow waltzes gave him a warm feeling all over. They had planned to go to the pictures, but the dance would be better if he could convince her. And besides, he wanted to prove to Liesl that she was wrong, that Róisín wasn't refusing to be seen with him because he was a Jew. Nobody from her community would be attending the cricket club dance, cricket being a Protestant sport, so there was no chance of her brothers seeing her. Catholics were forbidden from attending social events run by what they called 'foreign sports'. This was much to the disgust of the local Catholic boys he was friends with; they longed to go since the rugby and cricket club dances were not as closely monitored for close dancing as the parish dances held in aid of the new church roof. At those, Father O'Toole was in attendance, and affable as he was, nobody would dare risk even the slightest impropriety. Besides, they always had the local ceili band, so it was all fast tunes, jigs and reels and no opportunity for close dancing.

He remembered the first time he and Simon and a few of the others from the farm had attended the Catholic dance. Both Father O'Toole and Mother Raphael, the principal of the girls' secondary school in Newtownards, had been there. Father O'Toole chatted happily with everyone, but the nun had been beady-eyed and viewed all the male dancers with suspicion, especially seeming to reserve her most searing of stares for the Jews. None of the boys he'd gone with had had the courage to ask anyone up. It wasn't until it was the ladies' choice and Patricia Curran, a girl Erich had known since he arrived in Ballycreggan aged eight, asked him up that he finally got onto the dance floor. As they danced together, a complicated dance involving a lot of hopping around and no touching, the nun approached and slid her cane between him and Patricia, instructing them to 'allow room for the Holy Spirit'.

Patricia had invited him to walk her home that evening, a code for agreeing to a kiss, but Erich declined. The curate, Father McDonald, was well known for roaming the parish after the dance hoping to intercept courting couples in the ditches. And anyway, Patricia was a nice girl but not really his type. She wasn't a stunner like Róisín, nor was she as funny or smart.

Erich did a few other jobs and the hours flew by. He had to order more supplies for the Powells' project, and he checked their supply of paint, making a list of what they needed to stock up on. He then spent a pleasant hour working on the cradle he was making for Liesl's baby. Eventually, he locked up the yard and went home.

He lived mostly at Elizabeth and Daniel's, but he had a room at Ariella and Willi's house too. It was an odd arrangement, he supposed, but when his mother had turned up after all those years, she knew she couldn't uproot him and Liesl, so she settled in Ballycreggan and he and Liesl had two homes.

'Well, hello, stranger.' Elizabeth smiled as he entered the sitting room where she was reading a book.

He bent to kiss her, placing a hand on her shoulder. She placed her hand over his and patted the sofa beside her for him to sit down.

'Daniel is making some sandwiches, as I don't feel like cooking. Would you like one?' she offered as he sat down.

'I would. I'm starving.' He grinned. 'Count me in on the sandwiches, Daniel,' he called to the kitchen. He turned to face Elizabeth. 'So how are you? I called to Liesl. She's so relieved to be on holidays, as the school really took it out of her for the last few months.'

Elizabeth took off her glasses and placed them on her book. 'It really did, but she was such a trooper. She was very nauseous at the start, the poor girl, but hopefully that's passed now. Yes, I'm glad for the break as well. To be honest with you, I'd retire if Liesl wasn't having her baby, but it wouldn't be fair to let her take over the whole thing next year on top of becoming a new mother.'

'I can't imagine you retiring.' Erich smiled. 'You're part of the furniture of that school, and it wouldn't be the same without you.'

'Well, if I am a piece of furniture, I'm an old, battered and creaky one.' She sighed ruefully. 'The thing about schools is that they are ever rejuvenating, new little faces each year, older ones moving on. It's like a river, constantly flowing, and just like the pupils, the staff move on too. Remember when the Morrises retired and we were all wondering how on earth it would go on without them? And you know what? It just did. And I'll be the same.'

'Do you ever think it strange that Liesl settled down here?' Erich wondered. 'After all her education and travelling to Germany and everything? Don't get me wrong, I'm delighted, but I always thought when she went to university and then to Europe that she'd stay and have some big career over there.'

'I think Liesl was looking for something. She had to find where she belonged, and Kurt and all that happened were unfortunately part of that journey. But in the end, she found herself and realised here was where her heart was.'

'I could have told her that.' Erich chuckled.

'I know, we all could have. But some lessons you just need to learn for yourself. Now, how are you doing? I feel like I've hardly seen you all week, as you've all been working so hard. Are you all ready for the big trip to Biloxi?'

'I am,' Erich replied. 'I leave next month, so I want to get as many jobs finished up as I can, though Colm and Neil are doing really well. Neil has a real gift for woodwork. Willi is teaching him, and even he's amazed at how quickly Neil picks it up. And you know how hard it is to get a compliment out of Willi.' Erich chuckled again. 'And Colm is more into the physical lifting, as he's so strong. But to be fair, either one of them is happy to turn their hand to anything.'

Daniel appeared at the door with a tray of coffee and a plate piled high with sandwiches. Erich saw the unspoken conversation pass between him and Elizabeth.

'What is it?' Erich asked. Elizabeth had something on her mind, he knew it. 'If you've something to say, just say it.'

'Well, I know you like the boys,' Elizabeth said, glancing at Daniel again, 'but Daniel overheard them talking, and well, let's just say it was less than complimentary about Jews.'

'What did they say?' Erich was defensive now. He thought of the brothers as his friends – surely they weren't just pretending?

'Look, I'm still mulling it over,' Daniel said. 'They were outside having a smoke, and I happened to be up in the back loft so I could hear them. They were just joking, I think, but they talked about how we deserved our reputation for being tight and how we'd always do well no matter what the situation, the implication being that Jews will always survive because we exploit others, that sort of thing. The usual claptrap.'

Erich was shocked. Daniel would not embellish a story, so if he was saying it, it must be true. But Colm and Neil seemed so nice, and it felt great to have some friends again; he just couldn't imagine them saying things like that.

'So what are you going to do?' Erich asked quietly. He knew dismissing them was the obvious and probably only option.

'Well, I only took them on because Father O'Toole asked me to.

He's a relative of their mother's, I think, and she was worried about her sons going the way of their older brother. And as you know, finding apprentices was proving difficult. They're good workers, they're polite to the customers, and I can't fault them, but if that's the way they see us, then maybe we'd be better off without them.' Daniel sighed. 'It's nothing I haven't heard a hundred times before, but it's unfortunate.'

'It is, and that sort of thing is unforgivable. I certainly don't want you two or Willi working with people who hold such opinions, but I would say this,' Elizabeth interjected. 'I grew up in the Catholic Church. I don't have anything to do with any churches now, as you know, but I do know there is a blatant, almost inherent anti-Semitism within it. Those boys may truly dislike Jews, I don't know, but I heard so much anti-Jewish stuff as a child – anti-everything that wasn't Catholic, to be honest with you. And as you know, my mother didn't speak to me ever again once I married Rudi just because he was Jewish, and she wasn't the exception. So maybe they are just parroting what they've heard all their lives. It doesn't excuse it, but it might explain it.'

Daniel nodded. 'You might be right.' He turned to Erich. 'You know them better than we do. What do you think?'

Erich was torn. Of course he didn't want to be around people who hated him because of who he was, but he equally didn't want this defi-nition, his religion, complicating everything once again. It was back to what he'd said to Liesl. He could never tell anyone else, they wouldn't understand, but everywhere he went, every development in his life seemed to be through the lens of his faith, and it bothered him more than he ever let on.

'I don't know. I'm shocked, though. We always seemed to get along so well, and I never got the impression they were like that. But as you say...'

He tried not to be so sensitive as to imagine every slight as being because he was Jewish, but after all that had happened it was hard not to.

'So you think I should let them go?' Daniel asked.

71

'Well, maybe, but how about we wait until I get back from America at least? We need them until then. But after that we'll have to see.' He stood up, drained his cup and placed it on the tray. 'I better go and get ready.'

As he showered and shaved, he made his decision. He would have to ask Róisín out straight and demand she either make their relationship public or it was over. If she was secretly like her brothers and ashamed of his Jewishness the sooner he found out the better.

CHAPTER 10

*R*óisín kept up the chatter on the drive from Raggettstown. Erich pulled in before the turnoff for Ballycreggan.

'What's all this for?' She grinned, thinking he was going to kiss her.

Instead he turned and summoned all of his courage. This might be the conversation that ended the best relationship he'd ever had, but it had to be said. 'I want to go to the dance in Ballycreggan tonight, the cricket club one in the hall behind my brother-in-law's pub. Will you come with me?' He paused, then added meaningfully, 'As my girlfriend?'

'Ah, Erich, we can't – you know that. I explained... My brothers are so protective of me, they don't want me seeing anyone and –'

She looked distressed but he had to go on. 'Anyone? Or a Jew?' The words hung between them.

'Of course it's not that. You know it's not. It's just easier this way. We get to do what we want without everyone sticking their beaks into our business...'

Erich turned and faced forward, his eyes fixed on the empty road ahead. 'It's not easier for me. I'm tired of sneaking around, Ró, feeling like I'm some dirty secret. I am really proud that you're my girl, and I want the whole world to know it. I want to introduce you to my family, my friends, the whole lot. But if you can't do that, then there's no point in us continuing.' He hated saying the words, but he had no options.

'Erich, please, don't be like this. I love you – you know I do…' She was crying now.

'I love you too,' he said quietly. 'But either we are open and honest or we're finished.'

'But you know my brothers, how they are. They hate everyone not exactly like them. Remember I told you about Mei-Ling? The Chinese girl whose family had the laundry at the bottom of our street in Belfast? They wouldn't let me play with her because she was Chinese. They would not let us have a minute's peace, so they wouldn't, and she was just a wee girl like me.' she said earnestly.

'So we go somewhere else,' Erich heard himself say. He loved this girl enough to leave the village and the family. 'It's a big world. We could leave and start a new life.'

'You'd do that for me?' She sounded incredulous. He'd told her about Abigail and why he didn't want to go to Israel. 'Leave everything?'

'If you were willing to be open about us, then yeah, I would.' He turned to face her again. 'So will you come to the dance with me, as my girl?'

A single tear slid down her cheek. She just nodded.

He drove in silence, her hand in his resting on his knee. He pulled up outside the pub – the dance hall was at the back – and went around to help her out. She looked stunning in a red silk dress that clung to her curves and black patent high-heeled shoes. Her blonde hair shone, and she wore a little make-up, just enough to accentuate her full red lips and unusual eyes. She turned heads wherever she went.

He could sense her nervousness. She linked his arm as he paid for them to get into the dance and waited patiently in the darkest corner of the hall while he got them some drinks. The dance had a soft-drink bar only, but he snuck into Jamie's bar and got a little nip of gin for each of them to put in their lemonade.

'Are you trying to get me drunk now as well as killed, Erich Bannon?' Róisín managed a smile as she took her first sip.

'Just taking the edge off.' He kissed her ear. He put their drinks down and her hand snuck into his as he led her to the dance floor. Jamie had astounded everyone by arranging for the Clipper Carlton, the showband from Strabane, to play. They were much sought after, even in England, so once word got out, the hall was packed to the rafters. The band were playing 'Rock Around the Clock' with gusto as Erich and Róisín joined the heaving crowds, but then the tempo changed and the unmistakable opening riff of 'Unchained Melody' filled the hall.

Róisín glanced left and right, rigid in his arms.

'Relax,' he murmured in her ear. 'It's going to be all right. Nothing can happen. I'm here.'

She gazed into his eyes, her arms snaking around his neck, a move that would have had the Reverend Mother in a state of apoplexy had it been a church dance. He responded by encircling her slender waist and drawing her close to him. As they danced, he could feel her breath on his cheek.

'I love you,' she whispered in his ear.

The band went on to do three or four slow numbers, and Erich and Róisín never let each other go. Slowly she relaxed against him, her fear at being seen dissipating. She responded to him as his hands slid downwards, masked by all the crowds, to caress her bottom, moving her body even closer to his.

As the last notes of 'Mona Lisa' drew to a close and the band turned up the temp again with 'Shake, Rattle and Roll', Róisín suddenly froze. 'We have to go,' she said. She dragged him off the dance floor and out the back door.

'What is it? What's wrong?' he asked once they were outside.

'Bobby Craven was in there – he works for Fiach. I don't think he saw me, but he could have…' She could barely get the words out.

'So what if he did?' Erich replied calmly. 'It's not his business, Ró. You're a grown woman, and you can see who you like. Look, it will be a five-minute wonder. I'll go round to your house if you like, talk to

Colm and Neil, your mother, whatever, convince them that my intentions are pure and that you'll be fine.' He lifted her chin and bent his head to kiss her. As always, she responded, kissing him back passionately.

'You're right,' she whispered. 'I just need to stand up to them.'

'And I'll be right beside you.' He wrapped her in his arms.

'Can we go somewhere, just the two of us?' she asked.

He looked at her and saw the longing in her eyes, knowing it was reflected in his. Without a word, he took her hand and led her out through the barrel yard and into the lane behind the main street of Ballycreggan. He glanced up at the window of Jamie and Liesl's bedroom, but there was no light. Liesl had mentioned she was going to sleep at Ariella and Willi's tonight, knowing the dance would be noisy.

He put his finger to his lips and led her over the rough ground at the back of the pub. The track was only used for deliveries, and there were a few old cars parked there too. Under the starlit summer night, they picked their way until they were at the back of the builders' yard. Erich reached in his pocket for his key and fumbled until he found the one to open the back gate. He cursed that he'd never oiled the gate, as it creaked loudly when he pushed it.

He didn't want to risk waking Bridie, whose sweetshop was next door, so he left the gate open. They crossed the open-air yard, where lumber and machinery were stored neatly, and opened the door into the workshop. The large pink sofa destined for the doctor's waiting room looked inviting, and Erich led Róisín towards it.

'We don't have to –' he began, but she stopped him with a kiss.

Within moments she'd removed his jacket and pulled his shirt from his waistband, slipping it off his shoulders. Erich exhaled with desire as she ran her hands over his chest and back. In one move she pulled her dress over her head. She stood before him in her underwear, a teasing smile on her lips. He went to take her in his arms once more, but she wagged her finger admonishingly. 'No, you must watch the whole show first.' She giggled.

Erich lay back on the couch as she slowly removed all of her clothes. She was so beautiful. He'd never seen a woman naked before, in the flesh. Of course there were the magazines he and his friends had seen – someone had an older brother in the army and he'd nicked the magazines from him – but nothing could prepare him for the sheer beauty of this girl. Her skin was alabaster white, and her small pert breasts entranced him. She took the lead, and for a second he wondered if he was not her first, but then he instantly dismissed the thought. What did it matter? She was his now. As he took her in his arms and made love to her, he felt like nothing could ever go wrong in the world again.

Afterwards, with his jacket and a length of upholstery fabric that was being used for the new bar seats in Jamie's over them both, she lay with her head on his chest as he stroked her hair.

'That was my first time,' he admitted.

'Mine too,' she replied.

'Did it hurt? Like, I wasn't sure…'

'No, it was lovely.' She kissed his chest. 'You're lovely.'

* * *

ERICH WOKE to a loud banging on the workshop door and men's voices. He shook Róisín and jumped up, dragging his trousers on as she pulled her dress over her head. Within a minute, the door was broken down and Colm and Neil burst in.

'Get your filthy Jewboy hands off my sister!' Colm yelled as he shoved Erich in the chest, forcing him backwards. 'What the hell do you think you're doing?' His voice was low and threatening.

'Colm, I… What are you doing here?' Erich asked. 'Look, we can talk about th –'

Before Erich could finish the sentence, Colm smashed his fist into Erich's mouth.

'Colm! Stop!' Róisín screamed, but her brother turned on her then, slapping her hard across the face, sending her reeling.

'Get dressed, you dirty little tramp. I didn't believe Bobby when he told me, but he was right. Here you are, my sister, the Jewman's wee tart? I'm disgraced of you. Just you wait till Fiach hears about this,' he spat, grabbing Róisín by her hair. 'Get her out of here,' he barked at Neil, who was trying to calm Róisín down.

'Leave her alone!' Erich bellowed, running at Colm, punching him hard in the stomach. Colm was winded, but as he recovered, Neil grabbed Erich from behind and held him as Colm landed blow after blow. The last sound Erich heard was Róisín's screams.

CHAPTER 11

*W*as he dreaming, or was someone praying over him, chanting the familiar prayers of his childhood? The world slowly came into focus, though it was blurry. Erich tried to open his eyes, but the light was searing so he shut them again. He could hear voices. He tried to move, but even the smallest movement seemed impossible.

'Ah, you are awake. Welcome back.'

Erich recognised the voice – at least he thought he did. There was another voice, a woman, then a hand on his forehead. He could make out snatches of conversation. The male voice was deeper, and the female seemed to need something urgently. The light, even through his closed eyelids, made his head hurt. He tried to speak but nothing came out. He was horribly thirsty and needed a drink, but how to tell these people eluded him. He tried to speak again but made a croaky sound.

'Oh, darling, I'm so glad you're back. We were so worried.' That hand holding his made him feel like he was all right. A sponge or something wet was mercifully placed in his mouth. He tried to swallow but couldn't. The water that dripped into his mouth was cool and welcome. He could sleep again now.

The next time he woke, the light was gone and there were no voices, just a faint humming noise. Was he alone now? He opened his eyes but couldn't focus in the dark. He tried to sit up, but a searing pain in his back stopped him. Where was he? What had happened? His brain felt muggy; his thoughts were nebulous and fleeting. It was like understanding was just beyond him, only barely beyond reach but still too far to grasp.

'Oh, Erich.' A voice, gentle, soft. 'I'm so sorry. This is all my fault...'

Who was there? He opened his eyes again and this time turned his head to the right. He could make out someone with dark hair. He opened his mouth to speak, but she placed her hand on his head.

'Don't try to talk. The doctor said you're going to be fine. You just need to rest.'

Why did he need a doctor? What had happened?

It was bright again, the light permeating his eyelids once more. There were people around him, all talking. He could hear them more clearly now, but it was still hard to focus.

'He's doing well. We're keeping him semi-sedated now, just to allow him to rest and recover, but I think we'll reduce the dosage of sedative from today. His kidney is bruised but thankfully not ruptured, and there is no lasting damage to his spine. Internally, I'm happy there is no bleeding, and so while he looks bad, I know, his injuries will heal with a bit of rest and care.'

'Should we take him home?' Elizabeth's voice.

'Well, not for a few days yet. We'll need to ensure he's got pain management under control. Incredibly, only two ribs are broken, but there's a lot of soft tissue damage to his face and I want to be a hundred percent sure there is no damage to his kidneys. So as I said, we'll allow the swelling to reduce a little more, but I would think all being well, you can take him home towards the end of the week.'

'Thank you, Doctor.' His *mutti*. Knowing she and Elizabeth were both there made him relax.

'The police will need to talk to him. They've been asking when he'll be able to speak to them.' Daniel.

'Yes, I would imagine they would. Do they have any idea who did this?'

'We know.' Daniel's tone was hard to distinguish.

Who had done this? A flash of memory. Blows, a punch, a kick... and then nothing. Someone had attacked him.

He opened his eyes, keeping them open now, despite the brightness.

'Close the blinds.' Another voice. 'His eyes will be sensitive now.'

The room was plunged into gloom, and Erich found he could keep his eyes open. His mother's face was only inches from his. 'Oh, darling, thank God. I... How are you, my love?'

Erich couldn't speak but nodded. He was so thirsty. A nurse or possibly a nun in a white uniform and starched veil put a cup to his lips, and he drank greedily. It felt like his thirst would never be slaked. Long before he was ready, she took it away.

'I know you're thirsty, but we need to take it slowly.' She took his temperature and his blood pressure, then turned to Ariella and Elizabeth. 'You can give him sips of water but not a huge amount at once because it might make him nauseous. We'll be bringing this fine young man back to the land of the living slowly.' She smiled at him as she replaced the thermometer in the glass receptacle on the wall.

She left and Erich tried to sit up, but his body just wouldn't do what he wanted it to.

'Shush now,' Elizabeth soothed him. 'You're going to be fine – you heard the doctor – but you need to take it easy for a while, give your body a chance to heal.'

He tried to sit up again, and this time Daniel helped. Every part of him hurt, but they managed to set the back of the bed at an angle that he could rest against it, pillows propped behind him.

'Erich, I know you're still feeling bad, but can you tell us anything about what happened? We know it was the McAreaveys. They were seen around the village that night and they've not shown up for work. But why?' Daniel's face was creased with concern.

Through Erich's foggy brain, something told him not to say

anything. He couldn't anyway; it felt like his tongue was too fat for his mouth, and he couldn't form words.

'Leave it, Daniel,' Elizabeth admonished, and cast her husband a warning glance. 'He can explain when he's well enough, but for now he just needs rest.'

Daniel's back was to the bed now, his hands in his pockets as he stared out the hospital ward window. Erich knew by the stance of the man he loved every bit as much as he'd loved his father, Peter Bannon, that he was furious.

'It's all right, Erich. You'll be fine,' his *mutti* soothed as she cast a glance at Daniel's back. 'Would you like another little drink?'

He nodded, and she held the cup to his lips. He took as long a drink as he could before she took it away. At least now his mouth was feeling a bit more normal. He tried to smile but his face hurt too much.

'Are you comfortable?' Elizabeth asked.

'Yes,' he managed, though he was far from it. His back ached and it hurt to speak. 'What's the damage?' he rasped, his voice sounding alien to his own ears.

His mother and Elizabeth shared a glance.

'Tell me,' he demanded.

'You have a bruised kidney,' Ariella explained, 'and quite a lot of swelling to your lower back. You have two broken ribs, and your face is a bit the worse for wear. It looks bad, but it will be fine. The doctor is sure there is no long-term damage.'

Erich relaxed. Neither Elizabeth nor his mother would ever lie to him.

'They are giving you drugs to keep you drowsy' – Elizabeth took his hand – 'so you won't move about too much as you heal. That's why you feel so groggy – it's nothing to do with your injuries.'

He drifted off to sleep again.

It was dark when he woke. This time was not like the others. He was wide awake, and the pain in his body was intense. His muscles screamed for release. He tried to get up to move into a more comfortable position, but the movement caused him to gasp in pain.

It was clearer now – the night with Róisín, falling asleep, Colm and Neil coming in and finding them. He wouldn't confirm it to the police, though, as that would only make matters worse for her. He wouldn't press charges. If he said he couldn't remember, then at least maybe they wouldn't take it out on her.

Had she been to see him? He had no idea. He hoped so.

Bit by bit, the events of that night came back to him. The conversation in the car, the dance, her terror at seeing this Bobby someone, them alone together in the workshop. And then she was crying and screaming. Erich tried to stop them hurting her, and then Colm hit him. The next thing he remembered was waking up in the hospital. What day was it? When did that all happen? Time had lost all meaning.

CHAPTER 12

*E*rich sat in the armchair in the living room. A book was open in front of him, but none of the words were sinking in. He'd been home a few days and he'd heard nothing from Róisín. He longed to ask if she'd called or written, but he knew if she had, they'd have mentioned it. Liesl told him that she'd filled the parents in on his romance and her advice. She felt responsible since she was the one who had told him to make their relationship public. He hadn't confirmed the reason for the beating, but he was sure they could guess, and despite everyone wanting him to talk to the police and point the finger at her brothers, he wasn't going to do that. If he had any hope of seeing her again, he would have to stick to the line that he couldn't remember.

Daniel appeared at the door, a cup of coffee in his hand, and passed it to Erich. He'd been around the house more often than usual, which frustrated Erich. He knew it was because Daniel was worried about him, but they were down to three men again with the business, so he wished Daniel would focus on that and take the spotlight off him.

'Elizabeth thinks I shouldn't be pressing you, but I just don't believe you have no idea who did it.' Daniel was agitated. 'I think you're protecting Colm and Neil, though I can't for the life of me figure out why. Look what they did to you, Erich.'

Erich shrugged. 'I've tried – I just don't remember. I won't accuse someone unless I'm sure, and I'm not.'

Daniel fixed him with a gaze. Erich dropped his eyes first.

'Remember that time when you were about ten and you and Simon broke into Father O'Toole's glasshouse and ate all his strawberries?' Daniel kept his voice light.

'I do. And Mrs O'Hanlon went up to the rabbi and told on us.'

'She did, and Rabbi Frank called me and asked me to ask you if you'd done it. You and Simon were the guiltiest-looking pair of criminals I'd ever seen in my life, but you both swore blind it wasn't you.'

Erich smiled.

'I think Mrs O'Hanlon wanted me to give you a beating, but I could never do that. So I told her that I was dealing with it but that I would do it my own way. The rabbi got very angry with Simon and he was punished for stealing and for lying about it, but I just accepted what you said and sent you to bed. I said I would always believe you if you promised me that you were telling the truth, and you swore that you were. And do you remember what happened that night?' Erich could see from Daniel's face that this wasn't just a friendly chat.

'I do.' Erich gazed into the fireplace.

'You were so racked with guilt, you came into our bedroom at around two in the morning, in tears, confessing everything.'

Erich nodded. 'I had to cut the priest's grass with that rusty old mower every week for the whole summer as a punishment.'

Daniel smiled. 'You did, though I did sharpen the blades without you knowing after the first time.'

'Thanks for that.' Erich smiled ruefully.

'You know where this is going, don't you?'

Silence hung between them.

'I can't, Daniel. I would tell you if I could, but I can't.' Erich winced as he moved on the chair.

'Why can't you?' Daniel probed. At least Erich was admitting he was lying. 'Is it to do with Róisín? Are you trying to protect her?'

'Look, Daniel, I just can't remember, all right?' Erich stood up painfully. 'Now, can we change the subject?'

'No, Erich, we can't. Someone did this to you. I find you in a pool of blood in the workshop and no sign of our two apprentices, who happen to be the brothers of a girl you were seeing without telling anyone, and you refuse to explain what happened?' Erich could hear that Daniel was getting frustrated now.

'Please, just leave it, all right? It's nothing. I'm fine. A bit bruised and battered but all right. It's nothing to do with Róisín. She's a lovely girl and I really like her, more than I've ever liked anyone actually, and it will all be fine.'

'Erich, I –' Daniel wasn't having it.

Erich cut across him. 'Daniel, please. I need to get my life back to normal, and I won't even have a job if you don't go back and take care of the business. I don't need you here all day fussing over me – I have Elizabeth and *Mutti* for that.' He smiled though his face hurt. 'Please, go and hire someone to replace the McAreaveys at least and keep everything going. I'll be fine. I promise.'

Just then, the doorbell rang, and Elizabeth answered it. It was the postman.

'It's for you,' Elizabeth said as she entered the dining room. She handed Erich an envelope, a look passing between her and Daniel as she did so.

'Thank you.' Erich took it and waited until they both left before opening it.

Dear Erich,

I'm sorry how everything turned out. I never meant for that to happen. I hope you feel better soon. I think it's best if we don't see each other any more. It would never have worked anyway – we both knew that deep down – but it was fun while it lasted.

I'm actually getting close with a lad from near where I grew up. He's more my type, if I'm honest.

Best of luck,

Róisín

The pain of his injuries paled into insignificance. It was as if someone had kicked him in the gut. How could she say something like this? She'd said she loved him, she talked about them going away together, and now she acted as if they were nothing more than a silly fling?

He read the letter over and over. He actually felt like he might vomit. He had been sure she didn't come to see him because her brothers wouldn't allow it, but that she could just dump him so callously... How could she?

He crumpled the sheet of paper in his fist, refusing to allow the tears that formed to fall. He blinked furiously.

'Erich, are you all right?' Elizabeth was hovering.

'For God's sake, can I not get one second's peace?' he roared at her, for the first time in his life. 'Can everyone just get out of my life?'

He dragged himself out of the chair and up the stairs to his bedroom, where he slammed the door. Only then did he allow himself to cry.

* * *

ERICH HOBBLED DOWNSTAIRS the following morning after a fitful night's sleep.

Elizabeth was making porridge as Daniel read the paper. Neither one spoke as he entered the room.

'Elizabeth, I'm so sorry. I...I was upset and took it out on you. I should never have done that.' He hated that he'd hurt her, this woman who had never been anything but kind.

She turned and embraced him, taking care not to squeeze too hard.

Daniel looked up from the paper and gave him half a smile. 'So will you tell us now what is going on?' he asked, folding the paper and placing it on the table.

'I... Look, I just need to get away, get my head straight, you know? It's been a difficult time. I promise when I get back from America –'

'What?' Daniel interrupted incredulously. 'You're not going to

America now? Erich, that's insane! It's only two weeks away and look at the state of you! Absolutely not, no way.'

Erich stood in front of him, facing him. 'Daniel, you know I respect you and I'm so grateful for all you do, but I'm not a ten-year-old kid any more. I'm a grown man, and I'm going to America, simple as that. You and *Mutti* and Elizabeth and Liesl and whoever else you want to join the committee for the management of Erich can say what you want, but I'm going.' He took a slice of toast from the rack. 'Now, I need to go and see my sister.'

CHAPTER 13

*R*abbi David Frank read the letter again.

Dear Rabbi Frank,

I hope this letter finds you well. I have this morning reviewed the results of the tests we conducted last week, and I'm sorry to say that while the drug mechlorethamine did not have as profound an effect as we had hoped, I have grounds for optimism nonetheless. The tumour in your colon appears to be at a similar size to what it was three months ago, which would suggest to me that after an initial growth spurt, the progress of your cancer seems to have slowed, which is a bit of good news.

I know you said you would rather communicate by letter as the journey to the hospital here in Belfast is arduous, but I do feel it might be of benefit for you to come to see me so we can discuss your care henceforth.

Yours faithfully,

Dr Alan Perrin

The rabbi put the letter down and took off his glasses, pinching the top of his nose to ease the stress headache he could feel building. So this was it. This was how it would end. He didn't believe the doctor's optimism for one second; he knew it was the final act.

He sat back in his chair, listening to Frau Braun on the telephone talking to a contact she had in Germany. One of the children who'd returned to her family was deeply unhappy there and had written to the rabbi in secret, begging to be allowed to return to Ballycreggan. Sophie Hart was only eighteen months old when she arrived on the Kindertransport, a tiny little thing, and she'd grown up happy and strong on the farm. Her aunt had emerged in 1947, having survived Buchenwald, and offered Sophie a home with her. That was fine, and Sophie and the aunt got along well, but when the woman remarried, Sophie disliked the man intensely. The aunt had died in a road accident a few months ago, and Sophie was in the house with him alone, so the rabbi and Frau Braun were determined to help. She was almost seventeen years old but she needed rescuing, and he was determined to do it. The contact Frau Braun was talking to lived not too far from the town where Sophie lived, so she was going to ask him to go by there and speak to her. Sophie had another cousin near Nuremberg, a young woman in her twenties with two little children, and she'd said Sophie could come to her, so that was an option.

He folded the letter and placed it in the drawer. Only yesterday he and Frau Braun had had the conversation he'd been dreading. She'd come into his office and in her normal brusque tones offered him a room at her house. She was apparently buying the late Mrs Thomas's house; the town librarian had died last winter, and her two-bedroomed terraced house on the main street of the village was up for sale.

He had to admit the prospect of ending his days in a warm cosy house, in the company of such a fine woman, was tempting. The farm was draughty and cold in the winter, and more than that, it made him melancholy to walk around, reminiscing on the happiest time in his life, when the voices of children rang out, bright and hopeful. He thanked God every day for His mercy and goodness, for sparing him the camps, not because he was afraid to die but because his deliverance from Germany meant he could do important work with the children of the Kindertransport.

Growing up the only child of a taciturn and silent father, himself a rabbi, was a lonely life. His mother died when he was four years old, and he barely remembered her. He'd studied diligently, and when the time came, he became a rabbi. It was expected and no alternative was ever discussed, but he was happy in his life. When his father said there was a girl who was to be his wife, a daughter of the prestigious Bayer family, he was nervous and overjoyed. He knew exactly who his father meant, as he'd seen those girls before. One was very pretty. The other was plain, so he hoped it was the pretty one but dared not ask his father. The Bayers were devout Jews and attended his father's synagogue weekly.

He would never forget the day the shadchan brought him and his father to the Bayer house, a large ivy-covered mansion in the Charlottenburg area of Berlin. He was twenty-one years old and had never been so nervous. He was not used to talking to girls, in fact he had hardly ever spoken to any, and he had no idea what to say. His father had given the cryptic instruction to 'do as was expected of him'. He had no idea what that would mean and was too terrified to ask.

He was led from the front door into the fanciest hallway he'd ever seen, then into an equally ornate parlour. He'd tried to hide his disappointment. It was the plain one, Marta, that they had chosen for him. She was plump, with mousey hair and a broad nose, and her eyes barely met his even once as she sat between her parents.

The next time they met was before the rabbi as they married. To his astonishment, Marta proved to be a lovely wife. She was funny and gentle, and together they learned how to be married. He also learned how difficult and spoiled the pretty sister was, making her husband's life a misery with her constant demands and complaining, and he realised he'd definitely got the best end of the bargain. Marta grew in beauty in his eyes, and he would never forget the night she told him they were going to have a child. But it was not to be. His beloved Marta died from some complication of the pregnancy that was never fully explained to him – men were not to know such things – and so did their child. He thought he would die himself of the grief, not that anyone knew. He was a rabbi by then, with his own synagogue, and publicly he accepted his loss stoically. But each night, as he lay in their bed alone, he cried and demanded of God why He would have done such a wicked thing as taking his beloved Marta.

Would they have survived? Did her premature death and that of his son or daughter save them from a worse fate? He could never know for sure, but the thought gave him some comfort many years later.

He'd not been raised with the concept of love – it was not ever mentioned – but he knew, deep in his heart, that once before in his life, he'd been loved and had loved well in return. He'd never imagined that his life would take the turn it had, but he was grateful for it. The children of the Kindertransport who found themselves in this obscure corner of Northern Ireland had become his children, and he loved each and every one of them. And now they were gone, grown up, moving on with their lives, and he wished them joy and love and peace. And like any father, he worried about them. He hated to think of Sophie alone in a house with that man, or Charlie getting into all sorts of trouble with the law in London, or Benjamin Krantz, who had returned to Prague to be with his family but who was injured in a farming accident and was now disabled as a result. Likewise, his heart burst with pride when he got a photograph from Viola and Ben of their new baby, Paul, or he learned of the wedding of her sister, Anika, to an Israeli man called Samuel Guildenstern. Those children who'd spent the war years in Ballycreggan, safe and protected from the horrors of National Socialism, were his life and they always would be.

But for some reason he wanted to talk about Marta today. People knew he'd been married, that his wife died, but that was all he ever said. Now that he was facing his own end, something compelled him to speak her name.

Frau Braun finished her call. Things had been awkward since the conversation yesterday when he politely and with gratitude declined her offer.

He rose, the effort taking more out of him than it used to, and walked to her in the next room. He tried to walk every day, just a little, because though the effort required was greater with each passing day, he loved this land, the green lushness of it, the cool morning air, the gentle birdsong and, sometimes, if one listened closely, the crashing of the waves on the seashore half a mile away.

'Will you join me for a walk?' he asked as she looked up.

'Where?' she snapped. She was clearly still annoyed with him, and he felt terrible. She was a proud woman who'd shown such strength of character, and to ask him to move into her house would have been very difficult for her. She had built sturdy walls around herself to protect her feelings and had let them down for him, only to be rebuffed. No wonder she was snappy.

'Along the corner field?' He smiled. 'Please, Katerin?'

In public he called her Frau Braun, but sometimes when they were alone, he used her first name, and this was one of those times. She never called him anything. She knew his name was David, but he'd not been called that for so many years. His father rarely addressed him, and to everyone in Ballycreggan, he was just 'the rabbi'. The only person who called him David was gone to heaven long ago.

'Why?' She wasn't melting.

'Because it is a lovely day, because I am sad that I hurt you yesterday and because I want to talk to you about my wife, Marta.'

Frau Braun stopped rifling through the bunch of papers on her desk and stood up, making for the door. She took her cardigan from the hook and stood in the doorway waiting. 'Well, come on if you're coming,' she said.

They walked in silence as he tried to find the words. The truth was, this former Nazi's widow, a German who lived through that time when Jews were rounded up like dogs and placed on trains to be slaughtered inhumanely, was his closest friend. He was comfortable with the community here in Ballycreggan, and the Liebers included him in every family occasion and he was incredibly fond of them all, but Katerin Braun was special. She was thin and bony, and every one of her sixty-two years was there on her face for all to see. She'd been beautiful once, he could tell, but there was nothing left of the soft and gentle girl he thought she must once have been, at least externally. But inside, despite her gruff and often abrupt manner, she was good and kind and generous.

'The first thing I want to say is I am sorry,' he began as they walked side by side through the meadow that had once been full of cattle that provided milk for the children. 'You made me a generous offer, and I didn't respond properly. I said no, not because I don't want to share a home with you, but because I don't want you to have the burden of my care.'

She opened her mouth to object, but he silenced her with a raise of his hand. 'I am sixty-eight years old, and I am dying. The drug didn't work. Yes, I tried it.' He smiled. She'd been most vocal on the subject when he said he wasn't going to. 'It didn't work. So that's it. They have tried, but my time is up.' He shrugged. 'I got much longer than most, and I was able to help in a way I could never have done before Hitler, so...'

'I...' Her voice had lost its hard edge. 'Is there nothing else to try?'

He shook his head. 'I don't know. I doubt I will ask. The doctor says he has reasons to feel optimistic, but that's just what they say. He did say the tumour seems to have slowed down growing.'

'How long, do you think?' she asked.

'I don't know, but it doesn't matter, Katerin. I'm ready.' And he found he was telling the truth. He was ready to die.

'Tell me about Marta.' Her voice was barely audible.

He smiled. 'You and she would have got along well – she liked to tell me off too.' He chuckled. 'But she loved me and I loved her. She was always baking, and she would then moan about how plump she was and that I could eat her *lekach* forever and never gain a pound. She was crazy about animals too. I told her I didn't want a pet in the apartment, but one day she said she was walking by the river and a man was about to drown a bag of kittens so she had to take them home. So we had cats, and they loved her. They would curl around her in the kitchen, and in time I got to like them too. We were an arranged match, of course, and I thought I would have preferred her sister, Lena, but oh, she just *kvetch* all day long. Her poor husband, *oy veh ist mir*– he was a broken man from listening to her.'

Frau Braun smiled. Though she had no Yiddish, she knew what he meant.

'But Marta was so sweet. And you know, we were worried, because when we got married, neither of us had a clue about what happened in marriage, you know? Nobody told her, and certainly nobody told me. There was a Torah class for men about marriage, but the melammed, the teacher, didn't say anything specific, so Marta and I had to learn together. Month after month, nothing happened, no baby on the way, and I thought maybe we were doing it wrong. Then her mother came and gave her a talking to, explaining what to do. Poor Marta was so embarrassed, but she confirmed we were doing it right. And then one day, she told me that she was pregnant. Oh, the joy! But we couldn't rejoice too much. My father was happy, I think, but he never said so, and to be delighted as we were would be a source of *shanda* – shame – to him. So we watched in awe as her belly swelled with our child, and we waited for him or her to arrive. She said how she loved it, being pregnant, because for the first time, she was allowed to be fat. But I said she was never fat to me, that she was always lovely.'

'We are never happy,' Frau Braun said with a sad smile. 'I always thought I was too thin, no curves, just up and down. Women are never happy.'

'Well like she was not too fat, you are not too thin, but Marta was happy then, those months. And then one day I came home, a few weeks before the child was to be born, and she was gone. Her father came, told me she was in the hospital. I rushed there, but it was too late, she was gone, and the baby too. He or she was too small to be born, so they died in their mother's body. And I lost them both.'

'What happened to her?' Frau Braun asked.

'I don't know exactly. Something to do with the pregnancy, but they didn't tell me. To be honest, I was so heartbroken that I didn't want to talk to anyone or hear anything. I wanted to die and to lie beside her and our child forever.'

'That's terrible.' Frau Braun sat on a stone wall, and the rabbi sat beside her.

'Yes, terrible,' he agreed.

'But you had love once, and that's a good thing. It's something I never had.' She sighed heavily.

'I did, and she was perfect for me. Did you ever have feelings for your husband? Just because he was a Nazi doesn't mean he didn't have some good points, you know. It's all right to tell me you loved him if you did.'

'No.' Frau Braun kept her gaze on the horizon. 'He humiliated and abused me for all of our marriage. I wasn't pretty like my sisters, and I thought he loved me. In the early days, I was so proud of him. He was so handsome and all the girls wanted him for themselves, but I got him. I didn't realise, fool that I was, that he only wanted my father's money. Willi was the only good thing to come out of it, and he wasn't even mine, not really. He was the result of an affair between a servant in my house and my husband, but I insisted we take him as his mother could not care for him – she was just a girl. So we took him and raised him as ours.'

'I'm sorry you had such hardship, Katerin, but Willi loves you every bit as much as a natural-born son would,' he said, and then without catching her eye at all, went on. 'And I doubt you were not pretty. In fact, I'm certain you were, and you still are.'

She laughed. 'So this is the effect of the new drug, is it? Making you a charming liar?'

Her laugh was gentle and teasing and he smiled. 'I'm serious.' He turned to her. 'I should have been better. I should have explained when you asked me about moving to your house...'

'The offer still stands, and it will remain open,' she said matter-of-factly.

'You've done enough caring in your life, Katerin, and I don't know how my health is going to go – not well, I would imagine. I can't let you take care of me. It wouldn't be right. If I was healthy, then I would have said yes to your kind offer, but now, no.'

'So what?' she demanded. 'You'll fade away up here, all on your own?'

He shrugged. 'Until I can't manage any more, and then I'll go wherever they send old men to die here. But I won't burden you. I know you are offering in the spirit of charity and I appreciate it, but I can't let you.'

She stood up and he saw the fury on her face.

'If you think charity was what I was offering, then you, David Frank, are an even bigger *schmuck* than I thought you were.'

She stormed off, leaving him stunned and bemused. Nobody, Jew or Gentile, had ever called him a *schmuck* before.

CHAPTER 14

'Hi, Erich,' Jamie called from behind the bar. There were only a few customers dotted around, all thankfully engaged in their own conversations. 'Good to see you out and about, though you still look like you've done a few rounds with Sugar Ray Robinson.'

'Hi Jamie. Is Liesl here?' Erich asked, trying not to wince as he walked. The pain was much more manageable now, and as the weeks had gone on, he was slowly coming back to himself.

'No, she's up at Doctor Crossley's. Are you all right?' Jamie looked worried.

'Why is she gone to the doctor's?' Erich asked, easing himself onto a high stool at the bar. 'I called a few days ago and she never said anything?'

'Just a routine check-up. Nothing to worry about.'

Erich settled himself on the stool and nodded. Jamie and he were friends, luckily. He couldn't imagine Liesl married to anyone he didn't like.

'I'm fine. Can I get a...' Erich paused. He wasn't much of a drinker, but he needed one now. 'A whiskey please, Jamie.'

His brother-in-law looked doubtful. 'Of course you can if you want one, but you are probably on a lot of medication so maybe it's not the best idea? How about a lemonade or a cup of coffee?'

'Whiskey please,' Erich insisted.

'All right, but just the one. If anything happened to you, Liesl would skin me alive and your mother, Daniel and Elizabeth would then finish the job. It's just not worth it, mate.' Jamie chuckled and Erich tried to return his smile.

The thing everyone loved about Jamie was his eternal good humour and optimism. He loved life in Ballycreggan, and after a promising career in medicine came to an abrupt halt because he hated studying it, Jamie went to work in a bar in Dublin. His parents were horrified as they were sure they were making a doctor of their son, but it wasn't to be. Jamie was a natural publican. He had exactly the right temperament. He was courteous and friendly with everyone, and all were welcome, regardless of religion, an unusual thing in Northern Ireland where pubs tended to be designated either Catholic or Protestant. He was also a big man, standing over six feet four and built like a tank, so any messing or inappropriate behaviour was dealt with easily. Jamie very rarely had to resort to physically ejecting anyone, but it was widely known that should the need arise, he was more than capable.

Jamie poured Erich a small measure of Bushmills and pushed the glass towards him. After checking that all the customers were happy and well away from earshot he said, 'So are you going to tell me what the blazes is going on, and why you won't set the police on that pair of thugs? You have them all driven demented with worry over you – you know that, don't you?' There was a note of admonishment in his voice.

'I'm fine,' Erich said, taking a sip of the whiskey, which burned his throat.

'I know that. You're tough and you'll heal, but that's not what I mean.' Jamie started polishing glasses, restoring them to their place over the bar. 'And well you know it.'

'Don't you start.' Erich sighed.

'I'm not starting anything, but in the name of God, Erich, you can't think we're all so stupid to accept you have no recollection of anything that night? Liesl told me about Róisín finishing with you, so you've no reason at all now not to come clean. Look, I know you were mad about her, but maybe it's for the best that it ended. There was no future in it if that's the kind she comes from. Mine aren't much better, God knows, but at least they wouldn't beat someone up. Though come to think of it, I'm not totally sure my mother wouldn't resort to those tactics either.' He smiled ruefully. 'Look, all I'm saying is I understand, you know? But Liesl and me are the exception rather than the rule – most mixed couples never stand a chance. And now you're apparently still going to America?' He leaned over. 'Look, if you're in some kind of trouble, if they threatened you or whatever, you can tell me, you know. I won't report back if that's what you're worried about.'

Erich smiled. 'It's not that. I just want to forget it all ever happened, Jamie, that's all.'

'All right, but you still mean to only go to the States for a holiday, though, right? Not for good?'

Erich shrugged. 'I don't know. Maybe it's time. Everyone I know has moved on in some way. If not going to Israel, it's getting married and having a family like you and Liesl. Even Daniel and Elizabeth are talking about travelling, and *Mutti* and Willi are in their own little bubble of love, so maybe it's time I stopped hanging around on the edges of your lives and started living my own. I thought Róisín was the one. I was wrong, so maybe it's time to move on? I don't know.'

Jamie shrugged. 'Only you know the answer to that, Erich, but I will tell you this – they'll all be devastated if you decide to go to America for good. I'm not saying you shouldn't. If it's what you really want, then you should go for it. But I know they would never want you to think you were in the way. They love fussing over you – you know they do.' Jamie grinned. It was a running joke how Erich was like the golden boy.

'I know.' Erich sighed. 'I just don't know what to do.' He waggled the glass for another whiskey.

Jamie raised an eyebrow but took it from him. 'A very small one, and that's your lot.' He filled a half measure from the optic behind the bar.

'In America, honestly, Jamie, it's amazing. People from literally all over the world. Nobody cares who you are, what religion you are, where you come from. If you're willing to work hard and just get on with your life, then people let that happen.'

'It sounds great.' Jamie continued polishing glasses. 'Look, how about this? Go over for the holiday you planned anyway. I'll try to talk them down if they go mad – well, I'll talk to Liesl and she'll convince them to let you go without too much wailing and gnashing of teeth. Then see how you feel? You might love it and decide to stay, or you might miss us all here and want to come back. I think not saying anything about it possibly being long term is a good idea, for now anyway.'

Jamie poured two cups of coffee, one for himself and another for Erich. 'Drink that, or they'll smell the whiskey on your breath.' He pushed the cup towards him.

CHAPTER 15

*E*rich couldn't believe his eyes; he was really there. Even with all that was going on, he was overawed at the sight of the lady with her lamp, standing proud and green in the harbour as the ship sailed in.

But each time he felt the thrill of adventure, he felt a pang, thinking about Róisín.

He gazed over the railing at the metropolis. He'd never seen anything like it, so many buildings packed so closely together, each one taller than the next.

An American standing beside him clapped him on the back, clearly delighted to be back, and said with a triumphant smile, 'Welcome to the Big Apple. Your first time?'

Erich nodded. 'I was in America once before, but I never saw New York.'

'You're in for a treat, my friend. It's the best city in the world.' He clapped him on the back once more. 'Take a big bite!'

As Erich disembarked and had his paperwork stamped, he took it all in – the accents, the noise. Once he was out of the terminal, he just stood and gazed at New York life in all its manic energy buzzing around him. It felt like another planet compared to Ballycreggan.

Huge cars, yellow taxis mostly, pulled up every few seconds at the kerbside, disgorging passengers and collecting more. Out of one, Bill Haley was belting 'Rock Around the Clock' from a tinny radio, while in another a man yelled in some language Erich didn't understand and gesticulated rudely because someone took his parking spot. Meanwhile, Frank Sinatra was crooning 'Someone to Watch Over Me' from the radio of yet another. The sun was shining and girls wore more daring dresses than anyone would wear at home.

Erich loved every second of it. Everything was bigger, brighter, newer and just better. The war deprivations hadn't touched this shiny, happy land. Nobody cared that he was a Jew; he might as well have been blue for all the interest people had in that.

'Hey, cutie!' a girl called as she and her friend walked by. They wore a lot of make-up and dresses that would have scandalised the entire parish of Ballycreggan regardless of what religion they were. They stopped and stood in front of him, a blonde and a redhead, both wearing dresses that barely contained their large breasts.

'You new in town?' The blonde smiled. She reminded Erich of a cat. And he was very much the mouse.

'I am, aye. I mean...yes...I am. I'm just arrived from Ireland...'

'Oh, Glenda, you hear that? He's Irish! Say something nice for me, sweetie, and me and Glenda here will show you a good time in New York.'

'Thanks.' Erich swallowed. The last thing he wanted to do was get mixed up with these two; he suspected their interest in him was more commercial than social. 'But I actually am meeting someone...' Suddenly he wished that were true. He'd planned to spend two days alone in New York before going to Biloxi as he wanted to see the sights.

Glenda and her pal seemed intent on detaining him. She ran her hand down his arm and over his chest. 'You're a strong boy. I guess growing all those potatoes builds up muscles.' She nudged him suggestively.

He knew from his last visit that his accent seemed to make girls melt, and everyone he spoke to had some Irish ancestors and wanted to know if he knew them. He'd tried to explain about the North and South and the historical division of the island of Ireland, but it fell on deaf ears. The images of Ireland in the heads of these Americans was of green fields, old castles and cute villages, and nothing he said was going to change their minds.

He stepped away, out of her clutches, when he heard his name being called. To his astonishment, Bud appeared.

'Hey, Erich! How ya doin'?' Bud hugged him tightly. 'I was afraid I missed ya, buddy.'

'Bud! What are you doing here?' Erich was thrilled to see his old friend. 'I thought I was meeting you in Biloxi?'

'Gabriella thought a cute Irish guy might need backup in the big city, so she sent me to keep an eye on you. And just in the nick of time too.' He gave a wry smile in the direction of the two women.

'Ladies,' he addressed them, 'nice meeting y'all, but we gotta go.' He tipped his hat and picked up Erich's suitcase.

They crossed the street. There was a bar on the corner.

'Let's start with a beer and take it from there?' Bud suggested, and Erich grinned. He was really there.

'Perfect.'

They took two seats and Bud went to the bar, returning moments later with two cold bottles of Dixie Beer. They each took long draughts, the cold beer sliding down their throats and slaking their thirst.

'I love y'all over there in Europe, y'know I do, Erich, but man am I glad to be back here where beer is cold. I ain't never understood how y'all over yonder can drink that warm brown stuff. Urgh.' Bud shuddered.

'I'm not a huge lover of it myself, to be honest.' Erich smiled.

'So, buddy, how 'bout those gals, huh? The blonde with the pink dress, she looked like she was just about ready to eat you right up.' Bud winked and nudged him.

'You rescued me.' Erich laughed. 'I'm not used to girls being so terrifying.'

'You know they were hookers, though, right?' Bud took another long drink.

'I guessed.' Erich nodded. 'Lucky you showed up. God knows what they would have done to me, and me a poor innocent.' He winked.

Though Erich had only been ten years old when he met Bud, then eighteen, they'd always operated as equals. Bud had been stationed with the RAF at the Ballyhalbert station – his mother was British – and Erich and Liesl had befriended him and taught him German. A firm friendship between the Bannon children and Corporal Thomas Smith, or Bud as he was known, had developed and had survived his return to Biloxi with his Italian wife, who he had found wandering in 1944 in the bombed-out city of Caserta.

Erich sighed. The sun was setting over the harbour now. 'I'm really here, in New York City.' He tried to take it all in. 'And now you're here too, the icing on the cake. You didn't need to come, but I'm so happy you're here.' Erich nibbled the small crunchy snacks in a basket the barman had put between them. They were salty and delicious.

'What are these?' he asked.

'What?' Bud looked confused. 'I thought pretzels were German?'

Erich took another of the little snacks. The pretzels of his childhood were large knots of pastry, baked until crisp on the outside but soft inside. 'They are, but this isn't like any pretzel I've ever seen.' He laughed, then popped another one in his mouth. 'So was it all right to take some time off to come up here?' Erich knew Bud had been very busy with the family business.

'Course! I'm the boss now, Erich.' His friend grinned.

Bud's father had passed away last year, leaving the family fruit business to his son. 'My daddy was as likely to be found packin' peaches in his undershirt as he was mixing with the highfalutin bankers and whatnot, so nobody in our house got to get too high and mighty,' he'd often say with a chuckle. Bud was tall and thin and still looked eighteen really. His dark red hair stuck up at strange angles, and freckles dotted his nose. Erich thought he was one of the best people he'd ever met.

'So tell me all about this girl, the one you dumped my nice cousin for.' Bud turned to the bartender and ordered two more beers.

'Oh, that's a long, sad story.'

'I got all day.' Bud clinked his bottle off Erich's.

When Erich finished telling Bud everything, he felt better, unburdened.

'And it was her brothers who came round and beat you up?' Bud asked.

'Yes, Colm and Neil. They worked for us. I thought we were friends, but they obviously were raging that I'd slept with their sister. They're Catholics as well, so while a good Jewish boy isn't supposed to go around having sex with girls, there's a whole other level of shame and sin with them. And now she's broken it off anyway, so it was all for nothing,' Erich finished miserably. He finished his first beer and placed the bottle on the table.

'But you loved this girl?' Bud probed.

Erich didn't need to think about it. 'I did.' He sighed. 'I still do.'

They sat in silence for a while, and eventually Bud spoke again. 'I wish I had better advice for you, Erich, but her brothers don't like you none so I reckon you're better off, that dog won't hunt. I know it hurts like hell now, but you can't be with a girl whose brothers are gonna be waitin' for you with pitchforks. You need to watch your back there, buddy. Those guys sound like trouble to me.'

'It doesn't matter now anyway. She wrote me a letter, ending it all, saying she'd found someone else.' The words felt like sawdust in his mouth.

'I know it's hard, but you'll get over it. And a vacation is just what you need.' Bud grinned.

Erich nodded. Bud's cheerfulness was infectious. His heart was broken, but he was in New York City with his best friend, so life wasn't all bad. 'Absolutely, and now we can see it together. Are you sure Gabriella doesn't mind you just taking off on a skite with me?'

Bud laughed. 'I haven't heard that word for years. I didn't know what it meant for ages, but it's a great word to describe two guys on the town. I must tell Gabriella about it when I get home. I'm always remembering bits of things that happened all those years I was over there to tell her.' The way Bud spoke about his wife, it was easy to tell he was besotted with her. 'To answer your question, she'll be fine, glad to be getting rid of me for a few days. She's made a bunch of friends with some other GI brides in town, so they keep each other worn slap out with the yakkin' about how uncultured us Americans are.'

Erich knew that wasn't true, that Gabriella adored Bud. But he was happy she'd made some friends. Even in Mississippi, lots of men who'd served in Europe during the war had come home with British, French or Italian wives. Bud had explained to him that it didn't always work out. Sometimes the women, who were all caught up in the romance of the war and everyone in uniform, thought life in America with their new husbands would be so glamorous and exciting, but for many it was a leap too far. The distance, the differences in culture, the fact that the dashing young pilot was now returned to running the mom-and-pop grocery store, all was too much to cope with, and several went home, or at least ended the marriage by divorce.

America was different, no doubt about it. But that's what Erich loved about it. Sure, some bits were hard to take. The treatment of coloured people, for example, was truly shocking, especially in the South. He remembered being appalled when he came for Bud's wedding. But generally, the freedom, the lack of concern for who your family were or what your religion was, he found so refreshing.

'It's not uncultured here' – Erich rushed to defend America – 'just different. Europe is so old, so historic, and there's good things about that too, but it means people get really stuck in the old ways, doing things and thinking a certain way because that's what was always done. I don't like that way of thinking. Just because an attitude has had the tenacity to endure for centuries doesn't make it right or worthy of repeating, you know?'

Bud laughed. 'You're a one-off, Erich Bannon. I knew it from the first day I played soccer with you in the park in Ballycreggan. You're a deep thinker, my friend.'

Erich shrugged. Liesl was always the brainy one, the one who liked studying and went to university and all of that. He was more practical, so he never saw himself as an intellectual kind of person. 'Well, whether I am or not, I'd better start doing some serious thinking about the future, because I need to do something. Maybe it's time to get out of Ballycreggan, start again somewhere new.'

Bud opened his mouth to speak but closed it again. Erich saw the hesitation there. 'What?' he asked. 'You were going to say something?'

Bud rubbed his hand over the back of his neck, sweat trickling onto the soft collar of his plaid shirt. 'Well, I was just gonna say – and you can tell me to mind my business if you want – but remember when I thought I was in love with Talia?'

They rarely mentioned the woman who'd come to the farm with the Kindertransport. Talia Zimmerman had proved to be a duplicitous traitor who worked for the Nazis. Elizabeth uncovered her, but not before Daniel was found guilty of espionage and faced the death penalty. Talia had confessed in the end, thus proving Daniel's innocence, but it was a close-run thing. The Nazis had some contacts with the IRA at the time, both united in their hatred of Britain, and it was a dark time for the Lieber family. When Bud realised Talia was only using him for information about the RAF base, he was devastated.

'I do,' Erich said.

'And, well, I know how it all turned out, and she never wanted me for me, only for whatever information she could get outta me, but at the time I'd have done anything for her, and even if she hadn't been a spy. I was plumb crazy. But you know, I thought about it a lot, and I reckon she'd have made me miserable, and me her too.'

'So...' Erich was none the wiser. 'What's that got to do with my situation?'

'Well, just that sometimes we get so caught up in romances. Those girls are so damn pretty and they look at you and man – well, me anyway, I ain't got the good sense God gave a rock. Talia played me, I know she did, but I'll tell you, Erich, she did a mighty fine job of it. I'd have walked through fire for her. I just want you to try to make decisions with your head, not your heart. I'd hate you to give up all you have back there, those people who love you, just on a whim, y'know?'

'I will. Thanks, Bud. And I know what you mean.' He put his hand on his friend's shoulder. 'After my holiday here I'll go back and see the lay of the land. I honestly don't know how I feel… Well, I feel so many things. I know what you mean about thinking you're in love, that this is the one. I thought Abigail was that for me, but I obviously wasn't for her considering she went to Israel and never came back. But I really thought Róisín was it.'

They finished their drinks and Bud explained how he'd cancelled Erich's hotel – he'd called Elizabeth to ask the name of it – so that they could room together. He wanted to keep his turning up in New York a surprise, but it took a bit of planning behind the scenes. Erich realised once again what a great friend Bud was, and knew he was lucky to have him.

They took a taxi to the hotel Bud had booked on Park Avenue. It was so different to the hotels at home, which were all steeped in history and furnished with antiques. This hotel was all glass and steel, and everything seemed to gleam in the evening sun. The bedroom was enormous, with two huge beds and its own bathroom. Erich had never seen anything so fancy.

'This place must have cost a fortune, Bud.' He felt guilty putting his friend to such expense.

'Don't worry. We use a lot of these hotels for the business, and this is just one more.' Bud winked. 'This is a business trip. We're investigating new sources of apples and pears. Now, first thing, I reserved us seats on the boat tour of Manhattan in the morning. It's the best way to see the waterfront, where all the cruise ships and tugboats come in.'

'Thanks, Bud. I can't wait.'

They had a lovely dinner, catching up on all of the news and reminiscing on Bud's years in the RAF. They laughed at how obsessed with aircraft Erich and his friends were and how Erich was so proud of having Bud as a friend and guarded him jealously from the others, who would have loved to befriend a Yank too.

* * *

AFTER A GOOD NIGHT'S sleep in the biggest bed Erich had ever seen, and following a sumptuous breakfast, Erich accompanied his friend down the street to Battery Park. Was he really there? It sure felt like it. New York was hot and sweaty, noisy and crowded, everything Bally-creggan wasn't, and he loved it.

'I was here for a few weeks when I got demobbed,' Bud explained as they waited at the ferry point for the tourist boat, Liberty Island with the beautiful statue out in front of them. 'Since I served with the RAF, not the US Air Force, I got my walking papers in England, so I was free as a bird. And when that ship pulled into New York that day in 1946, boy, did I see the sights. I never thought I'd come back alive, but here I was.

'Then me and a bunch of guys from Tennessee went up to Times Square. There were some workin' gals there, you know what I mean? Just like your pair yesterday.' He grinned. 'But by then I was plumb crazy about my Gabriella, so I went to the movies instead. Ingrid Bergman and Bing Crosby in *The Bells of St Mary's*. The guys gave me a right old ribbin' after when they heard, thought I was some kinda choirboy goin' to a movie about a nun and a priest. But there was only one girl for me, and I wasn't messin' that up for one night with a hooker.'

'You were right,' Erich agreed. 'Honestly, Bud, I can't believe I'm really here.' He watched the ferries, pleasure boats and tugs all going about their business in the harbour.

'It's some city, all right. Those Yankees reckon they got the best of everything. We can give 'em a run for their money in lots of things, but they sure got one of the greatest cities on earth.'

Erich turned around and consulted the map in his hands. 'Wall Street is just a few blocks that way, and the New York Stock Exchange. And over that way' – he pointed in the direction of the East River – 'is the new United Nations building.'

'Seventy-five nations making sure we don't get ourselves in another mess and start shootin' at each other again,' Bud said quietly.

Erich knew Bud had nightmares about the things he saw in the war, the carnage and death, but he tried, like everyone, to put it behind him and move on with his life.

'It can't ever happen again, Bud, not after everything.' Erich was convinced.

'They said that in 1918, buddy, and look how that turned out.' Bud shrugged. 'But let's not worry about it for now. Here comes the boat.'

They boarded the cruiser, taking their places at the rail. Erich didn't want to miss a thing. As they rounded the bottom of Manhattan Island, they saw all the national flags at the UN building blowing merrily in the wind, the nations having committed themselves to world peace. Erich felt a lump in his throat. Surely it was over now, the slaughter and misery? Surely people learned there were no winners, only losers?

As they sailed under the George Washington Bridge, a massive structure going from New York to New Jersey, Erich closed his eyes and felt the hot summer wind on his face. He allowed the smells and the sounds of New York to wash over him.

Twenty minutes later, they disembarked and made their way up to 5th Avenue. Erich took it all in, the mounted police, the crowds, the glamorous shops that appeared so expensive he was terrified even to look.

They walked on, and the crowds and vibrancy of the whole scene were so exciting. Everyone was so well dressed, and the shabby coats and worn shoes of Ballycreggan seemed like a million miles away.

Bud stopped in front of Tiffany's jewellery store and spotted a selection of necklaces with a jewelled initial hanging from each one. 'I'm gonna get my Gabriella one of those,' he said.

'Shouldn't you check the price first?' Erich could hardly believe the numbers written on tiny cards beside each piece. 'It looks like a very expensive place.'

'She's worth it.' Bud winked and went inside. Erich waited on the street, the jewellery shop definitely outside his budget. Besides, he wanted to soak it all up. He didn't have anyone to buy a necklace for now anyway.

Bud emerged with his purchase and opened the little velvet box with the Tiffany's logo on the inside. The exquisite little 'G' was encrusted with diamonds and hung on a gold chain. It was beautiful.

Bud then reached into his pocket and handed an identical box to Erich.

'What's this?' Erich asked, confused.

'Open it,' Bud urged.

'Hey, you're a nice fella and all of that, Bud, but you're not really my type.' Erich chuckled.

'It's not for you, smartass,' Bud drawled. 'It's for Liesl.'

Erich opened the box and there was the same necklace, only this time the chain held an 'L'.

'She'll love it, I know.' Erich smiled. 'She and Jamie are coming to the States next year with the baby. She was saying how she wished she could come. She missed the wedding too because of her injuries after the fire, so she's determined. I told her I'd take care of the bar.'

'Well, that's just great. She and Gabriella will get on like a house on fire, I know, and I'm looking forward to meeting her husband. You like him, right?'

'Very much. He's a lovely fella, and he's mad about Liesl.'

'I can't imagine her married and now with a baby on the way. To me she'll always be the studious little girl with braids, fixin' to take over the world.'

'Oh, she's still a right swot,' Erich joked. 'She buys me a book every year for my birthday, and I've never read one of them.'

'You two are like chalk and cheese, all right. But when I was a green kid from Biloxi and I found myself over yonder thousands of miles from home with no family or friends, y'all opened your home to me. When Talia turned out to be a liar, it was your family that picked me up and put me back together. We may not be blood, but we're friends for life. So where to now?'

They walked on, turning into Herald Square and then entering Macy's, the huge department store. Erich had never been in a shop of that size. He bought Elizabeth and his mother a scarf each and a little outfit for Liesl's baby. The lady on the desk advised him to get something white, which could be worn by either a boy or a girl. He got Willi a cigarette case and some chocolates and coffee for Daniel.

They passed the statue of Atlas as they wandered, and Erich stopped to admire it. 'I feel like him right now,' he told Bud. 'The weight of the world on me.'

'But you don't got his muscles, buddy,' Bud joked, and Erich laughed too. 'Look, I know you're sad, but try to put it out of your mind for now and enjoy New York.'

Erich knew his friend was right. He might never again see this wonderful city.

They strolled through Rockefeller Center. The channelled gardens were a riot of colour, and the sunken plaza with its gold statue of Prometheus almost took Erich's breath away.

'Let's get somethin' to eat,' Bud suggested. 'I'm starvin'.'

They ate lunch in the outdoor restaurant and talked and laughed as easily as they'd done when Erich was a boy and they played football together on the green of Ballycreggan. They talked about Liesl and Jamie and their plans to buy a house of their own as well as everyone's excitement over Israel, and Bud told him of the miscarriage Gabriella had had before becoming pregnant with little Tommy.

After lunch they went to the top floor of the RCA building to get a bird's-eye view of the city. Erich couldn't believe how many people worked there. There were shops, restaurants, theatres, and even radio and television studios in the building. He put a quarter in the telescope and scanned the whole city, from the Hudson River, over Central Park, which looked like an oasis of green in a sea of concrete, glass and steel, all the way to Queens and Long Island in the east. He could see the Chrysler Building and the Empire State Building, the tallest building on earth.

'That's 1400 feet high, you know,' Erich told Bud excitedly. He'd bought a book of facts and figures about New York, and everything about the city delighted him.

'You sure love this city, don't you?' Bud smiled at his friend.

'I do. I can't imagine how exciting it would be to call it home, to see these sights whenever you wanted instead of green fields and crashing ocean and small villages.'

'It ain't nothin like Ballycreggan for sure.'

Bud chuckled as two girls giggled beside them trying to get the telescope to work. He showed them how and they smiled flirtatiously. They were both dressed in halterneck dresses that tied around their necks and were very low-cut. They would have been considered indecent at home, but here they blended into the glorious, glamorous canvas of the amazing city.

'Can we go to see Temple Emanuel?' Erich asked as they went down in the elevator. 'I'd like to tell Rabbi Frank I went there.'

'Sure. Maybe we should drop into St Patrick's too. You know, keep Father O'Toole happy?' Bud teased.

They walked all over Manhattan until their legs could take no more and finally arrived back to the hotel. Erich had had no idea of the size of the city and felt silly at thinking he could see it all in a few days. He'd never got to Queens or the Bronx or Brooklyn, and now it was almost time for them to go south to Biloxi.

The next day was going to be Madison Square Garden. Erich had seen the first boxing match televised in colour last year, with Joey Giardello taking on Willie Troy. It had been arranged by the lads on the football team that they would all get together for the big event at a pub in Belfast that had a television, and it would be great to say he'd gone there in person.

* * *

THE NEXT MORNING, after a huge breakfast of bacon and pancakes smothered in syrup, they set off for 8th Avenue.

'How about we take the subway?' Erich suggested. 'I know it's not far to walk, but I'd like to ride the subway just to say I did it.'

'Sure, Cinderella, you get to go to the ball.' Bud laughed.

The subway was so hot that people waited until the train was due and then rushed down the steps, minimising the time on the platform. Erich and Bud did as the locals did and boarded the train. Erich imagined all of the buildings and people over their heads as the subway snaked under the huge city.

The tour of the famous Madison Square Garden located between 49th and 50th Streets in Manhattan was so interesting. The guide explained that it was the third building of that name, built in 1925, and the first not located near Madison Square. P.T. Barnum had used the original site for his circus, building an open arena with no roof in 1874. Then a new building was erected to combat inclement weather and the names of the founders that tripped off the guide's tongue made Erich smile, men synonymous with this great city, J.P. Morgan, Andrew Carnegie, P.T. Barnum, Darius Mills, W.W. Astor.

The rest of the day passed in a blur. Erich and Bud took a trip to Coney Island and as they paddled in the water, licking ice cream cones, they admired the confident New York girls in their daring swimming costumes.

'What do you think they'd make of that on the beach at Ballyhalbert?' Bud murmured as two stunning looking girls in polka-dot bikinis strolled by, oblivious to their admiring glances.

'I think the rabbi would have a stroke and poor Father O'Toole would collapse of exhaustion from the number of masses he'd be asked to say to pray for the moral degradation of the nation.'

Bud guffawed at that and the girls turned and smiled at them. Erich blushed to the roots of his hair.

That night they went to Chinatown to eat, and Erich was introduced to a cuisine he'd never heard of before as he tried shark fin soup, chicken chow mein and dumplings. It was delicious and he tucked in as all around him men and women called to each other in Chinese, and even the shops had Chinese writing. He'd never felt so foreign in his life before and he loved every second of it.

The following morning, they boarded the train for Biloxi, the sounds of New York City still ringing in Erich's ears.

CHAPTER 16

*R*abbi Frank stood at the sink, his hands shaking so violently that he found it close to impossible to open the small brown glass bottle. He was taking the Percodan they'd prescribed at the hospital – he so badly needed it to take the edge off the pain – but he was overdosing and he knew it. He tried to be more frugal with the tablets, but functioning without them was not an option.

A car pulled into the farmyard and he glanced outside. It was Daniel. Katerin had moved to the village, and he was thankfully alone with his pain. It was so hard to manage it but even harder to keep it from her, and it was becoming increasingly difficult to hide the deterioration of his condition. At night he lay on his bed, his body racked with agony so intense it was impossible to locate it to one part of him, willing God to take him. He knew the end was close – it had to be – and he should say his goodbyes, but something was stopping him. He had missed two appointments at the hospital, knowing they would say it was time to be admitted. His doctor had written, suggesting another drug, but it was pointless he knew. It was time to go.

He watched his friend cross the yard in the August sunshine. The land was now overgrown with weeds that he was no longer able to control, like everything else.

He looked around the old makeshift kitchen. He and Frau Braun had done some kind of a job of downsizing the industrial-sized one, necessary to feed the forty children and fifteen staff at the height of the war, to something they could manage. They'd blocked off the large dining hall and were using only the top corner of what had once been a fifty-by-thirty-foot room. They had an oven and a gas hob, and Daniel had donated a refrigerator, though since they relied on the generator for electricity, it only worked intermittently.

He couldn't eat now anyway. He'd even taken to crushing his tablets because his ability to swallow was almost gone. His clothes hung from his skeletal frame, and he knew he looked awful.

'Shalom.' Daniel had let himself in. He'd been a resident there since the beginning and knew the farm like the back of his hand.

'Shalom,' the rabbi managed.

Daniel took in the pill bottle and the glass of water but didn't mention them. 'How are you?' he asked.

The rabbi shrugged.

'You don't look so good,' Daniel said quietly. 'You need some of those?' He nodded in the direction of the pill bottle.

'Yes, I...I can't open the bottle.' The words came out of his mouth slowly, each one hurting as much as each swallow did these days.

Wordlessly, Daniel went to the sink, opened the bottle, shook out two pills and gave them to the rabbi.

'Can you please crush them?'

'Of course. Is two enough?' Daniel asked, rooting in the drawer for a soup spoon and a teaspoon.

'Four,' the rabbi said. He sat on the hard chair and waited for Daniel to crush the tablets and stir them into the water. Obviously realising how difficult swallowing now was for the rabbi, Daniel only used a half inch of water and handed the rabbi the glass.

'Thank you.'

Holding the glass with both hands to make sure he didn't spill any, Rabbi Frank managed to swallow the mixture. It would begin to work soon; he just needed to wait. He longed to lie down. He rose each morning at six, as he'd done all of his life, but these days dragging his body into an upright position was proving more and more difficult.

'Come on, let's get you lying down until that stuff works.' Daniel stood before him and took the glass from his hands and placed it on the draining board. The rabbi willed himself up from the chair, but he just couldn't do it. He tried, but each time he failed.

Without saying a word, Daniel reached down. He looped one arm under the other man's knees and the other around his shoulders and carried him to the bedroom. The rabbi hadn't the strength or energy to object.

The rabbi's room was the smallest on the whole farm. He could have moved to one of the larger rooms – there were any number to choose from – but the small single bed with its iron frame and thin mattress, a locker with some books and a single wardrobe containing a few garments in either black or white were all he owned in the world; it was adequate for him.

Daniel placed him on the bed and removed his shoes, socks and trousers. He found a pair of pyjamas and dressed him in them. The rabbi felt like a baby, but he was too weak to feel embarrassed or shame that his old friend had to come to his rescue like this.

Once he was settled in his bed, the blanket pulled over him, Daniel left, returning a few moments later with a chair from the kitchen. He sat beside the bed. 'Are the drugs working now?' he asked.

The rabbi nodded.

'So you know this can't go on, don't you?' Daniel smiled. 'Frau Braun was down at our place this morning, and that's why I'm here. She says you won't listen to her and she's terrified you're going to collapse in front of her someday.'

As Daniel's words washed over him, the rabbi sighed, resting his head on the pillow as the drugs took effect. He was tired, so bone-weary.

'So here's what we're going to do. I know you don't want to go to the hospital and that you've missed appointments there. Yes, she's told us everything.' Daniel grinned again. 'Dr Crossley is coming up this afternoon. He'll examine you, and then we'll all three of us have a talk about what happens next. I understand you're a proud man, Rabbi, but you need us to help you and you have to let us do it, all right? This has gone far enough. It took all I could do to stop Elizabeth and Ariella marching in here, and if Liesl knew, she'd be here too. Frau Braun is fit to be tied she's so worried, which is coming out as bad-tempered, as you know.'

The rabbi managed a weak smile. 'She called me a *schmuck*,' he whispered.

Daniel laughed. 'I can imagine it. So I will protect you from the care and fussing of the women, but you need to do what I say, all right? That's the deal, otherwise I turn you over to them.'

The rabbi nodded.

'All right. I'm going to stay, and you can sleep now. I called to Dr Crossley on the way, and his wife said she'd send him after morning surgery, so he'll be here in an hour or so.'

For the first time in weeks, Rabbi Frank felt better. He couldn't have asked for help, but now it seemed it was happening anyway. He was too tired to object.

CHAPTER 17

Six weeks later Rabbi Frank could hardly believe the words the doctor was saying. He was sitting in the small but cosy living room of Katerin Braun, reading his book, when Doctor Crossley called.

Katerin hovered nervously, and he beckoned her in as soon as the doctor entered. The days of keeping everything a secret were over. He had very few memories of the days and weeks after Daniel had come to the farm and carried him to bed. He'd been transferred to a hospital in Belfast, and an operation had been performed. It was all done without his knowledge or permission, but he was glad they did it. The tumour was still there – the surgeon had never imagined he could get it all because of where in his bowel it was located – but he got a lot of it, and whatever the outcome now, at least he didn't feel so wretched.

When the time came to go home from the hospital, the Liebers, the Brauns and Katerin all offered him a bed. His friends, Father O'Toole and Reverend Parkes, also said they could put him up, but in the end, he asked Katerin. It had taken every fibre of his strength to ask, especially after the way he'd spoken to her before on the subject, but he did need care and she was the one he wanted to be around, despite their many differences of opinion on virtually everything.

Dr Crossley was explaining. 'I got a telephone call from Mr Anderson, the surgeon, this morning. He was awaiting the results of the tests they took just before you left hospital, and they just came back, he wanted to tell me how happy he is with the outcome. As you know, the surgery was simply to give you more time and to relieve suffering. I can see you are thriving here.' He grinned at Katerin, who flushed with embarrassment but could only scowl.

'So all in all, it's a good outcome. I think we're managing your pain better, are we not?' he asked, and Rabbi Frank nodded. The new medication was definitely easier to take and it seemed to take the edge off certainly.

'Yes, thank you. I feel better,' he confirmed.

'Well, feeling worse than you were would hardly have been possible, but that was due to a combination of overdoing things and not eating properly, as well as a somewhat haphazard approach to dosage and intervals.' The rabbi heard the admonishment in the doctor's voice. 'You were taking too much of the other drug without food, and it gave you an ulcer, which was bleeding.'

An unspoken conversation passed between the doctor and Frau Braun.

'So you need to follow the prescription exactly this time,' the doctor continued. He was a gruff man, who seemed at first to lack empathy, but Rabbi Frank had seen him provide care tenderly and with tremendous dedication to the children of the farm over the years, always for free, so he knew that the doctor was not really like that.

'But I'm sure now that Mrs Braun is in charge of your prescription and diet, things can only improve.'

'Indeed,' the rabbi agreed.

It had been hard to admit he needed help, harder still to move into the home of a widow, worrying what people would think. But to his astonishment, nobody cared, and everyone just seemed concerned for his well-being. For the last week since he'd been there, there had been endless cakes and casseroles dropped off and cards from the children at the school, and Father O'Toole and Reverend Parkes called every second day to check on him. He often thought, now that he had time for such contemplation, how the war had granted him a life full of people and love, where in peacetime his life had been one of solitude and loneliness. When Marta died, he buried himself in his work and his congregation and was, he realised now, very rigid and unapproachable. The care of the Kindertransport children had, as Ariella Braun had said, knocked the hard edges off him, and now, in his final phase of life, he found himself miraculously surrounded by love and friendship. Life truly was strange.

'So as well as looking much better, the results show that your tumour, while still there, is now smaller as a result of the surgery and seems not to be growing at the rate it once was. You'll be with us for a while yet, Rabbi,' Dr Crossley said cheerfully, extracting his thermometer to do his check-up.

Frau Braun withdrew then, leaving them to it.

* * *

As she heard Dr Crossley let himself out, Frau Braun finished adding cream to the mushroom soup she'd prepared. Elizabeth and Liesl were back to school now; a new school year had begun, and the days were getting cooler.

Willi had helped her to buy the little house in the middle of the main street, and she loved it. It was small but perfectly appointed, with a sitting room and a kitchen downstairs and two bedrooms and a bathroom upstairs. So far, the rabbi was able to make it up to his room unaided, incredible really considering just a few weeks ago, it seemed like he would die.

The operation and the spell in hospital, where they'd changed his medication and seemed to get him back to at least some version of his old self, had done so much good. As she stirred the soup, she replayed the conversation they'd had in the hospital, hardly believing it was real.

Those days after he was admitted seemed like a lifetime ago. Nobody was allowed in to see him, and then they called after ten days and said he could have a visitor, just one, and he'd asked for her. She felt ridiculously pleased and then silly at her foolishness. It had turned out to be the best day of her life, and she smiled at the memory as she took the bread from the oven.

The nurse told her on the way in that he refused to lie in bed wearing pyjamas and insisted on getting up and dressing properly each day. She'd gone into the room, and there he was, ten short days after Daniel had to carry him because he was so weak, in his black trousers and white shirt, his beard and hair neatly combed. She nearly leapt for joy to see him restored to health.

'Ah, Frau Braun, how are you?' he'd asked, as if they'd met in the middle of the street for a friendly chat.

'I'm fine. You're the one causing all of the fuss,' she said, sitting down on the only other chair.

'Regretfully, you are right.' The rabbi looked contrite. 'Poor Daniel found me in a bad way, and for that I apologise. I had let it go too far. I was trying not to be a burden and became even a bigger one as a result.'

'Yes, well, you are very stubborn and, frankly, stupid.' She'd been so worried, but it emerged as frustration. 'You have cancer, you need help, medical and practical, and yet you just reject all offers. It's not just stupid, it's selfish, because these people around you actually care about you and you're throwing their kindness back in their faces.'

'I am guilty, as you say, Katerin. I am so sorry, and I want to thank you especially. You have tried so hard to help me, and you're right – I'm a stubborn, proud old fool. You're absolutely right, I'm a *schmuck*.' He smiled and his eyes twinkled.

'Yes, well...' She'd been nonplussed at that; abject apologies were not his style. 'Perhaps I shouldn't have said –'

'No, you were right.' He inhaled then, as if gearing up to something. 'And if the offer of a room in your new home is still good, then I would be most honoured and grateful to take it up. If, however, you have changed your mind – and I would not blame you if you did – then of course I will make other plans. I don't want you to feel obligated in any way.'

She'd tried to interrupt, but he held up his hand to stop her and went on. 'Please, I have rehearsed my little speech to you all of these days, so let me finish or I will forget the important bits.' He smiled and she relaxed.

'A part of me didn't want the farm to end, and that's why I was holding on. They were the sentimental actions of an old man, who realised the end is nigh. My life, before the war, apart from the brief time with Marta, was uneventful, devoid of companionship, of love, of friendship. People respected my father and later me, and I served my people to the best of my ability. I would watch, you know, as they came to synagogue in Berlin, the families, and I would envy them going home to a Shabbat dinner, all sitting around the family table, sharing, loving, laughing, arguing, supporting. I never had that, and I'd resigned myself to believe that it was not something I could ever experience. But then the war came and I found myself here, this most unlikely of places, and without asking to be, I became the leader of the farm and the protector and parent really to all of these little ones. And though the circumstances were beyond comprehension and I still find it hard to believe it happened, those years were the happiest of my life. For the first time, I've known what it is to belong to others, to care for them in a way, not just as their rabbi but as me, as David, and I was afraid to let the farm go in case I lost that.'

'But what you have, that family now, all of us, we're not going anywhere,' Frau Braun explained. 'Of course the children have moved on, but that was going to happen. And they write. And seeing them so happy, that must make you proud?'

He nodded with a smile. Each child was emblazoned in his memory forever, and she knew he could not care more for them if he was their own father.

'And Daniel and Elizabeth, and Ariella and Willi, and your friends in Ballycreggan, they are your people, and nothing will change that now.'

'And you?' he asked quietly. 'Are you my person?' His voice was barely audible.

With the vulnerability and fear only barely overcome by a glimmer of hope, she fought back every urge she had to dismiss, to snap in response. A lifetime of never letting anyone in, of protecting herself by the construction of that hard impenetrable shell, made being open, being emotional, so difficult.

'Do you want me to be?' she managed, terrified she was misreading this.

'Very much.'

And so he'd come home to her house from the hospital, and without ever discussing their relationship further, they were now together.

She brought his lunch on a tray to the sitting room.

'Ah, Katerin, I could have come to the table. You don't need to wait on me – I should be waiting on you.' He stood up, much steadier on his feet than even a week ago. Weeks of living companionably side by side had passed, and she was so content knowing he was there. She prayed each night for another day, just one more. One day he would leave her, she knew that, but each night she thanked God for one more day. It was all she could do.

'It's fine. I need to bake some strudel for the church bake sale, so I'll need the table, and I promised Father O'Toole I'd have them ready by three.'

He took the tray and placed it on the side table, and as she turned to return to the kitchen, he called her back. When she turned, he was standing before her, a small leather box open in his hands. He offered it to her, and with a tentative smile, said, 'Katerin, I know I'm not much of a catch, as they say nowadays, but would you do me the very great honour of becoming my wife?'

Almost in a trance, she took the ring slowly from the box. She'd studied Hebrew during her conversion to Judaism when she first arrived in Ireland, and she read the inscription around the band slowly. *I am my beloved's and my beloved is mine.* The quotation was from the Book of Solomon, one of her favourites.

'Can you do this? I mean, you're a rabbi and I only converted...' She found the words were buried; she struggled to find them.

'Yes.' He nodded.

Katerin had told him before that she had never in her life been in love. She'd been infatuated with her husband in the early days, but that wasn't love. She loved Willi with all of her heart, but that was a mother-child connection. So the idea that she would now be standing in the sitting room of her own house in Ireland, being proposed to by a rabbi, both of them in their sixties, was as ridiculous as it was wonderful.

'I love you, Katerin. If you'll have me?' he said slowly.

'I love you too,' she whispered. 'I would love to marry you.'

He crossed the short space between them and stood before her, then ran his finger down her face. He smiled and she returned it.

'You are very lovely, especially when you smile,' he said.

'No, I'm not, but thank you for saying it.'

'You are. I've always thought so, even when you are angry with me, which is most of the time.'

They chuckled.

Slowly his arms went around her slender waist, and they were closer than they'd ever been. He was only an inch or two taller than her. It could have been awkward as it had been so long for either of them to have any physical intimacy with anyone, but it wasn't. He leaned towards her, his lips brushing hers, tentatively at first. As her arms slid around his neck, she kissed him back.

CHAPTER 18

'You know, don't you?' Ariella held her daughter's gaze.

The kitchen of Elizabeth and Daniel's house was bright and sunny, and Liesl and Ariella stood at the window, watching Elizabeth taking the laundry down from the clothes-line. The two women were as comfortable there as in their own homes. Ariella had embroidered the red and cream tablecloth, and the soda bread that was cooling on the rack had been made that morning by Liesl while Elizabeth did the laundry.

The fact that Ariella was Liesl's biological mother and Elizabeth was her adopted one might have seemed complicated to an outsider, but to them it was perfectly normal. Their family was united by love, loyalty and a history of shared adversity, blood ties were only one part of it.

The hens in the pen outside clucked loudly.

'Know what?' Liesl asked, knowing full well what her mother meant.

'Liesl, don't take me for a fool.' Ariella smiled. Although Liesl's tiny, red-haired, porcelain-doll-like mother might look naïve and inno-cent, she was anything but.

'I'm not. I just...' Liesl began, her hand on her swelling bump. It was an unusually hot day for late October, and the heat was making her uncomfortable. She sat down at the oak dining table. She, Erich and Elizabeth had eaten so many meals there, before Elizabeth married Daniel, before they knew Ariella had survived the war, when it was just the three of them, making do and keeping going in a world of dark uncertainty. Elizabeth and Ariella shared her and Erich easily, both women bringing different talents and traits to the relationship, and though Liesl adored her mother, in many ways she could relate better to Elizabeth. Elizabeth was calmer, less adamant about things. Ariella was determined and fiery and didn't back away from anything, including awkward conversations. Elizabeth was more diplomatic, more willing to see everyone's perspective. Perhaps it was that Elizabeth had been her mother in those more formative of years, from ten to sixteen.

Liesl willed Elizabeth back inside now. This was a perfect example of the differences in Elizabeth and Ariella. Daniel and Elizabeth knew Erich had confided in her, but they wouldn't press her, feeling that it wouldn't be fair. Ariella had no such qualms.

'Look, I understand the bond between you and your brother, I do, and I love it about you. When I told you to take care of him that day on the platform, you took that instruction so seriously, and I'm so proud of you. But we just can't understand why he won't go to the police about the McAreaveys. They're just getting off scot-free, and they could have killed him. Do they have something on him? Is that it?'

Ariella sat down opposite her. Liesl tried to focus on the brown porcelain wall clock over the sink. It had been in the house when they arrived, and was more Elizabeth's mother's taste than Elizabeth's. It had measured out faithfully each second and minute of their new lives as little Irish children, growing to adulthood under its ticking presence. Liesl did not want to meet her mother's eyes.

'No, I honestly don't know why he won't. He just told me that Róisín broke it off, that she was really sorry about what happened but they had no future. I don't know anything else, I swear.'

Elizabeth came in, a basket of laundry in her arms, and immediately Ariella jumped up and began to help her fold the sheets. The women worked together, as united as it was possible for them to be, and Liesl watched on, conflicted.

'Oh!' she exclaimed.

'What? Are you all right?' Elizabeth asked, alarmed.

Liesl smiled. 'Yes.' She massaged her bump. 'This little one has his or her daddy's kicking skills, I think.'

'Aww, can I feel?' Ariella placed the shirt she was folding in the basket and bent down beside her daughter, her hand on her belly.

'Oh, it happened again!' Ariella gasped delightedly.

Elizabeth stood back, smiling at the mother-daughter moment.

'Do you want to feel it?' Liesl asked her.

Ariella moved back to allow her in, and Elizabeth placed her hand on the spot where Ariella had felt the kick. She waited a few seconds but nothing happened.

'He or she's decided that's enough kicking for one day,' Elizabeth said, removing her hand.

It was something Liesl was acutely aware of, that Ariella had been through this whole experience twice and so was able to advise and empathise, whereas Elizabeth had only ever been pregnant once, a lifetime ago now, and had lost that child through a miscarriage. The last thing Liesl would ever do was exclude Elizabeth – she owed her everything and loved her every bit as much as her mother – but it felt like the pregnancy was separating them and it made her sad. She wished her baby would kick for Elizabeth.

'So, cup of tea?' Ariella asked, filling the kettle.

'Lovely.' Liesl smiled. 'I must just pop to the bathroom...again.' She sighed.

'Oh, I remember that. The summer you were born, it was so hot I couldn't sleep. I would get Peter to drag the sofa to the long windows of our apartment and sleep right by them, hoping for a puff of air. And then if I did fall asleep, I'd have to wake to go to the toilet every five minutes it seemed like.' Ariella chuckled at the memory. 'By the time you were born, I was so huge, I could hardly make it up the stairs.'

Liesl knew her mother didn't mean any harm, and of course she should share reminiscences of her pregnancies, but Liesl felt for Elizabeth. She'd only spoken once of the pain of losing her only child, and while she saw Liesl and Erich as hers too, it wasn't the same. It hadn't seemed to matter so much before, but now that Liesl was about to be a mother herself, it was all the more difficult. She'd explained her feelings to Jamie and he understood, but he thought she was imagining the fleeting look of remembered grief on Elizabeth's face every time she and Ariella spoke of babies and pregnancy.

'If you're going up anyway, can you pop this laundry on Erich's bed, please?' Elizabeth handed her some of her brother's shirts.

'Of course. All must be perfect for the little prince when he comes home,' Liesl teased.

She went into Erich's bedroom. The sheets were freshly laundered and the windows open to air the room so it would be ready for him when he returned. She opened a drawer to place the shirts inside when she spotted a letter. Normally she would never read a person's private letter, but she was worried too – did the McAreaveys have something on her brother?

Impulsively, she took the envelope and slipped the single sheet out. As she suspected, it was from Róisín. The murmur of muffled conversation between Elizabeth and Ariella in the kitchen was barely audible as she read.

Dear Erich,

I'm sorry how everything turned out. I never meant for that to happen. I hope you feel better soon. I think it's best if we don't see each other any more. It would never have worked anyway – we both knew that deep down – but it was fun while it lasted.

I'm actually getting close with a lad from near where I grew up. He's more my type, if I'm honest.

Best of luck,

Róisín

Her heart thumping loudly in her chest, she stuffed the letter back into the envelope and hastily resealed it, thinking quickly. The little madam! Liesl was furious. How dare she be so callous! Erich had let on that Róisín was contrite and as devastated as he was, but this cold, mean little note gave no indication of that. She replaced the letter, seething with indignation.

She needed to get away, to be on her own to process this information. She was a terrible liar, so she knew if she went back in and joined the conversation, immediately her mother would ask what was wrong.

She popped her head in the kitchen door. 'I just remembered that Jamie asked me to be home by midday because there's a brewery delivery and he needs me, so I better go. See you later.' She tried to leave but Ariella stopped her.

'Needs you for what?' she demanded, following her daughter out into the hall. Ariella was suspicious of everything these days, knowing Liesl and Erich were in league over something. 'Surely you're not lifting anything?'

'Oh no,' Liesl lied clumsily. 'Just to do the paperwork. He thinks they might have left him short before, and he needs to watch the delivery and tally it with the invoice…' Her voice trailed off. It was the most pathetic effort at a fib ever, but it was all she could think of.

'Right.' Ariella looked sceptical. 'No lifting or anything like that, all right?'

'See you later, Liesl,' Elizabeth called from the kitchen.

Liesl laughed. 'Don't worry, *Mutti*. Jamie won't let me lift a spoon – it drives me mad, to be honest.' Liesl was glad to change the subject.

'He's a good one, that boy.' Ariella winked and kissed her daughter's cheek. 'Bye-bye, little one.' She patted Liesl's belly.

Liesl took her brother's car keys from the hallstand. When she was sixteen, Daniel had taught her to drive in the fields around the farm, and though she and Jamie didn't have a car, they planned to get one.

She drove all the way to Raggettstown and stopped a woman to ask for directions to the McAreaveys' house. She was going to have this out with Róisín once and for all.

The tiny terraced house exuded poverty and deprivation, but Liesl was too angry to notice as she rapped on the door.

It opened and a small timid-looking woman stood there. She was in her late forties possibly. Her mousey-brown hair hung down in straggles underneath a headscarf, and a faded blue housecoat covered her tiny frame.

'Mrs McAreavey?' Liesl asked.

'I am.' The woman looked terrified and Liesl melted a little.

'I'm looking for Róisín?' she said, a little more gently.

The woman's face moved as if she were trying not to cry. She shook her head and went to close the door.

'Mrs McAreavey, I need to speak to Róisín,' she tried again. 'I'm Erich Bannon's sister.'

She had no idea if the name would mean anything to this woman. There was a good chance that Róisín never even mentioned Erich to her family.

'You'd better come in.' The woman stood aside and Liesl went in. The corridor leading to a back kitchen was tiny, and the whole house smelled of cabbage. 'Would you like tea?' she asked.

'No,' Liesl replied. 'No, thank you. I won't keep you. I just need to see Róisín, please.'

'You can't.' The words were barely audible.

'Why not? Is she at work?' Liesl asked.

The woman shook her head.

Liesl had no idea what, but something was very wrong. 'Mrs McAreavey, where is your daughter?'

The woman sat at the table and two fat tears ran down her face. 'They took her,' she managed.

Liesl pulled out a seat and sat opposite her, all fury dissipating in favour of a sense of dread. 'Who took her? Where?'

'Monsignor Doherty. He was a cousin of my husband's,' the woman whispered, as if saying his name aloud would summon him.

'I'm sorry, I don't understand. Is that a priest?' Liesl was baffled.

'Aye, a Monsignor. Colm and Neil said Fiach ordered it, so they took her.' Mrs McAreavey wiped her eye with the edge of her apron.

'Róisín's brothers ordered that this priest take her away?' Liesl was struggling to make any sense of it all. Perhaps the woman wasn't right in the head; she seemed very distressed. 'Where did they take her?'

The woman shook her head. 'I don't know. A home for girls like her, I suppose, down South. She'll have the baby there, and they'll have it adopted...' The woman's shoulders were shaking now, silent sobs racking her sparrow-like frame.

'Baby?' A sudden awareness dawned. 'Mrs McAreavey, is Róisín pregnant?'

'My poor wee girl. Her brothers, they beat her and then sent her away, I tried to stop them, but they...'

'Did they beat you too?' Liesl asked quietly.

The woman nodded.

She had to ask, though she was sure of the answer. 'And the baby's father is my brother?'

'Róisín loves him. Och, the tears she's cried over him. She tried to get to him, but they watched her, and me, every minute of the day. They made her write to him, saying it was over, and then, once they realised she was pregnant, they arranged for her to leave. I tried to stop it, tried to hide the pregnancy, but it was no good.'

'And you've no idea where she is now?' Liesl was trying to stay calm.

'No. I wish I did,' the woman said quietly.

'And your sons, Colm and Neil? Where are they?'

'I don't know. I've not seen them for days. England maybe. I don't know.'

'Is my brother in danger, Mrs McAreavey?' Liesl asked. She felt so sad for this downtrodden woman. She glanced around the tiny chilly kitchen. There didn't appear to be much food. She took out her purse. 'Please, take this.' She handed the other woman a ten-shilling note.

'I can't take your money, Missus,' she said with a force that surprised Liesl. 'My boys nearly killed your brother – Róisín told me – and I'm truly sorry for that. They... Well, I don't have any control over them. I haven't had for a long time. Fiach, my eldest, is the only one they answer to. So yes, I would think your brother is in consider-able danger. My sons are dangerous men, Missus...'

'Gallagher,' Liesl filled in. 'But please call me Liesl.'

'Sure you're only a wee girl yourself, and with a baby on the way

133

too.' She gave a weak smile. 'Aye, Fiach will not take this lying down, so please, tell your brother to be very careful and to get away if he can. He'll not be safe here.'

Liesl stood up. 'Here is my address and my parents' telephone number,' she said, scribbling the information on a piece of paper from her bag. 'If you hear from her, or find out anything, please get in touch.'

'Aye, I will,' the other woman said.

Liesl shoved the money under a tin on the table – Mrs McAreavey would find it when Liesl was gone – and left.

CHAPTER 19

*L*iesl started as Jamie appeared at the kitchen door. He crossed the room and turned the gas off under the pot that was burning.

'You could just say you don't like the flat – no need to burn it down.' He chuckled as he placed the blackened saucepan in the sink, where it emitted a loud hiss and a cloud of steam.

'I'm sorry,' Liesl replied, distressed. 'That's the second time I've done that, and it was your dinner too...'

Jamie took her hands and led her to the small Queen Anne chair Ariella had bought at an auction for them. Liesl loved it. It was bright-yellow velvet, and she was going to use it as a nursing chair for the baby once the time came.

The flat over the bar was poky and a little bit drab, but despite offers from their parents, Jamie and Liesl wanted to save for their own place together. Daniel had tried to object, but Elizabeth knew how important independence was to Jamie in particular.

Everyone was in agreement that Jamie had made an excellent job of the pub, but Liesl knew that though Jamie was grateful, he hated being beholden and wanted them to buy a house of their own.

Between her teaching job and his profits in the bar, they were almost there and were now beginning to look at places to buy. Jamie heard before anyone who was moving on, who was dying and what was for sale, as the local gossip was the stock in trade of the bar, and he'd been excited to report that there was a cottage going up for sale next month, right on the cliff overlooking the sea and only a mile from the village. His plan was that they would buy it and do it up. She wished she could share his enthusiasm. Normally she would, but she was out of her mind with worry about Erich.

It had been two days since she'd visited Róisín's mother, and she'd told nobody about what she'd learned, not even Jamie. But she had to do something. Erich wasn't due back until the end of November, and she couldn't wait that long.

'Don't worry about it. I'll make a sandwich or something.' He ran his hand over her hair, and she turned her face to his palm and kissed it.

'Liesl,' he asked, 'is everything all right? You've been…I don't know, distracted or something. I don't want to be mithering you, and I'm sure carrying a baby around is exhausting, so if it's just that, then tell me. But I'm a bit worried. If there was something on your mind, you'd tell me, wouldn't you?'

Liesl observed this man she'd married, and it struck her how odd it was that a boy, raised in County Kerry, thousands of miles from Berlin, could now be her closest ally, her best friend, her love. Their upbringings could not have been more different, and yet she felt a unity with Jamie that she'd never felt with anyone. She trusted him completely and knew she was safe in his arms. But there was a vulnerability to him as well that she loved. He didn't have all the answers. He was, like her, flawed, but it felt right with him, like they were two pieces of a jigsaw puzzle that fit perfectly.

'Is the bar busy?' she asked.

'No, the teatime crowd have been and gone, and the pickled regulars have to finish their dinner first for soakage.' He laughed. As a non-drinker, he had no moral problem with alcohol, but he found those who spent all of their time and money in his pub each night kind of sad. One of the regulars, Mattie Hancock, had explained to

Liesl one night – whiskey fumes nearly knocking Liesl out as Mattie spoke – how Jamie was the only publican in the world who tried to talk fellas out of drink. But it was true; he only served them up to a point and did not allow any rowdy behaviour. Jamie was known to make a man a sandwich and a cup of tea at night rather than giving him another drink, and when Liesl questioned the financial sense of it, Jamie explained that while it might not make him money – in fact it cost him – he couldn't look the drinker's wife in the face the next day knowing the condition he'd sent her husband home in.

'It's hardly your fault, though, is it? I mean, it's a person's own choice,' Liesl had argued.

'I know, but poor Mrs Hancock has enough to be dealing with, and Mattie coming in roaring drunk and waking the kids at all hours isn't right. So if I can do something to keep him someway under control, then I will,' Jamie had reasoned.

'I can close up for an hour if you like? Make you something to eat?' Jamie offered.

Liesl rested her head against the velvet chair. 'I'm not hungry. *Mutti* dropped in with soup a while ago. But I would like to talk to you.'

'Give me two minutes.' He sprang to his feet, his huge body dominating the small room.

As he went downstairs and she heard him shoot the bolt on the front door, she tried to formulate her thoughts. Within a minute he was back, and he dragged an old tapestry-covered chair with one wobbly leg over to sit in front of her. It had been in the flat when they arrived, and whatever pattern or design was once on it, had long been rubbed off by thousands of bottoms over the years. Everything they owned was second-hand or had been thrown out by someone else, but Liesl couldn't care less. She knit and sewed and made do. They were used to it from the war years, and they wanted to save every penny for their new home.

He sat opposite her, and her eyes took in the contours of his face, the slight stubble on his jaw, the bump in his nose from a break he'd sustained playing football, the copper curls untamed by the Brylcreem most men used. His eyes were sea green, and she often felt she could just sail away in them. She knew his toned, fit body as intimately as her own by now, but it never failed to excite her. He'd been delighted that pregnancy, rather than kill her desire for him, had in fact enhanced it once the nausea wore off.

'What is it, my love?' he asked, and she could hear the worry in his voice. 'Whatever it is, we'll manage it together. We've endured worse.'

He reminded her a lot of Daniel in the sense that he exuded a kind of rational calm. 'We've endured worse' had become a kind of catch-phrase. Neither of them enjoyed thinking about Kurt Richter, but those events had happened, and Jamie had been by her side through the entire ordeal. He'd broken her fall when she jumped from the window to escape Kurt, so her injuries, while still serious, were much less than they could have been.

Then Jamie's family had rejected her. He'd dropped out of college and they'd blamed her for that. He and his brother the priest, had barely spoken in years because Brendan so disapproved of Jamie marrying a non-Catholic. So for a young couple they'd had their fair share of hardship, but they weathered it by sticking together.

'I opened a letter addressed to Erich,' she began.

'And?'

'It was from Róisín.' She moved to sit more comfortably, wincing a little. The damage to her spine in the fall, while not crippling, did make being pregnant a little more challenging than it would have been had she not been injured.

'And what did she say?'

'Oh, Jamie.' Liesl sighed. 'I don't know what to do.'

She quickly told him how cold and mean the letter was and how she went round to the McAreavey house to give Róisín a piece of her mind.

'I can well imagine that.' Jamie smiled. Liesl could be fiery when necessary.

'But I couldn't because she wasn't there. She'd been taken away by some priest or something. Her mother is distraught.' Liesl paused. 'She's pregnant and the baby is Erich's.'

There was silence as Liesl waited for the news to sink in.

'Damn and blast it anyway!' Jamie ran his hand through his hair in frustration.

'What should we do? Erich doesn't know about the baby. Róisín's mother says her brother – Fiach, I think she called him, the one in prison anyhow – knows about it and that Colm tells him everything and that he's angry.' Liesl swallowed. Saying the words aloud made them real. 'I'm so scared for him, Jamie. What should we do?'

Jamie ran his hands over his stubble, deep in thought. Then he took her hands in his. 'All right, if this girl is in trouble – the phrase us Catholics use for pregnant without a ring on her finger – then that's very bad news.' Jamie's normally open and cheerful face looked worried.

Liesl went on. 'Her mother said she was taken to someplace, a mother and baby home, I presume, to have the child. And then something about adoption, but I didn't understand that.'

Jamie's eyes darkened. 'Remember Patricia Barry, who was in my anatomy class at UCD? Dark curly hair, really unusual laugh?'

Liesl remembered her. She was a lively girl with a great singing voice and always the last to leave the party. 'Yes, I do. What's she got to do with this?'

'Well, she just left college in the middle of second year. She was pregnant.'

'Really?' Liesl was surprised, but perplexed at what this had to do with Erich.

'Nobody mentioned it, as it isn't really something people want to talk about, but the Church – well, nuns really – have places where girls who find themselves in trouble out of wedlock are sent. They call them Magdalen Asylums, after Mary Magdalen, the fallen woman.'

'Yes, I'm sure that's the place Róisín was sent. The mother said a priest was collecting her. Why?'

Jamie looked awkward, as if he didn't want to explain. 'I met Patricia, bumped into her on the street in Dublin one day when I went down for Derry's graduation a while back, and we went for a cup of coffee. Liesl, those places...they're horrible. She told me that the nuns were so cruel, forcing the girls to work in a laundry, giving them very little food and no medical attention and calling them sinners. They are not allowed any contact with the outside world at all. They have to wear a uniform and change their names, and then, when the time comes to have their baby, they have to do so without any medicine for the pain and no doctors there to deliver the babies. There might be a midwife if you're lucky enough to go into labour when the one or two that work there might be on duty, but often not. And then, after a few months, they take the babies and have them adopted without giving the mother any say whatsoever. Patricia had to stay for another six months after they took her son away to work off the debt of her bed and board.' Jamie exhaled. Telling this harrowing story was hard on him. 'I didn't tell you at the time because you were just pregnant with our baby and I didn't want to upset you, but I know she's telling the truth.'

Liesl was incredulous. She knew the Catholic Church took a very dim view of sex before marriage, but surely this treatment wasn't commonplace. Perhaps Patricia had been very unlucky, the poor girl. She said as much to Jamie.

'No, they are all like that.' He gazed out the window, over her head. 'There was a place near us at home, the Good Shepherd Convent, and look, we all knew what went on there and nobody said it. I was up a tree near the convent wall one day – I was only a young fella – and I saw in over the wall. There they were, loads of girls, all pregnant, digging potatoes. They were all dressed the same in grey kind of dresses, and a nun was standing guard. I asked my mam when I went home, and she just said that it was nothing for me to worry about and that the girls in there got there by their own actions.'

'What? That's horrendous!' Liesl exclaimed, aghast. 'But how can they keep them there? Why don't the women just leave if it's so awful?'

'They can't. The guards would bring them back if they escaped,' Jamie said quietly.

'The guards... You mean the police?' Liesl couldn't believe what she was hearing. 'But that's impossible! I mean, they aren't criminals...'

'No, but that's the way it is.'

'And what about the babies' fathers, the boyfriends?'

'They are never consulted.' Jamie seemed sure. 'I remember one wet night, I was about thirteen, and there was a knock on the door. My mother was out at Benediction in the church – it was a Sunday night. Anyway, this fella arrived, soaked to the skin he was, only seventeen or eighteen. My father answered the door to him and I suppose took pity on him and let him in. I sat on the top step trying to hear whatever was going on. I only caught snatches of the conversation, but basically this lad's girl was in the convent and he'd worked and saved up enough money for them to go to England. He had the tickets for the boat and everything, and he wanted to go up to the convent and demand they release her. My father told him he was wasting his time, that there was no way they'd let her out. But he was determined, so my father gave him a dry shirt and trousers and a coat and let him off.'

Liesl was horrified at the story but didn't interrupt.

'About an hour later, he was back, drenched again, in tears. They wouldn't even open the door to him. My father was trying to console him when my mother came back and put the run on him, saying he should have thought of the consequences before he went around committing sins.'

Jamie sounded ashamed of his mother's attitude. Liesl wasn't surprised at Peggy Gallagher's behaviour; it sounded perfectly plausible that she would be so cruel.

'My father followed him out to the hallway and advised him to use his ticket and go to England, to start again and forget about her and the baby, that there was no hope.'

'And there was nothing he could do? Legally even?' Though Liesl didn't doubt Jamie's word, it seemed unbelievable that someone could be held prisoner like that.

'The Church and the state are kind of one and the same down South, Liesl. You wouldn't have noticed it so much going to Trinity, where no Catholics go, so you wouldn't have known many. But the archbishop of Dublin, John Charles McQuaid, has the ear of de Valera. He's always had it, and that's why the Irish state is very much a Catholic one. My brother Brendan nearly gave himself an ulcer trying to get himself appointed to the archbishop's staff. They'd be cut from the same cloth, Brendan and Bishop McQuaid, you can be sure. So if the Church says something, the state tends to back them up. It's kind of how it is.'

'So you think Róisín and my brother's unborn child are in a place like that?' Liesl was furious now.

'I do,' Jamie said quietly. 'In fact, I'm convinced of it.' He took her hands again.

She shook him off. 'Well we have to get her out. Maybe they'll get married or...'

Jamie tried to reason with her. 'Liesl, love, I know this sounds harsh, but there is no way on earth they are going to allow her to marry Erich. They just won't. And this is no world for an unmarried mother and her child. I know it sounds horrible, but maybe it's for the best?'

Liesl couldn't believe her ears. 'Are you serious? You of all people? I'm Jewish and we got married – how is it different for Erich?' She could hear the indignation in her voice, but she was horrified to hear him speak like this. She had been sure he would be as outraged as she was.

'I'm not defending it, Liesl. You're right, it's terrible, but it's how it is. All over Ireland there are places like that for girls like her, and the people who run them are very powerful.'

Jamie was trying to be reasonable, she knew.

'They have the backing of the state, the Church, the Gardaí, everyone. Nobody talks about it but people know. And I agree it's mad. She's not a criminal but she might as well be.'

'No, Jamie. Just no. I won't accept that. I can't contact Erich, tell him he's about to be a father but unfortunately the child's mother has been kidnapped by a priest and can't be found. Oh, and by the way, your child is going to be sent for adoption and neither you nor Róisín get a say in the matter. Can't you see how preposterous that is?' Liesl was fuming now, and though taking it out on Jamie was unfair, he was the only Irish Catholic in the room.

The flat felt stuffy and constricting, and Liesl stood up and opened the window. Then she closed it again because she realised this conversation was not one she wanted reported to the entire village.

'What is wrong with that Church of yours, with the people of your part of Ireland, that they allow this? Is sex such a shameful thing? Is the arrival of a new life so dreadful if the mother and father aren't married that it warrants that barbaric behaviour?'

Jamie tried to take her into his arms for a hug and to bury his face in her hair. She normally relaxed into him, his hugs making everything better, but now she was just too frustrated and angry. She wanted to scream, to rant, to find someone to blame. Poor Róisín, and poor Erich. This was awful.

She pushed away from him and sat back down on her yellow chair.

'Can I make you a cup of tea?' Jamie asked gently.

'No,' she snapped, then relented. 'No, thanks. I... We have to do something, Jamie. What about Father O'Toole? He's nice, and I think it was he who approached Daniel first about employing her brothers – doesn't he know the family?'

'I think he does,' Jamie agreed.

'Well, will we go up there now? Speak to him and demand that –'

Jamie didn't try to touch her again, but he spoke calmly. 'Demand what, Liesl? That he find her and release her? If he did that, which I can almost guarantee that he wouldn't, then what? Send her home to her mother? It was her family who sent her away. Or bring her here? Erich doesn't even know she's pregnant, and he had more or less come to the conclusion that the relationship was over before he left. You and I both know Erich is thinking of staying in America – he's done with Ballycreggan. So he doesn't love her. If he did, he wouldn't leave her, pregnant or not, now would he?'

'So what are you saying?' Liesl asked, daring him to say it.

'I'm saying that there's no easy answer here.' He sighed.

'You think we should just abandon her, don't you, that it's for the best?' Liesl couldn't believe what she was hearing.

'No, I'm saying we need to tread carefully and not go in there like a bull in a china shop issuing demands and accusations in a situation that really isn't our business.'

'Not our business?' Liesl was shouting now and didn't care who heard her. 'Are you serious? How can it not be my business? That child is my niece or nephew!'

'Ah, Liesl, would you calm down? Let's talk about this rationally...' He tried to take her hand, but she pulled it away.

She needed to get away. Jamie was just as bad as all of those lunatic Catholics. He was just like his horrible bigoted mother. Peggy Gallagher acted like she'd changed, but getting drunk the last time they visited and going on about their baby being raised in that horrible, mean, cruel faith... Well, she, and her son, and every single one of them, could just bugger off. Liesl left the flat, slamming the door behind her.

CHAPTER 20

*L*iesl got off the bus in Belfast. She'd taken the first one that had come along to the bus stop in the village after her dramatic walkout, and now she felt more than a little foolish. Storming off on Jamie like that was stupid, she knew. He wasn't defending the system, he was just explaining it to her, but her need to protect Erich ran into her bones; she could not let him down now. She needed to speak to him and she couldn't make the call from anywhere in Ballycreggan without the whole village hearing about it. It was nice, living in such a close community, but sometimes she had to admit it suffocated her.

When she was a student, she always imagined she would end up working in Europe, using her linguistics training, living an exotic life, but fate had other ideas. She didn't ever regret marrying Jamie, and he wasn't stopping her. He'd follow her wherever she wanted to go; she knew he would. But the experience with Kurt, the accident, had made her nervous. She wondered if rushing back to the village of her family was not what she really wanted but was just somewhere safe?

Anyway, now she had Erich to worry about. Her brother was in love with Róisín and her rejection of him broke his heart. The fact that she'd been forced to write that letter would surely give him comfort even if the rest of the story was horrific. If she didn't do something it might be the reason he stayed in America. He'd spoken to her about it before he left, and that was the attraction of America for him; he thought nobody would care what religion or nationality he was there. But he was wrong. It mattered everywhere. The core of all conflict, no matter where in the world it happened, was difference, with one group of people deciding they were better than another group – a better colour, a better religion, a better nationality. Her international studies had taught her that. It made no sense, but it was how it was, and Liesl doubted America was any different to anywhere else.

She went into a shop and asked for change for the telephone, then found a call box on the street. Luckily her address book was always in her handbag, which mercifully she'd remembered to snatch before leaving.

She should call Jamie first, but they didn't have a phone, and if she called her mother, she'd want to know why Liesl was in Belfast and what had happened. The same with Elizabeth. Then she had an idea. Bridie in the sweetshop had just got a phone and took great delight in giving Liesl her new number, insisting she write it down in her address book. At the time, Liesl did it to humour her. Bridie had always been lovely to them as children, but Liesl could not think of a single occasion when she would need to ring Bridie, whose shop was no more than thirty yards from the pub.

She dialled the number, and it was answered on the first ring.

'Good afternoon, Bridie's sweetshop, Ballycreggan. Bridie speaking. How may I help you?'

Liesl smiled at Bridie's telephone voice, in which there was no trace of her normally thick Northern accent.

'Hello, Bridie. It's Liesl.'

'Oh, Liesl love, are you all right?' Immediately she was back to herself.

'Fine, fine, Bridie, thanks. But I came to Belfast to get some material for curtains and I meant to leave Jamie a note because he was in the bar dealing with something when I left. I just remembered I forgot, so could you just pop over and tell him I'm in Belfast, that I'm fine and I'll be on the next bus home? You know how men get!'

'Och, I do surely. He'd be all up in a hoop thinking you'd done a flit, so he would.' Bridie guffawed at her own joke. 'I'll pop over right now, don't you worry, darlin'. And be sure you come home soon! A girl in your condition needs to rest and not be traipsing about the streets all day, do you hear me now?'

'I will, Bridie. Thanks very much. Bye now.'

'Bye-bye, Liesl love.' Bridie hung up.

Liesl then rifled through the pages until she came to Bud's address in Biloxi. She dialled the operator. 'Can you connect me to Mr Thomas Smith of 1365 Elmer Street, Biloxi, Mississippi, in America, please?'

The operator's voice sounded robotic. 'Do you have the number, caller?'

'Um, no, I'm sorry...' Liesl had never called anyone in America before. She'd rung her friend Millie once or twice in England and people had called the house from Israel, but this was new territory for her.

'I'll look it up. Please hold the line.'

There were several clicks and then the voice again. 'Putting you through now. Insert coins when the call is answered.'

'Th-thank you,' Liesl stammered, but the woman was gone.

There was a long tone, not like the double ring she was used to. On and on it rang, and she held the money in her fist, ready to insert it in the slot.

'Hello, the Smith residencia?' an Italian-accented woman's voice answered as Liesl fumbled to insert the coins. She thought it must be Gabriella, Bud's wife.

'Oh, hello! Um...my name is Liesl Galla –I mean Bannon. My brother is staying there with you – Erich. I wonder, could I speak to him?'

'Ah, Liesl, Ciao! Erich! One minute – I will get him.'

The phone beeped to insert more coins, and as she did, Liesl prayed she'd have enough.

'Liesl?' Erich sounded panicked. 'What's wrong?'

'Everyone is fine, Erich, don't worry. I just need to talk to you about Róisín.'

There was more beeping, and she put in all her remaining coins. This was news that should be broken gently, but she had no time.

'What about her?' he asked. 'Is she all right?'

'Yes – well, I think so. Look, Erich, she wrote to you and I opened the letter. I'm sorry but I was worried. Anyway, I went round to her house to have it out with her, how she could be so cutting to you, but I met her mother, who told me she's pregnant and you're the father and that she was taken away by a priest to some horrible place run by nuns and that the child would be taken away from her or something. Jamie explained they have those kinds of places in the South, and I didn't know what to do...'

There was silence on the line, nothing but the crackle. A bus's brakes screeched beside her, followed by loud honking of horns. A boy on a bike had narrowly missed being knocked down.

'Erich, are you still there?' she asked, pressing the receiver to her ear to try to block out the din outside the phone box.

'Yes, Liesl, I...I'm here. I... Did her mother say anything else, like how she felt about me or anything?'

Liesl's heart broke for him. 'She said Róisín loves you and that her brothers made her write that horrible letter. They kept her locked up, and then when they found out she was pregnant, they sent her away.'

'She loves me?' Erich sounded so relieved and happy despite the terrible situation they found themselves in now. 'All right, look, um... I don't know what to do either. I... Let me see if I can change my ticket and get home. I need to...' He sounded very far away.

'Do you want me to try to find her?' Liesl asked. 'Though Jamie says it won't be possible, I could ask?'

'No.' Erich sounded sure about that at least. 'You need to take it easy with the baby and everything. This is my mess, and I'll sort it out. But, Liesl...'

The line crackled and she missed what he said; it was so frustrating. She just caught, 'I want to handle this myself.'

'I won't tell anyone. Jamie knows, but nobody else.'

'Right, I'll try to change my ticket. I'll send a telegram if I can. Poor Róisín…'

'Erich, I know you feel responsible, and you are in as much as she is, but if she's not the one for you, you don't need to do anything hasty, you know, like marry her or something? These nuns will try to have the child adopted, it seems that's what they do, and maybe it's for the best?' She didn't believe it for a second – the idea that her brother's child would grow up thinking some other people were his or her parents was inconceivable – but she wanted him to know all the options.

'No. I won't abandon her. I love her, Liesl.'

More beeping.

'Erich, I don't have any more money. I'm sorry, I –' The line went dead.

She took the bus back to Ballycreggan as she promised she would and was relieved to see Jamie standing at the bus stop waiting for her. She got off, and he held her hand as they walked along the street. They waited until they were inside their little flat before speaking.

'I rang Erich,' Liesl said. 'I wanted to go somewhere I could speak to him without the whole parish being in on it.' Hetty Devlin, the postmistress, was known to eavesdrop on some of the more juicy conversations that had to go through her telephone exchange.

'And to get away from your clumsy Catholic husband?' Jamie raised an enquiring eyebrow.

'Well, I was angry, but it was unfair to take it out on you. You don't represent the Catholic Church, I know that, but I just… I'm sorry.'

Jamie helped her off with her light autumn coat. It was a pink one that she'd made herself and she liked it. So many maternity clothes were navy, beige or grey, like a woman carrying a child should fade into the background; she liked her coat making a splash. It drew some looks from the women more than the men, as if it was a bit unseemly to be so bright with such an obvious bump, but she didn't care. Her long dark hair also hung loose the way Jamie liked it, not tied back in a modest bun or roll as befitting a married woman.

Jamie refused to wear the dark trousers and white shirts of the men in the village, and he didn't even own a tie. He lived in sweaters she knit him in the winter and short-sleeved casual shirts in the summer. Elizabeth despaired of the worn corduroy or canvas trousers he wore daily, but Liesl loved that he looked so rugged and handsome and not stuffy and old-fashioned like most of the other men she knew. They were a slightly bohemian couple, and they got away with it because people liked them.

'So,' he asked, resting his arms on her shoulders and looking down into her face, a cheeky smile playing around his lips, 'are we friends again?'

'Friends.' She smiled and leaned up on her tiptoes to kiss his nose.

'Well, what did Romeo have to say for himself?' Jamie took a glass and filled it with cold water from the tap, sinking the full pint in a few seconds.

'Oh, don't you come over all judgemental on me, Mr Gallagher. We weren't exactly legal before we were up to all sorts in Horrible Hanratty's boarding house, if I recall correctly,' she admonished as she accepted a glass of water from him.

'Fair enough.' He grinned. 'Tea?'

'Please, and a slice of *Mutti's* apple cake from the tin. I'm famished.'

She eased herself into her yellow chair and looked around their living room while Jamie made tea. Was it only a few hours ago she'd stormed off?

Though buying a proper house of their own was exciting, a part of her would miss this first home they had together. The kitchen was a hodgepodge arrangement of a dresser and a table, a sink up on a makeshift timber frame and a gas stove that belonged in a museum. Daniel and Willi had offered several times to fix it up better for them, but there really wasn't any point. The sitting room, part of the kitchen really as it was all one big room, had her lovely yellow chair, an old brown velvet sofa that they both loathed because the springs stuck out and because of the horrid colour, and a huge red and gold Axminster rug Elizabeth insisted they take. Erich had bought them a wireless as a wedding present, a huge Bush set with all the important cities of the world listed on the glass front panel. It was cased in real mahogany, and the large dials allowed the listener to dial it to whatever frequency was necessary. Liesl kept up her fluency in French, German and a little Italian by tuning into the radio each night. Jamie worked until ten or eleven in the bar, so she found it great company.

Jamie placed the cup and slice of cake on the small side table beside her chair, and she took the cup and sipped gratefully.

'Right. From the start,' he said, sitting opposite her.

CHAPTER 21

*E*rich packed his bags, having first rearranged his passage home. He was cutting the trip short, but he had to find Róisín. The news that she was being held somewhere against her will was so distressing, and he needed to rectify the situation as soon as possible. Somewhere in the pit of his stomach, though, was a flutter of joy. She loved him, she was about to have his child, that letter wasn't what she meant, and there was nobody else.

He would have to tell the family too, once he got back. He would put Daniel and Willi on alert. He owed them so much – his life, in fact, and that of his sister. Daniel and Elizabeth had given them a stable and loving home in a time when the alternative was unimaginably horrific. And as for his *mutti*, well, she'd endured privations beyond anything anyone should be expected to just to be reunited with him and Liesl. He needed to keep them all safe, and if the McAreaveys had a grudge against him, which they did, they were in danger as much as he was.

He was going to be a father. Over and over, he said the words in his mind. He, Erich Bannon, a father. He'd supposed he'd become a parent one day, but it was not something he'd ever spent any time thinking about. He felt like a boy. His father had had Liesl when he was Erich's age, twenty-three, so it wasn't outlandish but he just couldn't imagine it. Liesl and Jamie having a baby was fine; they were grown up, married, with their own place and everything. But him? And Róisín?

He'd always felt there was plenty of time for that later, when he was…what? Older? Wiser? Well, as Bud might say, he'd better start wising up, and soon. This was a very grown-up predicament, and he needed to figure it out. His boyhood was behind him; it was time to step up and be a man.

The priority now had to be Róisín. She didn't deserve any of this. The thought of her being sent to some horrible place broke his heart. She was so beautiful and lively and full of fun; this wasn't fair at all. He knew neither Liesl nor Jamie would lie to him, but did such places really exist? It was hard to believe.

He would leave Biloxi in the morning and take the train journey to Atlanta. All he had to do now was tell Bud.

He found Bud chopping wood in the yard with his shirt off.

'Hey, Erich.' His friend smiled. 'Coming to help?'

'Afraid not. I need to finish packing. I have to go home, Bud, tomorrow.' Erich delivered the words sadly.

'What? Why?' Bud asked, dismayed. 'I thought you and me was fixin' to go exploring next week, and my Mama says we need to take you over there for a potluck, she wants to show you off to her ladies. If I don't deliver you she's gonna be madder than a wet hen.'

'There's been a development.' Erich cut across him.

'Tell me.' Bud led him to the steps and got two beers from the fridge he kept on the veranda, a decadent extravagance that never failed to impress Erich. They sat, side by side.

When Erich finished telling Bud all Liesl had said, he looked at his friend. 'So I have to go home, try to find her.'

'And if you find her, and it sounds like that ain't gonna be easy, what then?' Bud asked.

Erich finished his beer, placed the bottle beside him and rested his forearms on his knees, his eyes examining the wooden step between his feet. 'I've absolutely no idea,' he admitted finally.

'But you love this girl?' Bud probed.

'I do, very much,' he answered truthfully. 'And she loves me too it seems. But even if I didn't or she didn't, I can't allow her to be locked up like some kind of criminal and then have our child given to strangers. That can't be allowed to happen.'

They sat in silence for a while, and eventually Bud spoke again. 'I'd go back with you and help you if Tommy wasn't so little. You know that, don't you?' Bud sounded so sad he couldn't be there for his friend.

'Of course, and I appreciate it, Bud. But to be truthful with you, I don't even know where to start. I'm hoping if I can go to the priest who took her and explain that I want to take care of her and at least have a conversation...'

Bud raised one eyebrow sceptically. 'You need to watch your back there, buddy. Those brothers of hers sound like trouble to me.'

'Maybe they are. All Liesl knows is that she was taken to the South. That could mean anywhere from Donegal to Kerry. But if the priest sees me as genuine, maybe they'll let her out, or let me go to see her or something. I don't know.'

'So are you goin' back right away?' Bud asked.

'Yes, I sail the day after tomorrow. There's a train to Atlanta at 8 a.m. and from there to New York, that should get me there on time. I'll book a taxi to take me to the station.'

'Don't matter if you bound for heaven or hell, you still gotta change at Atlanta huh? I'll drive you to the station in the morning.' Bud chuckled.

'Ah, thanks, Bud, but there's no need. I'll be fine –...' Erich protested.

'Now you hush your mouth. I know I don't gotta do it, but we're friends, and I dunno when I'm gonna see you again. I wanna wave you off, like a broken-hearted sweetheart, wavin' my handkerchief.' He gave Erich a playful nudge and they laughed.

CHAPTER 22

he voyage back across the ocean was uneventful, and as Erich hoped, his cabin was a single one. He spent most of his time there, reading, or at least trying to, but he was never much of a book lover, and besides, he had too much on his mind. At night he saw her, Róisín, in a prison uniform, her hair limp and dirty, screaming and begging him to rescue her. He'd wake in a bog of sweat.

As each nautical mile brought him further away from the magic of America and closer to the reality of the mess they were in at home, he found himself torn. He longed to see Róisín again, but he was worried about the McAreaveys – not so much for himself, but for his family. He could not have them in danger.

Was he being naïve thinking that his family would be disappointed but supportive? Maybe they would be mortified and furious. He couldn't even try to imagine what the rabbi would say when he found out…if he found out. Maybe he should just handle this alone? Well, with Liesl and Jamie, but without the parents knowing anything?

He thought about it and made a plan. He would approach Father O'Toole on the quiet. The priest was a nice man and surely wouldn't stand for this imprisoning of an innocent girl. He must know where she was, and Erich could just go there and explain. He had money, so if that's what it took, he could pay, and once he got her out, they would leave, maybe go right back to America, away from Colm and Neil and the shadowy Fiach. Yes, he would have to leave his family, but Róisín and the baby were his new family now.

He went to the dining room for meals, sitting alone, and returned to his cabin afterwards. Apart from an occasional walk up on deck for some air, when he nodded in greeting to his fellow passengers, he spoke to nobody.

He had an overnight in Liverpool, docking late and sailing for Larne the next afternoon, and despite sleeping on the ship, he was exhausted.

It was a dull misty evening when the ship docked in Liverpool. He dragged his suitcase from the rack over the bed and donned his coat and the new trilby hat he'd treated himself to before the trip. The ticket had included a hotel stay, so he'd go straight there. He had very few memories of the first city he and Liesl had lived in with Elizabeth after she came to meet them as they got off the Kindertransport. He recalled a small red-bricked house on a long street of identical houses, and a night in a neighbour's bomb shelter as German bombs rained down on them from overhead. They'd come up the next morning to find their house flattened and all of their possessions gone. That had been the reason they moved to Elizabeth's parents' house in Ireland. If the Luftwaffe had chosen a different city, or a different street even, perhaps he'd have grown up Liverpudlian rather than Irish. It was an odd thought. His life had taken so many twists and turns, and none of the outcomes had been predictable, and here he was again, at another perilous juncture.

He buttoned his coat against the damp mist and pulled his collar up. As he stepped out of the ship onto the gangway, the sidelong wind, carrying salty spray, whipped at the side of his face. Was he basking in Biloxi sunshine only a week ago? It seemed hard to believe.

He gripped the rope on the side of the gangway and made his way down the laths of wood at intervals on the wooden walkway that stopped passengers slipping. In America it would have been glass and metal and something more sophisticated than timber and rope. He felt like he'd stepped back fifty years.

He stayed overnight in a hotel and sailed the next day for Belfast. He took the bus to Ballycreggan; thankfully it was almost empty and he didn't recognise anyone on it.

He looked up and down the village as dusk settled; the air smelled of the familiar turf fumes from the fires. He made his way to the parochial house. Fortune smiled on him, and he watched Mrs O'Hanlon from behind a belt of trees as she left via the back door for bingo in the community hall. With any luck he would get to speak to the priest alone and nobody would see him.

He crept to the back door and knocked. Within a few minutes, he saw the limping figure of Father O'Toole.

'Erich!' the priest exclaimed. 'The rabbi told me you were in America. What happened? Is everything all right?'

'Yes, Father,' Erich replied, addressing the priest as he'd always done. 'Can I have a word, please?'

'Of course! Come in.' The priest stood back and beckoned Erich in. 'Tea?' he asked.

'No, thanks.' Erich stood in the priest's kitchen, trying not to recall stealing his strawberries or cutting his grass as punishment when he was a child. He was a man now, and he needed to be seen as one.

'I'll get right to the point.' He exhaled. 'My girlfriend, your cousin Róisín, has been taken away somewhere. She's pregnant, and I want to find her and get her out of there.'

Father O'Toole seemed to visibly deflate. 'Look, Erich, I did hear, and I'm very sorry to learn about it. Róisín is a lovely girl. But I honestly have no idea, so I can't help you –'

'But you must know! It's the Catholic Church are locking her up, and you're a Catholic priest. What do you mean, you don't know? Of course you do!'

'Erich, please, calm yourself,' Father O'Toole pleaded. 'It wasn't me! It was another man, a Monsignor, and I had nothing to do with it, so I can't tell you –'

'Won't, you mean,' Erich interjected. He had been brought up to be respectful to everyone, but this was ridiculous.

'It's not like that. I feel terrible about even connecting the McAreaveys to your family. I had no idea what kind of people they really were. I only met the mother, my cousin a few times in my life. I knew the older boy was bad news, but I thought the younger ones were –'

'I don't care about them. Róisín is the only one I want to know about. They're irrelevant.' He did nothing to hide his frustration.

'Erich, please, listen to me.' Fr O'Toole was visibly upset. 'You do not want to make more of an enemy of them. Please trust me on this. Fiach McAreavey is a very dangerous person, and him being locked up seems to have had no impact on his influence. I urge you, please, let this go, for your own sake and for the girl's.'

'Are you mad?' Erich knew he was being rude but didn't care. 'She is carrying my child and has been whisked away someplace where they will treat her terribly and then take the baby, and you think I should do nothing?'

'Unfortunately, yes. There is nothing you can do – I wish you could see that.'

'I thought you were better than this, Father O'Toole, I really did.' Erich walked out into the night.

The lights were on in Jamie's pub and he wished he could call to Liesl, but the fewer people who knew he was back, the better, at least for now. He had to go to plan B.

Elizabeth had told him on the phone the incredible news that the rabbi and Frau Braun had somehow got together and were now living in the village. He knew the house, so he put his hat on, pulled his collar up and headed straight there, hoping he didn't bump into anyone.

The door to Frau Braun and the rabbi's was on the latch – nobody in Ballycreggan locked their doors – and he simply let himself in. He hoped the rabbi would still be awake, but if not, he would wake him.

Luckily he saw the light on in the little living room; the rabbi was always a night owl. He was alone, and Erich slipped quietly into the room. Another man might have got a fright or been angry at such an intrusion, but not Rabbi Frank.

He stood and greeted Erich, embracing him like a long-lost son. 'So you came back early?' he asked. 'We best be quiet, as Katerin is sleeping.'

Erich nodded and as quickly and succinctly as possible told him the story, including his futile attempts to get an address out of Father O'Toole.

'Can you speak to him, Rabbi, on my behalf? Get him to tell me where she is? He won't talk to me, but you and he are friends so he might tell you. I'm sure he knows.' Erich was trying to stay calm.

'Sit, please, Erich. Let's talk about this.' The rabbi gestured to the sofa. Reluctantly Erich sat. Now that he was there, he wanted to get on the case of finding her as soon as possible.

'Now, supposing I could get Father O'Toole to tell me – and if he says he doesn't know, then he is probably telling the truth. You might have to accept that. But just supposing he gives me an answer, what then?'

'Then I go there, find a way of getting her out, and we leave. I was thinking America.'

The rabbi nodded and gently tugged his beard, a gesture Erich remembered him doing all his life when he had something to ponder.

'And these brothers of hers, the ones that beat you up before, they are in the IRA, no?'

'Yes, they are,' Erich confirmed, trying to mask his frustration at the speed of the conversation. 'But we'll be gone before anyone here even knows, and –'

'And you think the IRA have no connections in America?' the rabbi asked calmly.

'Well, they probably do, but...' Erich didn't care about the brothers; why could the rabbi not see that?

'Erich, they definitely do, not probably. No, America is not the place for you. It would be too dangerous... Let me think.' He sat back down in his fireside chair.

'Look, I have money. I can –'

'Erich, my boy, please, calm down. I understand you are worried, and yes, I will speak to the priest for you, but you must act rationally, you must be clever. Think with this' – he pointed a finger to his temple – 'not this.' He pointed to his heart.

'All right, Rabbi, I'll try,' Erich conceded. 'What do you think I should do?'

The rabbi nodded slowly, his lips pursed in thought. 'One step at a time, but if I can get it out of Father O'Toole, and if you can liberate this young woman, then I think you should go to the one place on earth I can guarantee there are no IRA members.'

'Where is that?' Erich asked, intrigued.

'A kibbutz.' The rabbi smiled slowly. 'Here's what we will do, and this is all subject to a lot of ifs. But supposing you are successful in your rescue mission, then you fly to London and contact this man. There's a flight from Shannon Airport every day I believe. And from London, you'll be brought to Tel Aviv and then to the kibbutz.' He scribbled an address on a piece of notepaper, transcribing it from his address book.

Erich read it. 'Abraham Schultz. Who is he?'

'Mossad,' the rabbi said calmly.

'Israeli secret service? But why would they help me?' Erich was struggling to come to grips with what was happening.

The rabbi smiled. 'I have friends in all sorts of places, Erich. You should know that by now.'

'But we won't have any papers, passports and that sort of thing…' Of course, he would face the same problem going to America he realised now.

'It's fine. I'll sort it out. You don't need a passport to travel to Britain, and once you get to London, this man will sort out everything you need for Israel. You have my backing and you are a Jew, therefore, under the Law of Return, you have the right to Israeli citizenship.'

'And Róisín?'

'By the time you get there, Mr Schultz will know the entire story, so don't worry – he will arrange everything for both of you. Now, you'll need money.' He went to a small wooden box in his desk drawer.

'Ah, no, Rabbi, I have my own money...' Erich protested.

'Best you keep a low profile, Erich, stay out of sight, and walking into the bank is not how to do that. This is from a former friend of yours – remember Karl Kolitz, he goes by Charlie now of course? He sends me money for the farm. I don't think it's exactly the most legitimately earned money in the world, but he won't accept it back and I don't want to offend him in case he doesn't contact me again – he needs guidance – so I've been keeping it.' He handed Erich a large wad of rolled-up bank notes. 'So you'll stay here, in the spare room, and stay out of sight until I can talk to Father O'Toole in the morning.' He stood.

'And what about Frau Br...' Erich began. It was so hard to call her Frau Frank now.

The rabbi smiled. 'I will confide in Katerin. If she has proven anything in all these years, it is that she can keep a secret.'

'Rabbi, can you keep this between us? I don't want my family knowing anything – it's safer for them that way. I'll contact them myself once we are safely in Israel. If I can get Róisín out of there, that is.'

The rabbi nodded and patted Erich on the shoulder. '*Zayt mir gezunt un shtark.* Go sleep, pray. All will be well.'

CHAPTER 23

*R*abbi Frank walked with a cane now, taking one step at a time, but it was better than the alternative of being immobile and relying on Katerin for everything. He couldn't be much of a husband to her in his decrepit state, but he needed to do as much for himself as he could to make her feel like she wasn't drawing the very last straw. He opened their bedroom door and felt, as he had done every night since they married, the thrill of sheer love to see her there, under the covers.

Their marriage had been a small affair, as neither of them wanted a big fuss. They went to Dublin, to Rabbi Frank's friend and brother rabbi, Herschel Samuels, where the ceremony took place. They stayed that night in a fancy hotel, a gift from the Liebers, and enjoyed a lovely dinner. He had never felt so happy in his life and told her so.

She had dressed in a beautiful ivory cream dress and coat and wore a cream hat with a little net over her eye. He knew she and Elizabeth had worked on it for a long time, making sure it was perfect. Her hair, normally tied back in a bun, was in soft waves around her face.

'You are beautiful,' he'd said as the waiter left their plates on the table.

'Bah.' She dismissed the compliment. 'You don't have to say such things we both know are not true.'

'But it is true. To me, Katerin Frank, you are a beautiful woman and I am the luckiest man alive to have you by my side as my wife.'

She flushed red and tried to suppress a smile. 'Well, you scrub up all right too, I suppose, now that we've put some flesh on your bones,' she'd responded, the smile taking the sting out of her words.

'Well, I could hardly look any worse than I did a month or so ago, eh?' He then tucked into his fish with relish, his appetite fully restored.

Life as a married man was bliss, nothing short of it. He woke each morning to her there beside him, and she was, as nobody suspected, a tender and loving woman.

He woke her and gently told her Erich's story.

* * *

THE NEXT MORNING, Rabbi Frank knocked on the door of the parochial house, knowing Father O'Toole would be back from early Mass by now and finished with breakfast. Woe betide anyone, even a rabbi, who would have the audacity to interrupt the Reverend Father's bacon and eggs. His housekeeper, Mrs O'Hanlon, was a force to be reckoned with. She guarded the parish priest against the demands of his flock with alacrity, and nobody in Ballycreggan would take her on as an adversary.

The rabbi smiled broadly as the woman with iron-coloured hair and ramrod-straight posture opened the door imperiously. Her dislike of foreigners generally, and Jews in particular, was not far beneath the surface, but he was determined to keep relations amicable at least.

'Ah, good morning, Mrs O'Hanlon. I'm sorry to disturb you, but I wonder if I could have a quick word with Father O'Toole?'

She eyed him up suspiciously as if he might have a hand grenade in his pocket, her beady dark eyes raking his face for a hint of a clue about the purpose of the visit. The priest usually met the rabbi and the vicar in Masie's tea shop, a practice of which Mrs O'Hanlon deeply disapproved, so house calls were unusual.

'Well, he is only up from his breakfast this minute, so I don't know –' she began, but the large priest appeared in the hallway behind her.

'Rabbi Frank!' he called expansively. 'How great to see you up and about! And I hear congratulations are in order?' The priest made his way to the doorstep, allowing his housekeeper no option but to stand aside and permit the rabbi's entry.

The two men shook hands, and the rabbi nodded. 'Indeed, Katerin and I got married last week, but it was a quiet ceremony. Neither of us wanted a fuss.'

Mrs O'Hanlon managed to look even more censorious as he slowly made his way down the hall towards the drawing room. Clearly ancient foreigners marrying each other was another cause for ire.

'Mrs O'Hanlon, I wonder if you could make us some tea? And perhaps bring in some of those lovely buns you made this morning?' Father O'Toole smiled and was polite, and instantly her entire demeanour changed.

She beamed like a girl asked up by the town Romeo at a dance, and replied, 'Oh, certainly, Father, right away.'

She left, leaving the drawing room door ajar, but as soon as both men were inside, Father O'Toole shut the wide oak door firmly. He had not served as a parish priest for over fifty years and not learned something about human body language. His face told the rabbi that he knew the rabbi had something on his mind.

Rabbi Frank lowered himself into a brown and gold brocade Queen Anne chair beside the empty fireplace, and the priest took the identical one opposite. The room was full of statues, relics, saints' images and biographies of various religious people, and though it was a million miles from his own experience, the rabbi felt comfortable there. If someone had told him as a conservative rabbi in Berlin that his friends would one day be a Catholic priest and a Protestant vicar, he would have said they were mad, but life took all manner of twists and turns and one of those was why he was there that day.

'So what can I do for you, Rabbi?'

'You guessed it's not a social call?' The rabbi smiled.

'Fifty years hearing people's confessions gives you a nose for these things.' Paddy O'Toole shrugged. 'I hope it's not advice about the ladies you're after, though, because you're barking up the wrong tree with me, I'm afraid.'

Rabbi Frank chuckled. 'No, that's all fine, though denying you the comfort of a wife seems an unnecessary cruelty of your faith, I have to say.'

Matters of doctrine and faith were often discussed among the men, and the subject of Catholic clergy celibacy sometimes came up.

'I'm not sure Andrew would agree with you.' The priest shrugged.

Reverend Parkes' wife, the formidable Amelia Parkes, was a large blustery woman who had a penchant for dressing in lurid florals, making her look rather like a sofa with legs. She tolerated no dissention on any subject from her husband, the mild-mannered vicar.

'Ah, he wouldn't have it any other way,' the rabbi said.

Father O'Toole looked up as Mrs O'Hanlon appeared with a tray. She placed it on the side table and offered to pour, but the priest gently ushered her out. He filled two cups and put one spoon of sugar in one for the rabbi and a splash of milk in his own. He handed the rabbi the cup and went back to retrieve the small plate of buns, offering him one. 'They're quite delicious, I must say.' He lowered his voice, 'She may be a little sour sometimes, God knows, but her buns are lovely and sweet.'

The rabbi sipped his tea, a taste for which he'd developed only in Ireland, and took a bite of the bun. It was light as a feather and he enjoyed it before speaking.

'I have a problem and I need your help,' he began.

'If I can, I will,' Paddy O'Toole replied without hesitation.

'Well, you know young Erich Bannon.'

The priest nodded, an air of resignation settling over him. 'Of course. He was here last night, but then you know that.'

'I do. He came to me afterwards, very upset.'

Father O'Toole inhaled through his teeth, making a whistling sound.

'I know you told him that you don't know where she is, but I was hoping you could find out where the girl has been taken and hopefully intercede on Erich's behalf with the authorities there to release her. He'll have to deal with her family then, he knows that, but at least the girl and the child would be safe, and that's his main objective.'

The silence was thick in the room between the two men.

When Erich came to Rabbi Frank and told him the story, he'd been sympathetic. The old rabbi he was back in Berlin would have been appalled, or at least disappointed, but not now, not after all he'd seen. Erich and this girl were young and in love, and they found themselves in the same position as so many young couples all over the world. Why should the natural expression of that love between a man and a woman be associated with such shame and guilt? Erich Bannon was a good person, and he assumed this girl was too – Erich wouldn't have chosen her if she wasn't – so why not let them be happy? He knew he was not like other rabbis now, and he didn't care. The war and life in Ballycreggan had taught him that all there was left after everything else was kindness. The time for judgement and recriminations was over; it was time to help and support.

'It's not that easy, Rabbi, I'm sorry to say.'

'Why not? Do you know this priest, the one who took the girl away?'

Father O'Toole nodded slowly. 'Not really. He's Monsignor Doherty. He's on the McAreavey side of the family, and he's *politically* aligned that way too, if you know what I mean? I'm related to the girl's mother. Either way, I can't do anything for you, my friend.'

'But why not?' The rabbi was confused. He'd known Paddy O'Toole since he arrived in Ballycreggan seventeen years ago and knew him to be a kind and compassionate man. 'Erich wants to marry this girl who is expecting his child. Surely that's what the Church and the family want for her and the baby, a husband and a stable home? I don't agree with locking girls up who get into trouble, but maybe it's a kindness in the long run if they have no man and no way to support the child, I don't know. But that's not the case here. Look, I know they probably won't be thrilled about him being Jewish – we've come to expect that. We Jews are used to it...' The rabbi paused, seeing the hurt in his friend's eyes. 'Not here, not in Ballycreggan,' he rushed to correct himself. 'Of course not. We've been welcomed with open arms. But in general, we all have come to expect that most Christians won't want a mixed marriage. To be honest, there was a time I wouldn't have wanted it either, but you know as well as I do that life knocks the edges off your firmly held beliefs. For every rule, there are a hundred exceptions, and in this case, the boy loves her, he thinks she loves him, and they want to be together and raise their child. Why would anyone object to that? They're willing to leave, to go abroad if that is what the family demand.'

Father O'Toole stood and walked to the window, his huge hands thrust in the pockets of his black trousers. 'It's a very complicated situation, Rabbi, even if the girl in question wasn't a member of a very prominent republican family with links to organised crime in Britain and the United States.' He sighed heavily. 'But when she is...'

'These McAreaveys are bad news – we know that. Look what they did to Erich. But we can't allow them to bully us. Surely you can see that?' Rabbi Frank was getting frustrated now.

'They are more than bad news. They are dangerous murderers, and they would think nothing of killing Erich, or anyone else connected to him, if things don't go their way. I'm really sorry for both of them, genuinely I am, but Erich won't be living happily ever after with that girl, and that's a certainty. If I tell you, I'm just putting that family in even more danger, and I feel responsible enough as it is asking Daniel to take them on.' The priest turned and sat back down.

'But Erich met her before those people came to work for Daniel, so that's not your fault.' The rabbi tried to get through to his old friend.

'I don't see it like that, but either way, Rabbi, once a girl goes into that system, it's out of our hands. I've had dealings with them myself over the years, with parents insisting their daughters go away and have the child. They can return then, maybe even marry or emigrate, without the stigma or responsibility of a child out of wedlock. I know it sounds cruel, and I suppose it is, but there's no place for an unmarried mother in our world. It's harsh but true.'

'But surely if they got married...' The rabbi couldn't believe what his friend was saying.

'Rabbi, listen to me. They would never release her to a Catholic, let alone a Jew, not in a million years. She and the child are their property now. And even if he did get her out, which is, as I say, close to an impossibility, what hope would they have? The McAreaveys have tentacles all over the world through their connections, literally everywhere. A man that double-crossed an uncle of this girl's escaped to Australia – imagine, all the way to Australia – and he was found floating in the Darling River in New South Wales a month later. Erich and the girl, and even the baby, would be in such peril. I couldn't do it to any of them.'

'But you can tell me where she is?' Rabbi Frank wasn't convinced.

'Yes, but to do so would put all three of them in grave danger. I just couldn't –' he began again.

'Well, the thugs might be able to find them here, or even America or Australia, as you say, but I can put them somewhere they will be safe. So please, just tell me where she is?' The rabbi locked eyes with his old friend.

'There is nowhere safe from them – they have contacts everywhere. You're not listening to me. There is no place they could go. Trust me, I know...'

Rabbi Frank smiled and stood, placing his hand on the priest's shoulder. 'You may well know all about your world, but trust me, I know mine. These criminals have influence everywhere, and I believe it, but you have never been on a kibbutz, my friend. And I can stake my life that even the McAreaveys don't have people in the Negev desert.'

'I don't know. I know I sound weak and pathetic, but I would have their blood on my hands...'

'Paddy, listen to me.' The rabbi needed him to understand. 'We, the Jews, are united now. That was our problem before – people saw themselves as German or French or Italian before being Jewish. But if

Hitler has taught us anything, it is this – we must stick together, protect each other, pose a united front. Whatever is done to one of us is done to us all. I have contacts too, you know, and I can place Erich and the girl in the care of our people. They will make sure they get to Israel safely, and when they are there, they will watch and keep them safe.'

'Are you sure?' the priest asked.

'Positive. Nobody will get within a hundred miles of them.'

'And what about the Liebers, Ariella and Willi, you even?' Paddy O'Toole asked.

'We'll be alright. We've had our fair share of adversity and we survived. We live a nice peaceful life here now Paddy, but don't forget what we've endured, we are tougher than we look. Please, trust us.'

The birds gathered on the telephone wire outside the parochial house, as in silence, the two men watched the familiar scenes of the village going about its business.

Eventually, Father O'Toole sighed. 'It's St Gerard's in Leitrim. Run by the Bon Secours order.' Each word was dropped like a stone.

'You are sure?'

He nodded. ' Quite sure. Her mother asked me to help. I tried to buy the girl some time. She could have gone to England to another cousin of ours, but Fiach wanted her gone and the Monsignor stepped in. That's where he sends them all...'

Though the rabbi had such time for his friend, he had to say what was in his heart. 'It's a cruel system and one your church will live to regret, but not, I fear, before it's too late for so many. You're a good man, but as I know all too well, all it takes is for good men to stand by and say nothing in the face of wrongdoing to enable unspeakable horrors.'

The priest stood and took the rabbi's hand. 'I know, David, I know...' He sighed, and the rabbi could see the pain there.

CHAPTER 24

*R*óisín McAreavey had grown so used to answering to the name they'd given her that she'd started to think of herself as Mary. The body she once had seemed no longer her own; her back ached and every muscle cried out from overuse. At least the nausea had subsided a little thankfully; that was dreadful, and the nuns showed not the slightest shred of sympathy. One of the other girls said it usually wore off after the first three months.

Vomiting was met with derision and fury on the part of the nuns, because of the time it took out of her working day. They often didn't even allow her to change her stained smock, a grey shapeless thing all the so-called penitents wore, making her work all day with the smell of vomit.

Her blonde hair had been cut tight into her head by Sister Patrick; apparently she was too vain and should focus on repenting her sins rather than on her reflection. She'd teared up the first time she saw herself in the window of the refectory, but she didn't let them see. Stoic subservience was the key to survival.

Other girls were more resistant than she, but it got them nowhere except harder work and more abuse. Kathleen, a girl she'd become friendly with, had advised her to keep her head down, do as she was told and just get it all over with. Girls who didn't do that often were transferred to the county psychiatric home after their babies were born, branded insane or unmanageable, and so ended up much worse off.

Her baby. Except it wasn't. The nuns repeatedly told them that they were sinners, morally corrupt women who could not be trusted with the care of a child. Their babies, when born, would be adopted by good Catholic families and given a proper life despite their less-than-ideal start. Their mothers had no choices; it wasn't up for discussion.

Some of the girls had their little boys and girls taken while they were at work, the distraught women returning to the dormitories with eyes swollen from crying, but the crying did no good.

Part of her hoped they'd take her little one right away. She couldn't bear to be one of the girls who nursed their child for weeks, even months, only to go to the nursery one day and find them gone, never again to see them.

She tried not to think about the future, focusing on the present only as she removed the last of the weeds from the ground. The crop of vegetables was exhausted so the earth was to be hoed and prepared for reseeding, she tried to keep going. She longed to fall into bed and rest, just to fall into a dreamless sleep. The work in the vegetable garden was arduous and relentless. The autumn was well and truly gone, and the bitter winter wind gave her chilblains on her fingers. Her knuckles were red and raw from pulling weeds, and her knees had developed a thick layer of tough skin from constant kneeling on the gravel paths between the vegetable rows.

Sister Marie stood a few feet away on the porch of the potting shed, out of the wind and the rain, watching...always watching. Her long black habit reached all the way to the floor, and a large beaded rosary hung from a belt at her waist. She wasn't the worst of them; she allowed the girls to stand in the shed if the rain got too heavy, and sometimes even lit the paraffin heater there. If Sister Patrick, or Mother Agnes worse still, found them inside, there would be trouble, but Sister Marie often took the risk. She was younger than the other nuns, and had a kind face.

Nobody knew each other's story. It was forbidden to discuss their lives prior to coming to St Gerard's, so all anyone knew was a false name and the fact that they were all in the same boat – pregnant and unmarried.

'Are you all right, Sister?' Róisín dared ask. The nun seemed to be wincing in pain.

'Yes, I'm fine. Carry on with your work,' Sister Marie responded, not unkindly.

Róisín returned to her weeding, but moments later the nun seemed in further distress. Being the nearest to her, Róisín was the only one who could see what was going on. 'Are you sure, Sister? Should I call someone?' As Róisín walked towards her, the nun turned and threw up in a flower bed.

She straightened up and wiped her mouth with her handkerchief. 'I'm fine. I get sudden violent headaches and they make me nauseous, but I'm all right.'

Róisín led her into the potting shed, where rows of terracotta pots stood bearing plants in various phases of germination. She went to the tap and filled a glass of water. The nun accepted it gratefully, swallowing the cold liquid.

'Do you still have the headache?' Róisín asked. 'I could go and get you something from the sick bay?' She knew Mother Agnes was beyond stingy with any pain relief for the penitents, but surely she would allow her sister nun something to ease her suffering?

Sister Marie shook her head. 'No, it's fine.' She caught Róisín's eye. 'Thank you, but I'll just offer it up.'

That was Mother Agnes's response to everything: Offer up your pain in compensation for all the wrongdoing in your life. Róisín thought she must treat the nuns under her command the same way.

Róisín led the sister to the only stool in the room, put there for the supervising nun in the event of girls working in the shed, and took her hand. 'Let me try something,' she said.

Nervously she squeezed the fleshy part of the nun's hand between

172

her thumb and first finger. Within seconds she could see the lines of pain disappear from the young woman's face. She increased the pressure and the nun sighed in relief.

'How did you do that?' the sister asked in amazement. 'The pain is gone.'

Róisín smiled. 'It's part of Chinese medicine. That pressure point in the hand is connected to the head, so if you apply pressure there, it relieves headaches.'

'And how on earth do you know that?' The nun smiled.

Róisín considered whether she should tell the truth.

'Please, tell me,' Sister Marie prompted.

'I had a friend in Belfast, when I was a wee girl, Mei-Ling was her name. Her parents had a laundry at the end of our road, but her daddy used to do Chinese medicine on people. He was cheaper than the doctor, and people used to swear by him. He told my mammy to do this for my da when he had a hangover, for the pain in his head.'

'Amazing.' Sister Marie seemed genuinely fascinated.

'I tried it on my boyfriend one night. He'd been working with a compressor all day and his head was pounding from the noise, so I did it on him and it worked too.'

'What was your boyfriend's name?' Sister Marie asked.

Róisín was shocked. There was to be no mention ever of anyone before life in St Gerard's. It was as if the women there fell from the sky, with no past or future.

'Erich.' Róisín tried not to cry; she'd not said his name aloud for months.

'And he's the baby's father?' The nun nodded at Róisín's abdomen.

'Yes. But he doesn't know about the baby. My brothers made me write to him and break off our romance. They made me tell him I had someone else.' She continued the pressure on the nun's hand.

'If he did know, how would he react, do you think?'

Suddenly they were just two young women having a conversation, not jailer and prisoner.

'I think he wouldn't want me in here, but it's complicated. My family – he's Jewish, you see – would never accept him. I love him, though.' She heard the catch in her voice.

'And does he love you, do you think?' the nun probed gently.

Róisín could only nod. She had to believe he did, but she didn't trust herself to speak about him any more; she'd surely cry if she did.

'We'd better get back, but you can squeeze like this whenever it gets bad and it will relieve the pain.' Róisín showed her and released her hand.

'Thank you, Mary. It's such a relief.' The nun smiled and her face transformed. Róisín realised she was much younger even than she'd first thought. The habit made it hard to judge.

'It's Róisín, and my boyfriend is Erich Bannon.'

She slipped back to her spot at the vegetable patch just moments before Sister Patrick came on her rounds.

CHAPTER 25

*E*rich sat glumly in the dining room of the Bush Hotel in Carrick-on-Shannon. It had been a completely pointless journey.

Jamie was right. He couldn't even get past the gates of the convent. The entire place was inside a wall, smoothly plastered so unclimbable. He'd tried visiting the parochial house and was met by a dour house-keeper who claimed to know nothing of the mother-and-baby home. The priest was unavailable, and her look suggested he had displayed the utmost audacity in even asking.

Do you have to have a face like a bag of hatchets to be a priest's house-keeper? he wondered. *Mrs O'Hanlon is the same, like a Rottweiler guard dog.*

The waitress placed a pint of beer in front of him and removed the almost untouched plates of food that was now cold.

Erich smiled his thanks at the young waitress and then became lost in thought again. He'd asked around – a few farmhouses were within a few miles of the desolate convent, though all around was just bogland – but nobody seemed able to help.

The convent itself was barely visible through the high black wrought-iron gates, a red-brick, solid three-storey building at the end of a tree-lined avenue. There was no sign of any human life whatsoever. There was at least a twelve-foot wall around the perimeter, under which grew thick briars and brambles, making even getting within six feet of the wall close to impossible. And even if he could break in, what then? Pull a pregnant woman out over that wall into the briars?

'Can I get you any dessert, sir?' the waitress asked as she approached the table.

She looked around twenty, and Erich thought it might be worth a shot; he had nothing to lose. 'No, thanks, but I wonder if you could help me?' He smiled.

The girl blushed. 'If I can.'

'My girlfriend is being held in St Gerard's. Do you know it? A convent near Leitrim Village?'

The girl nodded slowly. 'I do know it.'

'I need to get her out of there, but I went there today and there was no way of getting in, even past the gates.'

The girl looked anxiously around the almost empty dining room and then spoke, her voice low and furtive. 'Even if you could get up to the door, they'd not give her to you. A few years ago, a lad came here, to the hotel, in the same predicament. He managed somehow to get in past the gates, and he got up to the door and knocked and knocked. When he came back here, hours later, his knuckles were cut from knocking and banging on the door for ages. He said some men eventually came – I don't know who they were, caretakers or something, I suppose – and dragged him out and threw him outside the gates again. Nobody comes out of there, sir, not till she's put out by the nuns.'

'But that's ridiculous! She hasn't committed a crime!' Erich instantly regretted the force of his words. The girl had recoiled and it wasn't her fault. 'I'm sorry, I didn't mean to startle you. It's nothing to do with you, of course, but it's just so insane. They can't just lock people up – it's not right. What if I went to the police?' he suggested.

The girl shook her head. 'It would do no good, sir. If anyone does escape from there, the guards bring them back.'

'How come you know so much about it?' Erich asked on a hunch. Something about the girl suggested she knew more.

A barman who'd been chatting around the other end of the bar suddenly took an interest in their conversation. Erich spotted it immediately and interjected, 'So do you have cream or ice cream with the apple pie?'

The girl looked relieved. 'You can have either, sir, or both if you like.' She began to scribble something in her notebook.

'Right, one apple pie, with ice cream, please.'

'Certainly, sir,' the girl replied as the barman drifted back to his customers. She tore off the page of her notebook, folded it quickly and tucked it under Erich's saucer. Then she was gone.

He opened the note.

Christy Costello, Photographer, Quay Rd.

He slipped the paper in his pocket and accepted his dessert from someone else who was serving.

Everyone said that the South was different to the North; the Catholic Church ruled supreme there. Everyone who knew, and who he trusted, said the same thing: Those places did what they did with the full backing of both the Church and the state. Seeing the startled look on the young waitress's face when he'd even asked about it confirmed it.

He didn't want the dessert but took a few bites before retiring for the night.

* * *

ERICH STOOD outside the small business that seemed to be housed in an extension to a sizable house. The only thing to identify it as a commercial entity was a small brass plaque on the pillar that read 'C. Costello Photography'.

He lifted the latch on the gate and walked up the gravel driveway. Either side of the path, well-pruned shrubs and manicured lawns thrived. He went to the side where he presumed the photography business was and knocked.

A voice from inside called, 'One minute, I'll be with you.'

Shortly afterwards, the door opened and a short, slight man wearing a floor-length apron and gloves opened the door. He was bald on top but around the back of his head was a band of grey curls. He had twinkling blue eyes that seemed full of merriment. 'Sorry, I'm up to my elbows in the darkroom. How can I help?'

'I...' Erich began, unsure of how to start. 'I'm not sure if you can or not. My name is Erich Bannon. I was given your name by someone, and she seemed to think you could help.'

'Intriguing.' The man smiled. 'Do you want some photographs taken?'

'No, not that. I was making enquiries about St Gerard's. My girlfriend is in there – well, she might be. I'm not sure. I think she is, but I can't get in, and I need to get her out.'

An unreadable look shadowed the man's face, and momentarily he stood aside. 'You'd better come in,' he said, and ushered Erich into a studio. There was a velvet sofa and an armchair, what looked like huge white umbrellas and several lights on tripods.

'Have a seat,' the man offered. He went into another room and returned moments later without the apron and gloves. He wore a bright turquoise shirt with a yellow and turquoise tie and dark trousers. 'So who are you again?' he asked, sitting opposite Erich.

'My name is Erich Bannon.' Erich noted the slight furrow to the man's brow.

The photographer nodded. 'And why are you here?'

'As I mentioned, I think my girlfriend is in that convent, St Gerard's, and I need to get her out of there.'

'And why come to me?' Mr Costello's demeanour had changed; he seemed less jovial and more troubled.

'A waitress in the Bush Hotel.' Erich caught the man's eye, hoping he was doing the right thing. 'When I asked her about the convent – I was there yesterday and to say it's impenetrable is to understate the situation – she said there was no way of getting anyone in or out, but then she scribbled your name on a piece of paper and here I am.'

Mr Costello exhaled through his nose and clearly wasn't happy. 'That was Joanne, my niece. Look, I can't help. She's right. Those nuns run that place –'

'Like a prison, I know. But the girl I want isn't a criminal and it's not right that she's being kept against her will.' Erich tried to keep the frustration out of his voice.

'Are you Catholic?' the man asked, eyeing Erich carefully.

'No, I'm a Jew,' Erich said quietly.

The photographer exhaled loudly through his teeth, an unreadable look crossing his face. 'What does she look like?' he asked wearily.

'Well, her name is Róisín –'

'They won't call her that. She'll have been given another name.'

'Well, she's blonde, and her eyes are two different colours – one is blue, the other green. She has a dark freckle just under her lip, she's tall, and she has a Belfast accent.'

'And how far along is she?'

Erich did the calculations. The cricket club dance was in June, and it was November now. 'About five months.'

The man thought for a moment. 'I...I take the photographs up there.'

The admission pained him, Erich could see, but he didn't know what the man meant. 'Of the girls?' he asked. Why would the nuns be taking their photographs?

'No.' Mr Costello's eyes were downcast. 'Of the babies. They need them for the prospective parents to see what they're getting ahead of time, and for passports, you see. Most of them go to America to be adopted, so they need a passport picture.'

'And you take them?' Erich tried to keep the note of accusation out of his voice, but he failed.

'Look, I know what you must be thinking, that I'm as bad as the rest of them being part of it, but if I don't do it, someone else will. I know you don't want to hear this, but in the case of most of those girls and their kids, it's for the best. What business has a single girl trying to raise a child on her own? This is not a kind society to the mothers or their offspring, and this way the kids get a decent home and the girls get a new start. But it's hard. I hate going up there. They send for me around once every three months, and I do all the ones that are ready.'

His expression told Erich that he knew how shocking the words were. 'Ready for sale.' Erich couldn't help himself.

'Well, you could say that,' the man agreed miserably.

'When are you next due to go there, Mr Costello?'

The man shook his head. 'Well, I was to go last week but I had two weddings to do, so I had to put it off.'

'Could you go today? And at least find out for sure if she's there? And if she is, give her a message from me, that I'm trying to get her out?'

'You won't be able to.'

That sentence again. Erich was sick of hearing it. 'Well, I have to try. But first I need to know for sure that she's there.'

Mr Costello stood and sighed. 'I'll try, but I wouldn't be anywhere near the girls that haven't given birth yet. Some of them think, God love them, that they'll be given the picture to remind them – I think that's what the nuns tell them. They only let the mothers hold them because babies are less inclined to cry if they can sense their mothers, better chance of having them adopted if they are happy looking.'

'That's barbaric!' Erich was outraged now. Girls forced to pose with their children only to have them stolen from them?

'It is, but as I say, for most of them, it's for the best. But a girl who has a man wanting her and the child, well, that's different.' He fixed Erich with a gaze. 'You do want them, don't you? I need to be sure, because it's a big risk me even asking.'

'I want them, both of them, very much. I love her and I want to marry her.' Erich needed this man to understand just how much this meant to him.

'Well, look, I'll go up this morning. I'll see what I can find out, all right?'

'Thank you, Mr Costello. I'll wait and come back this afternoon if that's all right?' Erich felt a slight hope. At least he would be one step closer to finding her.

'Christy, please.' The man took his coat from the coat stand inside the door and began gathering a bag with cameras and several lenses. 'Right. I should be back' – he checked his watch – 'around three?'

'I'll see you then.' Erich shook the man's hand. 'Thank you.'

The photographer shook his head. 'Don't thank me yet, son. There's a bloody big wall and some fairly ferocious nuns between you and your girl yet, and better men than me have failed to get a young one out of that hellhole, so don't get your hopes up. But I'll try to find out if she's even there anyway. Tall, blonde, from Belfast, two different-coloured eyes?'

'Yes.'

'Well, that'll be helpful right enough.' He gave a smile. 'I'll see you later. And best come round the back. We don't want the local tongues waggin', starved for a wee bit of gossip, so they are.'

Something struck Erich. Though his life had been blessed with the kindness of strangers, he wondered why someone like this man would risk the wrath of the Church, and possibly even the police, to help total strangers. Though it felt rude to ask, he had to. 'Why are you helping me?'

The man gazed at him, as if trying to memorise his face, or find something there. 'When I was a young fella, things were bad here, very bad, with the British and all of that, you know?'

Erich nodded. The Irish War of Independence and the subsequent Civil War formed one of the bloodiest chapters in an already brutal history of this small beautiful island.

'I was down in Cork, apprenticed to a photographer down there. Anyway, one night at a dance, I met a girl. She was a beauty, but more than that, she was so passionate and so worked up about the struggle for Irish independence that she got me involved too. She was in Cumann na mBan, you know, the women's army, and we spent the years of the War of Independence together, and after, during the Civil War too.'

Erich was confused as to what this had to do with him and Róisín.

'She was a Jew – there were loads of them in Cork at that time. Her family and others fled to Cork after the Limerick pogrom of 1904. And she... Well, we found ourselves in a similar position to you and your young lady.' He looked abashed. 'But she was terrified to tell her family, not just that she was expecting but that it was with me, a Catholic. We'd planned to run away together, but...well, we never got that far.'

Erich could hear the pain in his voice. 'I'm sorry,' he said. 'Did her family not allow it?'

'No. She was injured during the burning of Cork by the British in December 1920, and she lost the baby. Her mother sent her to live with some relatives in England, I think, or possibly America, she had cousins there, and I never heard from her again. Rachel was her name, Rachel Abrahams. I spent the next few years either in jail or on the run, so I hadn't much to offer her anyway, but...'

The two men stood silently, lost in thought. It was such a sad story, and a familiar one.

'Thank you for helping me. I really appreciate it,' Erich said quietly.

The photographer just nodded sadly. 'As I say, I'll do my best but I'm making no promises.'

Erich walked back to the hotel where he had yet to check out and went to his room. He sat on the bed. It was going to be a long time till three. He tried to read but found he couldn't concentrate. Different scenarios went round and round in his head.

What if she wasn't there? Where would he look then? He'd never experienced anything so covert, so secretive. It was as if they operated outside of the law, outside of society; they were a law unto themselves.

He'd never actually met a nun. He'd seen them from a distance but had never spoken to one. Father O'Toole was his only experience with Catholic clergy, and because Ballycreggan was largely a Protestant area, that version of Christianity seemed to dominate village life. That said, he never sensed too much animosity there; people were happy enough to live and let live for the most part. It was a different story elsewhere in Northern Ireland, though; religion dominated everything. Róisín had some terrible stories of sectarian hatred in her childhood.

Once again he found himself at the same thought crossroads. What was the point of it all? Religion just divided people, created barriers where none were needed. He was a Jew because he was born to a Jewish mother; he didn't choose it. Róisín was a Catholic for the same reason. Bud's family were Baptists and nice people but completely convinced theirs was the right way. He'd had to endure an aunt of Bud's explain at great length how devastated she was to discover her daughter was dating a Mormon; he was too polite to point out that religion was a stupid thing to divide people over. To claim one belief system was right and another wrong seemed nonsensical to him – none of them spoke to him. He was comfortable in his faith culturally, and it did give him a sense of belonging, but did he believe it, any of it, on a doctrinal level? He didn't know. And right now, he didn't care.

Supposing he did, by some miracle, liberate Róisín from the clutches of the nuns, was Israel the right option? He could see the rabbi's point; they would be safe there, as even the McAreaveys couldn't penetrate a kibbutz. But wouldn't a kibbutz be full of people emphatic in their faith? He certainly wasn't that. And Róisín was like him. Being Catholic was her culture, but did she believe in transubstantiation or the existence of angels and saints? He suspected she probably didn't. So there they were, two young people united by love and the new life they made together, and yet the world around them just saw a Catholic and a Jew. It was mad.

He thought about how to get her out if she was there. Offer a bribe? How would he even get to talk to someone to do that? Perhaps Christy could intervene on his behalf, ask the boss nun, whatever she was called, if she'd sell Róisín to Erich? Had it come to this? If it weren't so serious, it would be laughable. And why would they take his money if they had American couples queueing up to take these babies? What did they do with the money anyway? Were nuns not supposed to be poor? The whole thing went round and round until he thought he was going out of his mind.

The walls were closing in on him, so he went out for a walk. Carrick-on-Shannon was a busy town, with lots of shops and people coming and going. He wandered aimlessly until he came to a small quaint jewellery shop. It wasn't Tiffany's of New York, but they had some lovely necklaces and brooches nonetheless. He stopped, looked in the window, took a breath and went in.

CHAPTER 26

*C*hristy set the tripod up in the wood panelled room. It was warm and beautifully decorated, and he knew in stark contrast to the living quarters of the poor misfortunate girls he encountered there every three months. He smiled as the next young woman entered, her baby on her hip. 'Ah, isn't he a smashing little lad.' He said the same to everyone, but the girls beamed with pride in their babies and it felt good to make them smile, even for a moment. He wanted to allow them that bit of parental pride.

'His name's Joseph, after my brother who was killed on the buildings in England.' The girl's accent was southern, Cork or Kerry maybe.

'Ah, I'm sorry for your troubles, but his namesake is a fine bonny lad, isn't he?' Christy made cooing noises and the baby beamed.

'He likes you,' the girl remarked, sitting where she was told.

'Ah, sure, I'm so mad looking. I think they think I'm a clown out of the circus.' He chuckled, and the baby gave a gummy grin again. He used that exact moment to take the picture. It was lovely, and he'd be snapped right up. It was vital that no trace of the mother appeared in the photo, so he'd enlarge the head and shoulders of the baby in the cutting room.

'Maybe he'll go to a circus someday,' the girl said, and the loss expressed in her voice was palpable. She sighed raggedly, the breath like hope leaving her body. She kissed the top of her son's head.

Christy tried to allow the mothers to stay as long as possible – time cuddling their child was restricted to be almost negligible, in this as in all things – but the nuns had a strict in-and-out policy. They did everything they could to minimise the time the mothers got with their babies. He knew that if the women cuddled their babies while nursing them, the children would be weaned early and given a bottle.

'I'm sure he'll have a lovely life,' was all Christy could say. It sounded pathetic, he knew, but what else could he do? At least today it was the nice young nun supervising the photographs, Sister Marie; it was often that old trout Sister Patrick, who had a face to turn milk sour.

The girl stood and walked out of the room, knowing it might well be the last day she would ever see her child. Once they were weaned and their pictures taken, it was only a matter of time.

Christy was about to go out and call the next mother in when he realised the nun was crying. 'Sister? Are you all right?' he asked. He rarely engaged the other nuns in conversation but Sister Marie was different, she had a shred of humanity about her. They'd spoken about it before a few times.

She looked mortified. 'I'm sorry, Mr Costello. I...I just hate this. It's so cruel. How can they do it?'

He went down on his hunkers in front of her and took her hand in his. 'I know. It's very hard, and tisn't the life for everyone. Do yourself a favour, Sister, and get out of here. There's nothing in this place but tears and heartbreak. Would you not go out to the missions?'

'I was sent here, but...' – she tried to compose herself – 'I just don't know how many more times I can take a baby from its mother. I... It's so hard.'

Christy hated to use her like this – he believed she was genuine – but he might only get one chance. 'Is there a girl here, tall, from Belfast, with two different-coloured eyes?'

Sister Marie nodded. 'There is. Mary, she's called here, but her real name is Róisín. Do you know her?'

'I have her boyfriend at my house. He's going to try to get her out,' Christy murmured, terrified one of the other nuns would walk in. 'Though I told him it would be impossible, I promised him I'd try to find out about her.'

'If I get her to your car, can you take her now?' The nun's eyes lit up.

'What?' Christy fought panic. 'I didn't mean…I suppose I could try, but how would you…'

'Don't you worry about that. Could you run out of film or something, say you need to go back now? I'll go and hide Róisín in the boot of your car – is it open?'

'It is but…' This was all going too fast. If they caught him… He stopped. So what if they caught him? He'd lose the job he hated anyway? Nobody had given him and Rachel a chance all those years ago, but maybe if someone had, he might have had a very different life, with a wife and kids of his own, instead of spending his days taking pictures of families and going home to an empty house every night. He made his decision. 'Do it. I'm parked by the graveyard wall.' He glanced at his watch. 'You have fifteen minutes. I'll go to the Reverend Mother now, make something up.'

Sister Marie disappeared, and he went in search of Mother Agnes, who was in her beautifully decorated, warm office. A cup of tea and a slice of cream cake were on her desk. No such comfort was offered to the poor misfortunes in her care.

He knocked on the open door and she looked up, her glasses perched on the end of her nose.

'Mr Costello, is everything alright?' she asked.

'Reverend Mother, would you believe it? The bulb is blown in my flash, and I thought I had a spare but I don't. I'm so sorry about this.'

She looked at him with merry, kind blue eyes, and if he didn't know better, he would have thought she was as sweet as honey.

'Ah, Mr Costello, the good Lord sends these things to try us.' She smiled.

'I can do no more now without the flash, but would you like me to come back later today or will tomorrow do?' he asked, fervently hoping he sounded convincing; that woman had eyes that could see into a man's soul.

'Oh, I wouldn't dream of dragging you back today.' She gave a girlish laugh. 'Not at all. Come back tomorrow when you're rested, and we'll get the rest of the job done.'

He stood there. He'd surely only left Sister Marie a few minutes ago; he needed to give her time. 'Ah, that's very kind of you, Mother. I actually came straight here and I had no time for lunch, so I'll be glad to get my dinner early.' He hoped she'd take the hint.

'Oh, dear Lord, we can't have that.' She clapped her hands and rang a bell. A woman in her sixties possibly and wearing the same drab smock of the others appeared. 'Assumpta, fetch Mr Costello a cup of tea and some cake.'

The woman nodded and retreated from the room. The Reverend Mother had offered no please or thank you. Christy remembered the woman. Her real name was Molly O'Riordan, and he'd played football with her brothers years ago. They had all grown up together, and he remembered she was a great horsewoman. She'd been one of the girls in trouble. They'd said the parish priest was the father, and she was kept after her child was born and never left. He wondered if she recognised him; he'd not seen her in thirty years.

He made idle chit-chat about the weather and the resignation of Winston Churchill earlier in the year, and soon Assumpta was back with the tea and cake on a tray.

She placed it down, and as she did, Christy met her eye. The Reverend Mother was peering down the corridor, looking for someone to berate, no doubt, and Christy took his chance. 'How are you, Molly?' he asked quietly.

'Hello, Christy.' She smiled. Several of her teeth were missing and what were left were rotten and retreated.

* * *

RÓISÍN HAULED the heavy wheelbarrow full of weeds and pebbles across the garden. The tyre on the barrow needed air, but the caretaker refused to do it. It was as if they wanted to make a hard life even harder on every single level imaginable.

Sister Carmel was on duty today; that was something. She was blind as a bat and around ninety years old, so she didn't drive them on like cattle.

As Róisín tipped the barrow of weeds and stones onto the heap behind the milking parlour, she heard a voice hiss, 'Mary.'

She looked around but nobody was there. Then she heard the voice again. 'Mary, over here.' It was Sister Marie.

Róisín stepped into the smelly milking parlour where the herd of Friesians were brought in twice a day to be milked by hand. At least she'd not been assigned to that job; the smell turned her stomach.

'The photographer is here. He came today and asked me if I knew you, and he said to tell you your boyfriend, Erich, is trying to get you out of here.'

The mention of Erich's name alone sent Róisín into a panic. Could it be true? He was trying to rescue her? She longed for nothing so much as that, but even if it could be done, her brothers would surely track them down and kill him. 'Where is Erich? Is he here?' she asked urgently.

Sister Marie spotted another nun heading their way, and she ducked behind a wall just as Sister Kevin rounded the corner.

'You there! You have no business in here – you're on garden duty. What are you doing in the milking parlour?'

Sister Kevin was mean and terrifying and the best advice was to not cross her path.

'I...I'm sorry, Sister. I... My barrow has a flat wheel, and I was looking for something to pump it up with,' she stammered.

'A likely story. Go directly to Mother Agnes this minute and tell her I sent you for being in the milking parlour when you should be weeding. See what she thinks of such insubordination.'

'But, Sister...' Róisín protested.

'Do not argue with me, girl! Such attitude of superiority is what

189

got you into the sorry state you are in. Go.' She pointed out the other end of the milking parlour to the back door of the convent. The Reverend Mother's office was on the first floor.

Róisín walked as slowly as she dared, knowing Sister Kevin's eyes were on her back the whole time.

To her astonishment, Sister Marie flew around the corner into the cobbled courtyard between the milking parlour and the back door of the convent. 'Mary, Sister Patrick needs to speak to you urgently. Come this minute.'

Sister Kevin heard the exchange and moved with remarkable speed to join them. 'What's this about?' she snapped at the younger nun. 'I was sending this penitent to Mother Agnes.'

'Oh, I'm so sorry, Sister, but she is needed now. I'll send her right back as soon as Sister Patrick is finished dealing with her.' Sister Marie grabbed Róisín roughly and began to drag her.

'I see you're causing trouble in more areas than one, young lady,' Sister Kevin sneered. 'Well, once a problem, always a problem, I suppose. Take her, Sister Marie, but mind you send her directly to Mother Agnes afterwards.'

'I will, Sister. You can count on it.' Sister Marie tried to look stern as she turned back to Róisín. 'Get on with you! We can't keep her waiting all day. Sister Patrick has enough to do without waiting on the likes of you.'

'Yes, Sister.' Róisín tried to look meek as she was led away.

Once they were around the corner, Sister Marie pulled her into an alcove and reached under her voluminous habit. She extracted a dress and a pair of shoes. 'Quickly, put these on.'

Unquestioning, Róisín pulled off the smock and pulled the dress over her head. It was too short and didn't zip up all the way as her breasts were larger now, but she didn't care. She shoved her feet into the shoes, also too small.

'Now put the smock on again over it, just in case. Quickly, through here.' Sister Marie took a small key from her pocket and opened the padlock on the garden gate.

'How did you get that?' Róisín asked incredulously. 'I thought

Mother Agnes never let the keys out of her hands.'

'She doesn't. Mr O'Brien is a bit less careful, though.' Sister Marie giggled, and she seemed so young.

'Lucky they employed a caretaker as old as Methuselah then.' Róisín smiled and slipped through the garden gate. 'Where are we going? Is Erich here?' she whispered, barely daring to believe it.

'No, he's in town. We're going to put you in the boot of the photographer's car. He knows about it, so all you have to do is lie still until you get out of here.'

The two women made for the graveyard, made so much closer now by taking a shortcut though the wall.

Róisín could feel her heart thumping as they walked quickly, and she prayed fervently. *Dear God, don't let them catch me. Let me get out. Please, Jesus, just keep me safe for the next while.*

The photographer's car was where he said it would be, beside the graveyard wall. It was a reasonable size, a blue Ford Popular. Sister Marie opened the boot, and within seconds Róisín was inside. The nun threw a tartan rug over her.

Róisín fought feelings of panic at being enclosed in such a small space, and she struggled to breathe. 'I can't...' she began, but the nun pushed her gently down into the boot.

'You'll be all right,' Sister Marie said quietly. 'It won't be for long, and you'll be free.'

'But what about you?' Róisín held the door of the boot open a crack. 'You told Sister Kevin that Sister Patrick wanted me. They'll find you out...'

'Don't worry about me. I'll be fine. I don't think this is the life for me anyway, so I'm leaving. This was my last kick at the gate. Good luck, Róisín, and your little one.'

'Thank you, Sister Marie. I –'

'Delores. My name is Delores McGann.'

'Thank you, Delores, and good luck to you too.'

The nun closed the boot over her, and moments later, Róisín heard feet on gravel; she was walking away.

She tried to breathe normally, tried to visualise Erich's face and not think about the tiny space into which she was locked. She prayed the photographer wouldn't be long, and that nobody would check the car. She didn't know if they did that or not. There were very few visitors to St Gerard's so it was possible that they did search cars, but she had no way of knowing.

She tried to listen for the sound of approaching feet on the gravel. Would she be able to tell if it was him or not?

'Good afternoon, Sister. God bless the work.'

Róisín thought she was going to vomit. Her guts churned and twisted as she heard the unmistakably soft and deceptively kind voice of Sister Patrick.

'Ah, Sister Patrick. Yes, I was just pruning the cyclamen in the sisters' cemetery. We'll have nice colour there for Christmas.'

The second voice sounded like Sister Finbarr. She was a nice one. She loved gardening and had taught Róisín a lot about plants and vegetables. She took care of the lawns and tall hedges and preferred to do it alone, so she didn't interact with the penitents as much as some of the others.

'Indeed. It's always lovely to walk in there, at any time of the year. You do a beautiful job of it.'

Róisín was sure they could hear her heart thumping from where they stood just feet away by the sounds of it.

The nuns' cemetery was strictly off limits, but rumour had it that it was an oasis of colour and flowers, a beautiful place in complete contrast to the grey drabness of the rest of St Gerard's. The penitent and infants' cemetery, on the other hand, wasn't even a proper graveyard. It was outside the wall of the nuns' enclosure, and all each baby or mother got was a mark on the wall beside the hole they were buried in. In the six weeks she'd been there, eight babies had died. No explanation was ever given, and oftentimes the mother wasn't even allowed to go to the burial.

More footsteps.

'Ah, Sisters, how are you both? Getting fine and chilly now, isn't it?' A man's voice, cheery. This must be the photographer.

'Good afternoon, Mr Costello,' Sister Patrick responded. 'I take it you've completed your tasks today?'

'I did indeed, Sister, though I blew a bulb so I'll need to come back tomorrow. Mother Agnes was most understanding. I'll have those all ready for you by the end of the week. I can have young Jeremy, my nephew, deliver them once I've developed them.'

'Very good, Mr Costello. And be sure to furnish us with the bill as well.' Sister Patrick sounded positively charming. Róisín wouldn't have believed her capable.

'All in good time, Sister. There's no rush,' the man said, opening the car door. She heard him place what she assumed were his bag and cameras on the back seat.

'Would your delicate equipment not rattle about on the seat there, Mr Costello?' Sister Finbarr asked. 'I could find you a box if you like, and you could put them in the boot for safety?'

A slight pause. Róisín willed the man on, urged him with the power of her mind to remain calm.

'Ah, not at all, Sister. I put them on the floor there, and sure with the potholes I drive slowly all the way.'

'How about a box of vegetables? We have some lovely sprouts and winter cabbage?'

Dear God, no, Róisín pleaded. A box of vegetables would surely have to go in the boot.

'Well, that's so kind of you, Sister, but I'll tell you, my sister does all the cooking for me, being a bachelor, and my brother-in-law has a huge garden himself, so trying to get through it all, we are. And I eat at the hotel a lot – my niece works there – so it would only be a waste.'

Even from inside the stuffy boot of the car, she felt the awkwardness of the conversation.

Neither nun responded to his rejection of their vegetables.

'Right so, thanks again. Now I best be off and get these in the darkroom. God bless you, Sisters.'

She felt the weight of another person in the car, and then, mercifully, the engine started up.

She didn't risk moving but tried to pull the rug over herself even more. It wouldn't pull. A terrible thought struck her – it was caught in the door of the boot. What if a corner was sticking out? Would the nuns stop him to tell him as the car went past where they stood? Again she fought the urge to vomit. She tried pulling the rug once more, but it was definitely stuck in the door of the boot.

The car rolled slowly down the gravel path, and she felt him turn the car onto the driveway. She exhaled. They must not have noticed.

This road was smoother, and the wheels didn't crunch so much. Were they out of the nuns' sight? They had to get through the gates first. Mr O'Brien was probably down at the gates, ready with the key to open them momentarily and then lock them up again immediately.

The car rolled on and then slowed.

'Ah, how are you, Bill?' the photographer greeted the caretaker, a local man. She figured he'd have known him all his life.

'Christy, 'tis yourself. How'd you get on above? Did they give you the tea and cake?' Mr O'Brien chuckled, a wheezy rattling sound.

Róisín heard the creaking of the huge metal gates.

'Oh, indeed they did, the finest of cake.'

'Let me just have a quick look in the boot here. Some of them young wans do be up to all kinds of tricks, and the Reverend Mother says we must check everything going in or out.'

'Jays, Bill, I'm under savage pressure altogether. I'll have to go. My sister has an appointment in Castlerea, and I'm late to drive her.'

'It won't take a second, Christy, and sure she'd skin me alive if anyone got out.'

'Yerra, they'd have no chance, Bill. I put my stuff in there not ten minutes ago, and there was nothing in there, only old newspapers and stuff. Listen, I'll get you a pint in Mac's on Sunday after Mass, but I'll have to go now. Good luck!'

The engine revved, and they were on their way without waiting for Mr O'Brien to answer. Róisín allowed herself to exhale. The car picked up speed, and she felt the right-hand turn onto the main road. She had been so distraught on the way there with that creepy

Monsignor that she barely noticed where they were going, and now she wished she'd been more observant.

The drive seemed interminable. Then they slowed down and the car went over some uneven ground before coming to a stop. The photographer got out and opened the boot.

'Right so, you nearly got me murdered, so it better be worth the great love story.' A short grey-haired man grinned, and his eyes were kind.

He helped her out of the boot and quickly ushered her into the house. 'Right, your man is below in the Bush Hotel in the village. He's to come back here at three, but we're a bit early. How about you go into the bathroom here and have a wash and tidy yourself up a bit? My niece is about your size, so I'll run to my sister's next door and borrow something better for you to wear. And then you two better get as far from here as is humanly possible, because once them nuns work out how you escaped, all hell will break loose, I can assure you.'

CHAPTER 27

$\mathcal{A}$ s Erich returned to the hotel from a long walk by the river to kill some time, he almost collided with the girl who had served him at dinner the evening before.

'Oh, there you are!' She smiled. 'My Uncle Christy is looking for you. You're to go right there.' She was puffed out and had clearly been running to find him. 'And bring everything, he said.'

'Why?' he asked her. 'What's happened?'

'I don't know. I'm just to give you the message.'

Erich went to his room, bundled his things into his small suitcase and paid his bill, then rushed to the other end of town to the photographer's house.

Christy opened the door and gestured that he should enter. There, in front of him, stood a thinner version of the girl he remembered, apart from a noticeable bump and hair cut so short there was hardly any of it left. But it was definitely her.

'I'll leave the star-crossed lovers to it, I think. I need a pint.' Christy smiled. 'Now, there'll be a car here in a few minutes, so be ready to go, and the best of luck to you.'

'Christy, I… Thank you.' Erich took Christy's hand in both of his. 'I can never repay…'

'My pleasure, lad. Now, look after her, do you hear me?'

'I will,' Erich assured him, and he was gone.

He and Róisín stood, facing each other for a long second, neither knowing what to do. Erich opened his arms and she walked slowly towards him, then rested her head on his chest. He closed his arms around her. She looked so thin, so fragile.

'Oh, Róisín, I was sure I'd lost you,' he murmured into her shorn head.

'Erich, I...I...'

He stood back slightly from her, towering over her, and with his thumbs he wiped the tears from her face. 'It's all right, darling. Everything is going to be all right. You're here now with me, and I promise nothing bad is going to happen. I'm going to take care of you and this little one.' He tentatively placed his hand on her swollen belly. 'I...I can't believe it. We're going to be parents, Ró, you and me. It's amazing, isn't it?'

She nodded. 'They made me write that letter. I never would have _'

'I know, sweetheart, don't worry. I know what happened, but it's all right now. I love you, and we're going to be together if that's what you want?'

'Very much. But what about Fiach? Erich, if he catches us, he'll kill us.'

Erich smiled. 'He hasn't a hope of finding us where we're going.' He quickly filled her in on the plan for Israel, and she visibly relaxed.

'You always wanted to travel, so now's your chance.' He grinned and kissed her nose.

'This morning I was thinning turnips, and now I'm going to fly to Israel.' She looked up at him. 'Am I dreaming?'

'No, not dreaming. It's happening, and the nightmare is over.' He drew her to him once more and kissed her tenderly.

As the car pulled up outside, she pulled on a coat Christy had found for her that fastened over her belly and disguised her condition and a hat to cover her head.

The drive down to Shannon was torturous. The man driving asked no end of questions, and Erich had to make the whole story up as they drove along. The car stank of some kind of animal, and the man himself also had a cavalier attitude to personal hygiene. He prattled away endlessly as they pulled out onto the main road to Limerick. He was kind, though, and offered them several sweets that had been languishing in the bottom of his coat pocket. Erich recoiled, trying to hide his disgust, but to his amazement, Róisín accepted, and after picking the fluff and goodness knew what else off them, happily sucked the sweets.

The man told them all about the local area, stories of kings and queens and evil British governors, of rivers that ran red with blood as the Irish fought for their land and their birthright. He regaled them with tales of sightings of púcas and ghosts and fairies and odd happenings going back to his great-grandfather's time. Needing a break from tour guiding, he then began the questioning of his passengers.

The jabbering that needed no response had allowed Erich to formulate a plausible story. He said he was German, which was kind of true, though he no longer referred to himself as German, and that his wife was also German and spoke no English, which spared Róisín answering any awkward questions. He mentioned that they were on their honeymoon and were going back to Germany now that they had seen Ireland, and the man who had been driving them around all week had to go home suddenly because of a family emergency. Erich had never told so many untruths in his life.

The driver, who they learned was called Bird for some unexplained reason, seemed happy enough with his explanation as to who he and Róisín were and so began again with his own diatribe. This one involved an interminable relating of an argument with his brother, a man called Duck, about a gate or a fence or a goat. Apparently the battle was bitter and terrible things were said and done, aspersions cast and insinuations made, all of which were taken deeply personally. The slights mounted on either side in this drawn-out tale of fraternal rivalry, a 'who said what to who' type saga, and so Erich was greatly relieved when they pulled into Shannon Airport.

'And you've no luggage, only that small bag?' The man looked sceptically at Erich's overnight case as they stood on the pavement outside the terminal.

'Oh, we had. It's being shipped. We bought a lot of things, so we got our baggage sent ahead,' Erich lied again.

'Ah, right.' The man seemed happy enough with that. Erich gave him a decent fee for the transport, at which his eyes lit up.

'Ah, there's no need really,' he said, stuffing the notes in his pocket. 'I owe Christy a favour since he took a picture of myself and my brother two weeks ago.' He pulled a battered and dog-eared photo from his pocket to show them. Beaming out were the driver and a man indistinguishable from him. Both had eyebrows like hedges and jowly, fleshy faces.

Erich couldn't help it. 'Is this a different brother?'

'A different brother? Sure, haven't I only the one brother?' The man seemed perplexed.

'Oh, right, so this is Duck?' Erich asked. He could feel Róisín squeezing his hand as she tried not to giggle.

'Aye, Duck, me brother.' He spoke like Erich was a little slow on the uptake.

'Oh, I just thought you and he had fallen out?' Erich asked.

'We did,' the driver replied innocently.

Erich laughed. 'Bird, it was a pleasure to meet you. Thank you for the drive.' The men shook hands, and Róisín smiled.

'Good luck to you now in your married life together.' With a theatrical bow, Bird got back into his smelly car and drove away.

* * *

THE FLIGHT to London was later that day, and they bought two seats. Erich thought about phoning home but decided against it for fear Hetty Devlin would listen in.

He settled Róisín in a corner of the airport where they could see the doors just in case the McAreaveys had discovered her absence and

199

had someone looking for them. He bought two sandwiches and two cups of hot tea, and they sat side by side, talking quietly.

They had a two-hour wait, so it was fraught, and he was sure the hands of his watch had never moved that slowly before.

He told her about his trip to America, and Liesl's visit to her mother. Róisín was worried for her mam, but Erich tried to reassure her that Father O'Toole, now that he knew the situation, would keep a close eye on her.

Liesl's baby was due soon and he would miss it, but this was more important. He wished he could contact his family, and he would once he was safely out of the country, but for now they had to keep as low a profile as possible.

At one stage, a rough-looking man entered the airport and seemed to scan the waiting area. Erich and Róisín slunk down in their seats, but he left again, allowing them both to exhale. Eventually they were called forward and shown to their seats on the aircraft.

'Ah, Mr Green and Miss Clark.' The air hostess checked their tickets, using the names they had assumed. 'Seats 14A and 14B.'

Róisín had never flown before and Erich had only once, but they had too much on their minds to be excited. They just needed to get airborne and then they would be safe.

'Almost there now, Ró,' Erich reassured her as she gripped his hand tightly.

The pilot came on the public address system and welcomed them aboard, then explained the route the flight would take and the altitude they expected to reach. Róisín's eyes were squeezed shut as the mighty engines roared to life and the plane began its taxi to the runway.

'You're going to miss it if you don't open your eyes,' Erich whispered in her ear, kissing her cheek as he did so.

'I'm terrified, Erich,' she admitted.

'Of flying? Or of your brothers or for the baby or what?' he asked.

'All of it!' she gasped.

'Me too.' Erich winked, and they both started to laugh.

The plane gained momentum and suddenly they were airborne. Everyone else gazed out the windows or looked nervous, but nobody was in fits of hysterical laughter like the handsome young couple in row fourteen.

Eventually when their mirth subsided, she leaned against him, sipping the orange juice the hostess had given her.

'I didn't think you'd come,' she said quietly. 'I didn't even know if you knew about the baby. And, Erich, I know you've said we can go to Israel, but I don't want you to feel like you have to stay with me. I'm so grateful to get out of that place, but I lied to you and my brothers are...'

Erich didn't answer but stood up in the aisle and reached into his pocket, extracting the little box he'd bought that morning in Carrick-on-Shannon.

To the amusement of their fellow passengers, who could see what was happening, he knelt down in the aisle and reached for her hand. Her other hand flew to her mouth in astonishment as she saw what he was doing. He opened the box, and there on the blood-red velvet was an exquisite diamond ring.

'Róisín, will you marry me?' he asked quietly.

Tears filled her eyes and spilled down her hollow cheeks. 'Are you sure?' she asked.

'Well, I'd hardly be on my knees on an airplane over the Irish Sea if I wasn't, would I?' He grinned. 'I love you, and I want to take care of you and our baby. And whatever the future holds, I want to face it with you.'

'Then yes.' She beamed, a trace of the old spark there. 'I'd love to.'

He slipped the ring on her finger and announced to the plane, 'She said yes!'

The entire aircraft erupted into applause, and the air hostess managed to produce two glasses of champagne.

A few moments later the pilot's voice crackled over the intercom. 'Ladies and gentlemen, we will shortly be starting our descent into London Heathrow. I would ask you to fasten your seatbelts and for the cabin crew to prepare the cabin for landing. In addition, I would like to extend my and my crew's congratulations to Mr Green and

Miss Clark travelling with us today, who got engaged in the last few minutes.'

More applause, and Erich and Róisín looked at each other. Luckily no passports had been needed, so they'd made up names to travel under just in case. Erich leaned over and kissed her. 'It's going to be fine, I promise,' he whispered, cupping her face in his hands.

She nodded, her eyes locked with his. 'I love you,' she whispered.

'I love you too,' he replied.

CHAPTER 28

*L*iesl waited until Jamie was gone to work before deciding to clean the windows. She knew he'd object if he saw her, but she was going mad just sitting around. Her mother was calling later that morning. She knew they'd arranged a rota of allegedly random visitors, ostensibly so she wouldn't be alone.

Each morning and afternoon, Liesl had a caller – Willi, Elizabeth, Frau Braun or Bridie from the shop. Her mother visited every day, and that was lovely. They talked about the new baby, and Ariella told Liesl about when she and Erich were born. Both of her mothers, as she saw Ariella and Elizabeth, were as close as sisters, and there was no rivalry. However, Liesl knew her mother enjoyed those times when it was just the two of them.

Sometimes they spoke about Erich and tried to imagine his new life in Israel. They were both worried about him, but from his frequent letters and occasional telephone calls he seemed happy enough. He'd made new friends and he and Róisín were a good match. She knew he was sad to be missing the birth of the baby and he was lonely for Ballycreggan and everyone here. They'd been inseparable since they were put on the train in Berlin in 1939 and life without him was somehow empty.

She shook herself out of her maudlin thoughts and decided to take advantage of her rare time alone. She filled a bowl with soapy water and pushed a chair up to the window. She washed the windows and polished them with newspaper till they shone. Satisfied, she climbed down off the chair. She had no idea where the sudden burst of energy had come from, but she was happy it had.

The house looked lovely. The cushions Elizabeth had made matched the curtains, and Daniel and Willi had laid a beautiful wooden floor. Their new home was beautiful, just what they wanted. It was a sandstone cottage perched on the cliff, just a mile outside the village but with uninterrupted views of the sea. It was three bedroomed and had a little garden. The Gallaghers were on the way up from Kerry, wanting to be there for the birth, and they had toyed with the idea of having Jamie's parents to stay with them, but Jamie had vetoed the idea. He knew his mother of old and was positive she would get on Liesl's nerves. Elizabeth tactfully agreed and insisted on hosting them. They told the Gallaghers the guest room wasn't ready yet.

Liesl and Jamie's new home had been owned by the Paisley sisters, an eccentric pair who had a fifty-year-long romance with two Welsh brothers but nobody ever took the relationship further than long-distance love. Penny had died of pneumonia last winter, and her sister, June, followed her within weeks, of a broken heart, people said. The two boyfriend brothers, now in their eighties, came over for the funeral and were inconsolable. It was all very emotional.

The house was well cared for if a little old-fashioned, but Willi and Daniel had worked day and night to get it up to a more modern standard.

The stove had been lit since before Jamie went to work, and Christmas was around the corner. He'd made her promise that she wouldn't try to decorate the house alone. The Gallaghers were arriving that afternoon, no doubt laden down with food and all manner of Christmas fare, but Liesl didn't mind. She'd even told Jamie that if the baby hadn't arrived, she would go to midnight Mass with him and his parents.

As she stood at the sink emptying the water, she felt a strange dragging sensation, followed by a small gush of liquid down her legs. She gripped the sink as a pain the like of which she'd never experienced before gripped her abdomen. She needed to get to the telephone. Jamie had had one installed in their new house in the first week so she could keep in touch with Erich. As she tried to cross to the hallway, another stronger pain stopped her in her tracks. Her mother had explained that first labour could take a long time and not to panic, so she tried to remain calm.

She managed to get to the telephone and rang Hettie. 'Hello, Miss Devlin, it's Liesl. Can you call Jamie for me, please?' she asked, trying not to gasp. The pain was not unmanageable but it was strong.

'Certainly, Liesl, one moment.'

She waited, hoping to hear her husband's voice, but it was Hettie who came on the line again. 'I'm sorry, Liesl, he's not answering. Do you want to try again later?'

'No,' Liesl said, fighting panic. 'Can you get my *mutti*? Or Daniel?' Elizabeth would be at school.

'Of course, dear. Is everything all right?'

'I think the baby is c-coming...' Liesl groaned as the pain caused what seemed like spasms in her belly.

'Oh, dear me! Right. Oh, stay where you are. I'll get Dr Crossley as well. Just stay on the line, dear, and I'll get someone out there to you right away. And I'll send someone to fetch Jamie.'

'Thank you,' Liesl managed. She needed to sit, to lie down, something. She needed Jamie; he was the only one she wanted.

She kept the telephone off the hook and got to the sofa. She was wet and needed a change of dress and underwear, but she couldn't face the stairs to their bedroom so would just have to wait.

Within minutes, she heard brakes screech outside and Daniel and Willi burst in.

'Oh, Liesl, are you all right?' Daniel rushed to her, and he and Willi helped her into a sitting position and then to stand.

'I want to get upstairs, to my bedroom. I need...' she managed with no embarrassment. The two men helped her upstairs.

'I've delivered puppies and a donkey foal before, so I'm sure it will be fine,' Willi joked. He could always make her laugh. She giggled as the pain subsided, only to build again.

'What do you need?' Daniel asked, sitting her on the bed.

'A nightie, in the drawer there.' She pointed at the ornately carved oak chest in the corner of the sunny bedroom that overlooked the sea. Daniel extracted it while Willi held her hand, not wincing as she squeezed it at each pain.

'These pains are coming quickly for a first-timer,' Willi said gently. 'I think you might be closer to meeting your baby than we think.' He shot a look at Daniel.

'All right, darling. Doctor Crossley is with someone out on the peninsula and they don't have a telephone, so he might be a while, but your mother is on the way. Jamie went to Belfast to pick his parents up from the train.' Daniel tried to keep his voice as low and as calm as possible. 'So for now it's just us. But don't worry – everything is going to be fine.'

Liesl tried not to cry out as the pain now seemed to seize her entire body. Willi rubbed her back and gave her sips of water as Daniel took off her dress and slip and pulled the nightie over her head. Together they helped her onto the bed, dry and more comfortable at least.

The minutes ticked by and she found sometimes standing was easier. As each wave came, she placed her arms on either Daniel or Willi's shoulders, leaning on them as the contraction crashed over her. She groaned and sometimes screamed with the sheer intensity of it. Willi kept up an encouraging flow of conversation, even making her smile with his jokes, and Daniel's quiet strength calmed her.

To everyone's relief, eventually they heard Ariella's voice on the stairs. Seconds later she burst into the room, Frau Braun on her heels.

'All right, men, out you go! This is women's business.' Frau Braun ushered them out, but not before they each planted a kiss on her cheek.

'Oh, darling, are you all right?' Ariella asked.

'It hurts, *Mutti*,' Liesl gasped. 'I want Jamie.'

'I know, *liebling*. He's on his way, I promise, but it won't be long now, I think.'

Frau Braun went to the end of the bed and checked between Liesl's legs. 'I can see the head,' she said triumphantly.

'I want to push,' Liesl managed as another ferocious wave crashed over her.

'You do that, darling. Here, hold my hand and push as hard as you can.' Ariella wiped the beads of perspiration from her daughter's brow as Liesl bore down hard.

'Good girl, Liesl! Well done. Not too much more – the head is out and the shoulders are coming now...' Frau Braun called.

Wave after wave, the contractions came, and with each one, Liesl pushed harder until she felt she could do no more.

'One more big push, Liesl, just one more. You can do this! Come on, almost there...' Frau Braun encouraged her as Ariella climbed onto the bed beside her daughter. With one arm around Liesl's shoulders and the other gripping her hand, she kissed her temple. 'Come, my love, one more. Let's meet this little person, eh?'

Liesl was so exhausted that she felt she could drift away, but her body surged once more and she bore down for all she was worth. Then she felt it, that instant release, the baby sliding out of her body. And then the pain was gone.

Silence, then a loud wail.

'It's a little boy, Liesl! Oh, he is perfect, a perfect son.' Frau Braun's old wrinkled face was wet with tears as she cut the cord and wrapped the baby in a flannel sheet that was lying in preparation on the dresser. She handed Liesl her son.

Liesl gazed in adoration at him, taking in his scrunched-up face and fine head of reddish hair. 'He's beautiful,' she breathed, kissing his head. 'Oh, *Mutti*, look, isn't he just perfect?'

Together the three women admired the new arrival. Liesl couldn't take her eyes off him. After a while, Frau Braun took him. Ariella helped Liesl into a fresh nightie, changed the sheets, tied Liesl's hair back and washed her face, while Frau Braun put a napkin and a long white gown on the baby.

Once Liesl was sitting up and feeling fresher, Ariella allowed Daniel and Willi into the room to admire their grandson, and both men too were transfixed.

Frau Braun went downstairs to make Liesl some tea and toast.

'Let me introduce you to your family, Peter Gallagher.' Liesl caught her mother's eye and saw the look of love there. She had asked Jamie if the baby was a boy if he would mind if they named him after her father. Of course he agreed, but they'd kept their plan a secret.

Liesl smiled as she spoke to her son. 'So this is complicated, but basically you have more grandparents than most little boys.'

A commotion downstairs interrupted her. Jamie had arrived and he thundered up the stairs, with his parents and Elizabeth behind.

'Now we can introduce you to everyone properly.' Liesl smiled.

Jamie crossed the room, gazing in wonderment at the sight.

'Well, you missed the drama, but here we are. Peter, this is your daddy.' Liesl held her son out for Jamie to take, and with trembling hands, the big Kerryman took his infant son in his arms.

'Liesl, he's...he's so beautiful.' Jamie could barely get the words out. His voice choked and tears pooled in his eyes.

He took him across the room to where his parents stood. 'Look, Mam, Dad, isn't he smashing? This is Peter. And these are some of your grannies and grandads, Son.' Jamie chuckled.

Peggy was transfixed. She held her little finger out and the baby gripped it. She turned to her husband. 'Look, Donie, our grandson.'

'He's a smasher, all right, an absolute smasher,' Jamie's father agreed.

Jamie went back to the bed as Peter let out a howl.

'I think he's hungry,' Liesl said with a smile. 'We've had a busy few hours.'

Frau Braun appeared with a tray, and in a tone brooking no argument ushered everyone but Jamie out. Elizabeth leaned down and kissed the baby's head before leaving. 'Welcome to our family, Peter. We are very happy you're here.'

They all retreated, leaving Jamie and Liesl alone with their baby, who suckled happily at Liesl's breast as they both watched in delighted amazement.

'I'm sorry I wasn't here,' Jamie whispered.

'I'm not.' Liesl grinned. 'Frau Braun – I don't think I can ever get used to calling her Frau Frank – was amazing and so was *Mutti*.'

'Was it awful?' he asked, clearly half afraid of her answer.

Liesl shook her head. 'Yes. And it was the best thing that has ever happened to me.'

CHAPTER 29

*R*abbi Frank gazed into the fire as Katerin drew the curtains. The wireless was on in the background, playing some old romance serial his wife loved. He teased her about her romantic streak, but it was one of the things he loved most about her. He knew her in a way nobody else did, especially now since they'd married. She was gradually allowing him to see the real Katerin, a woman of passion and mischief, beaten down by years of an abusive marriage and a hard life. Seeing her smile, watching her learn to accept a compliment without some sharp quip to counteract it, feeling that rush as she reached for his hand or brushed a crumb off his beard, gave him joy he never thought possible. He longed to live in a way he hadn't before, just to be with her. He was grateful for each day. He felt that he'd been given a reprieve by God, here at the last hour. That day Daniel found him would surely have been his last had his dear friend not intervened. He owed his life to Daniel, and more than that, he owed him for this magical time, this precious relationship. He was determined to make Katerin feel like the most loved woman in the world for whatever time remained for them.

They'd enjoyed a wonderful Channukah and Christmas with the Liebers and the Brauns, celebrating both traditions, the only note of sadness being the absence of Erich, but little Peter was such a delight and such a welcome addition it was a joy filled affair. They'd even joined the entire village on New Year's Eve in the village green where everyone held hands at midnight and sang *Auld Lang Syne* to ring in 1956.

Their home, a terraced two-storey on the side of the main street that really felt like theirs, was decorated simply. He'd nailed the ornamental casing of the mezuzah to the right-hand doorpost, and several people had stopped to ask him what he was doing as they passed on their way to getting their groceries. Though his flock was ever dwindling, it was nice to explain to the neighbours about the Shema prayer rolled up on parchment and held within. He showed them how it was customary to touch it as one entered the home and then kiss one's fingers. They seemed genuinely interested, and he often commented on how often in Ireland he found himself explaining aspects of Judaism to people, far more than he'd ever done in Germany. Perhaps that was how the whole thing was allowed to happen, because Gentiles were so separate from Jews. Maybe if they opened up to each other, were more forthright about their faiths, it wouldn't be so easy to dehumanise, to kill.

'What's on your mind, *schatzi?*' she asked, placing a cup of cocoa beside him.

He smiled at the pet name she'd started calling him in private. It was a term of affection he'd heard others use but never imagined anyone would call him. He gratefully took a sip of the cocoa.

'I'm thinking about Daniel and the whole family.' He sighed.

'Has something happened?' she asked, sitting in the opposite fireside chair facing him.

'No, not that I know of. Erich and Róisín are getting on well at the kibbutz. Erich wrote to me, thanking me for everything and saying that even though it was a strange new place and so hot, he was enjoying it. Amazingly one of his friends – remember Simon? Well, he met a girl from that kibbutz last month at some event and is thinking of moving there, so Erich and he will be reunited.'

'So what's the problem?' she asked.

'Just the worry, I suppose. He likes it, and Róisín is being well cared for and she's happy enough, but she's not Jewish. And reading between the lines, I think Erich won't stay there long term. He's dying to see Liesl's new baby. And if he leaves, then Róisín's family will surely be after them. Father O'Toole told me how the McAreaveys sent someone to the convent and demanded to know who released her. He said he told them he didn't know where they went, but as Father O'Toole says, that family have tentacles everywhere.'

'So they can't come back?' she asked.

'No. It would seem not. I know the family are putting a brave face on it, but they miss him and he misses them. Liesl's baby is getting bigger now, and he feels like he's missing out. And Liesl wants her brother here to meet his nephew. It's like a forced exile.' He sighed, leaned back on the armchair and closed his eyes. Though the medication was working much better now, he didn't have the stamina he once had and tired more easily.

'But there's nothing we can do, is there?' she asked.

'Maybe. Probably not,' he replied, not opening his eyes.

'David...' She used his name only rarely, and when she did, it was normally music to his ears, but this time he could hear the admonishment there. 'What are you up to?'

He smiled, a half-lopsided grin that she found hard to resist.

'How many more times must I tell you, you are a foolish sick old man. Please do not begin meddling in things you should not meddle with.'

He knew she spoke out of concern, though she sounded so frustrated with him. He suppressed a chortle.

'Promise me you won't stick your nose in any further. I know they are lonely for Erich – we all are. And now with the new baby, it would be lovely to have the whole family together.' Her tone softened. 'Willi and Ariella won't have a child, so I'll never be a grandma, but I feel we are a little like honorary grandparents to the Bannon children's children after all we've been through together.'

He knew how such an admittance of vulnerability cost her; it was part of the gradual chipping away of the walls of protection built over decades. He wanted Erich back in Ballycreggan for her as much as for anyone. That family meant the world to her, and to him as well. There might just be a way, but perhaps she was right. He was meddling in things that could rapidly get out of control, so perhaps it was best to let sleeping dogs lie?

'I think they feel the same way, Katerin.' He leaned over and took her hand. 'The war was the worst thing to happen to our people. The world will never again be the same – so much loss, so much pain and suffering. But for us, you and me, I feel bad saying it, but my life has been so enriched by Ballycreggan and the Liebers and the children. And then, into my old long life, comes you. I'd never considered even for a second that possibility that I would find a family, let alone love, at this, the last act, but I have. And it astounds me the blessings God has piled upon me. I feel unworthy of such joy, and I want to find a way to repay these people for their kindness to me. And for them, being together is central to their happiness. It is why Erich never chose to go to Israel when all of his friends did. He thought it was a crisis of his faith, but I never thought that. Erich didn't want to go to Israel because he wanted to stay with his family. He lost his father, that is true, but what that family – the cobbled-together group of strangers who became an unshakable unit – endured created a bond of love so unbreakable that they hate to be apart. The Jewish people need the Promised Land to feel part of something, to feel safe, to feel that they belong somewhere that will never turn on them, to try to repair the deep fractures in their families and in their hearts, to be surrounded by people who understand and who can help to make them complete again. But he is different. And so he won't ever truly be happy in the Promised Land, or America either for that matter. And for as long as he is gone, the family here in Ballycreggan will always feel like a part of themselves is missing, and it will remain so, a gaping hole of loss, until he returns. He's a Jew, but for Erich, Israel is not home – Ireland is.'

'So what's your plan?' she asked, and he was relieved to hear the resignation in her voice. If he was going to succeed, he would need her help.

'Well' – he stroked his beard – 'I've been thinking. What do you need when the bully has a big stick?'

His wife looked confused. 'I don't know. What do you mean?'

'You need a bigger stick.' He smiled and explained his plan.

CHAPTER 30

iach McAreavey stepped out of the small door cut in the much larger one of Walton Gaol to see the handsome well-dressed man he'd been told to expect leaning against a beautiful burgundy-coloured Bentley with chrome trim. The man was younger than he'd envisioned for someone with such a reputation.

'All right, Fiach?' the man asked. His accent was pure cockney, from London's East End, but this, like everything else about him, was not as it seemed. He beamed as if he and Fiach were old friends. He took Fiach's bag and placed it in the boot. Fiach had never seen this man before, but he didn't need to; his reputation as the head of one of the largest organised crime families in England was enough.

Fiach nodded and got into the car. The man slid in beside him and tapped the screen to indicate to the driver that he should pull away.

'So, how ya been, mate?' the man asked. 'Did His Majesty treat you all right this time?'

Fiach wasn't fooled by the friendly demeanour. 'Fine.' He hated this, but it had to be done.

'Now then, I know you got things to do and that – don't we all, mate? So I'll get right to the point.'

Fiach looked down at his fingers, broken in several places now. He doubted they would ever look normal again. The prison doctor was neither competent nor caring.

'Firstly, right' – the man rubbed his chin – 'sorry about that.' He nodded in the direction of Fiach's mashed-up hand. 'My boys, well, what can I say. They's not the smartest, know what I mean?' He tapped his temple. 'But then, that's how come they winds up in there.' He jerked his head to indicate the grey looming prison behind them. 'I'm blue in the face, I am, from tellin' them, don't get caught, but do they listen?' He shook his head as a mother might as her children run across a clean floor in muddy boots. 'Anyways, they was a bit heavy-handed, if you pardon the horrible pun, and for that, I apologise. I've got a bloke in Harley Street, a surgeon. He'll sort you out. Tell him I sent ya.'

Fiach made a non-committal noise. He knew his role now was to listen, not to speak.

'So here we are. Now, the reason I come all the way up here to talk to you myself, in person, though I hate the North, bloody miserable place, is 'cause we need to be crystal clear, y'know?' He smiled again.

Clearly this time he wanted a response. Fiach nodded.

'Now,' he went on as the car sped through the Liverpool streets, 'my boys tell me that you're some kinda little mini gangster and you reckon you've got some influence. And I don't doubt it, my friend, I don't, a good-looking lad like you. And all you Irish is a bit, well – let's just say it, shall we – a bit aggressive, and so this line of work is ideal for ya.'

Fiach raged inside at the condescending tone but knew better than to show it.

'And don't get me wrong, mate. You do whatever you want. I ain't got no interest in this.' The man waved his hand dismissively at the city, wrinkling his nose in disgust at the large silos on the docks. 'But for some reason, about which I care absolutely nothin', mind you, you've got into a bit of a feud with a bloke called Erich Bannon, and that, I'm afraid, has got to stop.'

Fiach said nothing, keeping his eyes firmly on the back of the passenger seat. They were headed away from the city now, deeper into the docklands and further from people. Fiach's heart began to beat even louder, but he couldn't show fear. This man was infamous for the inventive and gruesome ways he dealt with anyone he considered an enemy. The very last thing Fiach could countenance, even for a second, was to make an enemy of him. Fiach knew a feud would mean all-out gangland war, and it was not one he stood even a ghost of a chance of winning. He'd made connections over the years, it was true, and there were those who feared him, but he knew that he was no match for the man sitting beside him, and he wasn't stupid enough to give him cause to start anything.

'So Erich and his girl are goin' to come home from the Promised Land – you know where that is, right? The land promised to my people by God himself?'

Fiach nodded. 'I do,' he murmured.

'Good. That's important that people know that, see? 'Cause we've had enough to be dealin' with, y'know what I mean?'

Fiach nodded again.

'So this Erich and I – well, I know him, and I know his rabbi. Him and me is mates, actually, and he's worried about the lad. Course he was, some tough bloke like yourself after him. Who wouldn't be scared?' The man chuckled. 'Now, this old man, this rabbi, was so worried, him and his old missus had to come all the way over to London to visit me, to tell me their tale of woe. Now, this rabbi was very good to me when I was a nipper, much better than I deserved, to be truthful about it, and he's never asked me for nothing in return, not once. So when he asks me a favour, I want to help him, don't I?'

The man lit a putrid-smelling cigarette and turned his head to Fiach as he spoke, blowing the foul smoke into his face. 'Now, I know my lads had a word with you in there, and I understand you got the message that you'll allow Erich and his girl to come back safely to Ireland. So I'm just tying up any loose ends where that's concerned, just in case any bits of how this is gonna go down are unclear to you.'

Fiach had no choice but bear the insults. He kept his eyes firmly on the back of the seat in front of him, desperate to keep his expression neutral. The man took two pulls from his cigarette and threw it out of the window.

'Now, you and me isn't goin' to fall out over this, are we? So we're clear, Erich Bannon, and all of his family and all of that, are entirely off limits to you. You let 'em be, let them live their lives happy ever after, and everythin' will be all right.' The upward cheery inflection in his voice suggested a simple transaction. ''Cause I will not be happy if I hear even a whisper of something going wrong for anyone to do with him. Now, Fiach, what you gettin' out of this little arrangement, I hear you ask.'

The man turned in the seat, pivoting his whole body now towards Fiach, his immaculately cut charcoal suit moving easily on him as he did so, and put his finger under Fiach's chin, moving Fiach's face around to look squarely into his cold grey eyes. The man was so close that Fiach could see the shadow of beard on his shaved jaw, the pores on his sallow skin, his perfectly coiffed dark hair, his manicured fingernails. The mingling aromas of his own sweat, the man's cologne and the cigarette smoke combined with the terror to churn his guts.

The car had stopped at the quayside; there was nobody about. The journey had started at dusk, but by now night had fallen and the dock was illuminated only by an odd yellow streetlight, the one nearest to the car flickering on and off. The arctic wind outside was buffeting even the sturdy car as it stirred up white horses on the dark sea. The only noise was the clinking of chains coming from a deserted cargo boat moored alongside the dock.

'The answer,' the man said slowly, his eyes never breaking contact with Fiach's, 'you thick Paddy, is nothin' at all.' He reached over and grabbed Fiach's mangled hand and squeezed hard. Fiach knew better than to scream, despite the excruciating pain.

'But I will not rain my wrath down on your Irish head, provided you keep your end of the bargain. But if anything – and I mean anything at all – happens to Erich or his girl or their family, then we have a very big problem. Do we understand each other?' the man asked quietly, releasing the hand.

'Yes, Mr Kolitz. I understand,' Fiach whimpered.

Charlie Kolitz patted his cheek patronisingly. 'Good lad.' He then nodded to the driver, who got out and opened the passenger door.

Fiach fought the panic – was he going to be killed anyway?

The freezing wind rushed into the warm car, and Charlie Kolitz shivered dramatically. 'Out ya get, mate. You know the way back, don't ya?'

Fiach nodded and climbed out of the car.

CHAPTER 31

*E*rich watched as Abigail and Róisín strolled up from the orchard, chatting animatedly. Abigail had announced that she'd got engaged to an Israeli man called Eli and she was madly in love and over the moon. They'd come to visit from Haifa, and Erich had been thrilled to see her.

He and Róisín were hosting a dinner in their house tonight, an unusual event as they normally ate communally, but they'd got special permission because Abigail and Eli were visiting. Erich had been to the market to get supplies. He actually loved life on the kibbutz, much to his amazement, and Róisín was really happy there too. She'd made lots of friends, and though the heat nearly killed both of them, they were enjoying life. They liked the food, most of which they had never seen before, and nobody pushed Róisín on the religious aspects. Erich practiced and found comfort and strength from the camaraderie of his faith. He and Róisín had married in London, at the Israeli embassy, to ensure her right to go to Israel, and so she had never set foot inside a synagogue, nor had she any desire to.

There was an energy at the kibbutz, a sense of being on the ground floor, of creating something for future generations, that he couldn't help but embrace. The work was hard but satisfying, and his building skills were much in demand. But neither he nor Róisín wanted to commit to the life permanently. It wasn't just homesickness, though that was a huge factor, and now that Liesl had had the baby, he desperately wanted to get back. But neither of them agreed with the way children were raised communally on the kibbutz, and the concept of ownership of anything was not allowed, even clothes or shoes; everything was shared and everyone had access to it all. While Erich could see the benefits, he didn't want to live like that.

He stood on the veranda overlooking the valley, shielding his eyes from the relentless sun. Date palms to the right, wheat in the middle covering the valley floor, olive trees growing up the other side – every spare inch had been cultivated, clawed back from the voracious desert, made profitable. Animals were raised for milk, meat and cheese, and there were chickens and fowl of all sorts. Everyone and everything on the kibbutz had a purpose, and it all worked in harmony most of the time.

Simon was there, and they worked together. He was courting a girl whose entire family was gassed in Dachau. Seeing people with numbers tattooed on their arms every day, and hearing the stories first-hand, brought what had happened to his people home to Erich in a way he could never have experienced in Ireland.

As Erich chopped the tomatoes and cheese for the salad, one of the children came to the door. 'A letter for you.' The child grinned and ran off.

Erich tore open the envelope, sat down at the scrubbed wooden table and read.

My dear Erich,

Thank you for your last letter. Yes, we are all doing well here, though the temperatures are a little lower here, I should imagine. Liesl and little Peter are doing very well, and every time I see him, I am reminded of the words from the Talmud: 'With each new child, the world begins anew.' You too soon will welcome new life. Ah, how precious that is.

Now, I am writing with some news. It is now safe for you to return to Ireland should you so wish. There is no further threat to your or Róisín's

221

safety. I cannot say how exactly I can make such a claim, but you will have to trust me as you always have.

Please give my best wishes to Simon and any others from Ballycreggan that you encounter and remind them that their old rabbi loves to hear from them, so to spare a moment in the construction of the Promised Land for him.

I look forward to seeing you in Ballycreggan soon.

God bless you.

Rabbi Frank

Erich could hardly believe it. They could go home.

* * *

LIESL COULD BARELY HEAR the words her brother was saying on the telephone. 'Erich, slow down and speak really slowly. The line is terrible.'

Jamie's parents had decided to visit, again, much to her horror. They'd arrived as a surprise, and she and Jamie had to feign excitement when both knew the reality; if they'd asked if they could come, he would have put them off.

The time when his mother had got so drunk and demanded her grandchild be raised as a Catholic had not been forgotten. Liesl knew Peggy Gallagher was mortified; Jamie's father had written to Jamie explaining how she was racked with guilt and embarrassment, and when they visited when Peter was born it had not been mentioned. But the fact was that they were the baby's grandparents, like it or not, so they were currently installed once again with Elizabeth and Daniel. They were mad about the baby to be fair and wanted to spend as much time with him as they could.

Peter was sleeping peacefully in the cradle that Erich had made for him and Liesl was loving the time in their new home with their son. The weather was bitterly cold, even for late January, and everyone was predicting snow next week.

Her brother spoke again, this time slowly, and she caught most of it.

'Rabbi…letter…mother…Fiach…message to come…'

She tried to make sense of it. 'You got a letter from the rabbi, is that it?' she asked.

'Yes, with a message...' More crackling.

She exhaled in frustration. 'Erich...' She was about to try again when the line went dead. She called Miss Devlin in the exchange.

'Can you try to reconnect me, please?' she asked politely.

'I'll try, Liesl, but the fault is at Erich's end. One moment...'

Liesl heard a few clicks on the line. 'Hello? Erich? Are you there?'

'Liesl?' He was back.

She sighed. Switching to German, she said, 'You know there are ears listening in, so tell me in German.'

Erich normally didn't use his German at all except when speaking to their old family friends the Richters on their rare visits to Ireland, so she was pleased to hear a fluency in his speech that had been lost.

He chuckled, '*Sicher*, Róisín says I speak German and Yiddish to keep her in the dark.' He laughed again and she was relieved to hear it; she'd thought he'd telephoned with bad news.

The line was better this time, and though he did sound like he was down a well, at least she got every word.

'Liesl, I was ringing to tell you that we're coming home. I got a letter from the rabbi and Róisín's had a letter from her mother. Fiach said to tell us that he holds no grudge, and that he's happy for us and will be leaving us alone.'

She hardly dared believe it. She missed her brother more than words could say, and the idea of him in permanent exile caused her deep pain. But could this be true?

'But why the sudden change of mind? He didn't surely just wake up one morning and decide all is forgiven?' She longed to believe it but it seemed implausible.

'I've no idea, and I don't care either. He says the debt is lifted and there is no bad blood between us. Look, I know it's a risk, Liesl, but what else am I to do? Stay here, hiding, forever? People have been so kind, everyone really, and having Simon here now as well – it's great. I like the work, and the women are so good to Róisín – they don't care at all that she's not Jewish – but my heart isn't here. I'm an uncle, and I want to be there for Peter, and for you and *Mutti* and Elizabeth and everyone. And Ró misses home too. She can't stand the heat here – her skin can't take it – and we both just want to come home.'

'And how's she doing with the pregnancy?' Liesl asked. She prayed the longing to come back to Ballycreggan wasn't clouding her brother's judgement.

'Good, really good, actually. She's such a trooper, Liesl. She just gets on with it, even though she's in a puddle of sweat most of the time and has no idea what people are saying. She works in the nursery, taking care of the little ones while the mothers are at work, and she really loves it. She's a natural with babies. When we get home, she'll be such a great help to you with Peter, and when our baby arrives...'

Her brother was going to be a father. Little Erich. It was hard to picture, but it sounded like he and Róisín were happy together, so that was wonderful.

'So she's due in March?' she asked.

'Yes, we think around then. So my child will only be a few months younger than yours. Can you believe this is happening, Liesl?' She could hear the emotion roughening his voice. 'Us as parents.'

'It's wonderful and I desperately want Peter to grow up with his cousin, but, Erich, I'm scared. What if it's a trap?'

'Ró and I have talked about it. We don't think it is. There's no way the rabbi would let that happen, and we want to risk it anyway.'

'All right. Well, better than all right, it's wonderful news. But please be very careful and watch your back. Once you leave the kibbutz, leave Israel, you will be outside of their protection.'

'I will. Liesl, I just can't wait to see you all.'

'We've missed you too, little man.' She smiled as she used the pet name Daniel had given Erich when he first met him.

'See you soon then,' Erich said, and the line went dead again.

She hung up the phone.

Liesl smiled as she pictured Hetty Devlin's face. The woman had actually had the audacity to admonish Liesl when she bumped into her in the library for speaking in German to her brother over the last couple of months on the telephone. She claimed it was against regulations for the Department of Posts and Telegraphs or some other such nonsense, when everyone knew she was just furious that she couldn't listen in.

'Coo-eee!'

Liesl's heart sank. It was her mother-in-law. Normally when she had to meet Peggy, Jamie was there, but now he was in the bar and she was alone.

'Hello, Mrs Gallagher.' Liesl tried to look pleased to see her. Jamie's mother had never invited her to call her Peggy, so to her face Liesl addressed her as Mrs Gallagher.

'Ah, Liesl, there you are, looking radiant, God bless you. And how's my little pride and joy?'

Her loud voice woke Peter and he started crying. Liesl gritted her teeth as she lifted him, but he was instantly snatched away by Peggy.

She'd let herself in; the half door was on the latch anyway. She now cast a judgemental glance around the kitchen. The breakfast ware was still on the table despite it being almost midday. Jamie and Liesl both slept late, him because he didn't get back from the pub until after 1 a.m. most nights, and she because she waited up for him to have a cup of cocoa before bed. Peter was trying to turn night into day, sleeping during waking hours and wide awake at night, and they were both exhausted.

The older woman sat down, cooing over the baby, who was at least content now that he was up in arms.

Liesl ran the tap and added some dish soap to the water, her hackles up. The very sight of her mother-in-law set her nerves on edge. Where on earth was Jamie? She wished Peggy hadn't called; she wanted to think about Erich's news.

'So I came here this morning, Liesl, to have a little chat with you, woman to woman.'

Something about the wheedling nature of her tone made Liesl put up her guard. What did she want? And she'd deliberately come when she knew Jamie would be at work, so something was definitely afoot.

'Oh, yes?' Liesl asked, her back to Peggy as she washed the dishes.

In general, Liesl avoided any alone time with her mother-in-law, feeling safer if Donie or Jamie was about.

'Yes. And firstly, can I say again how very sorry I am about how I acted at the dinner with your family? I do not drink, as you know, never touched it, but it didn't agree with me and I think I said some regrettable things. To be honest, I don't remember.'

You don't remember? Liesl thought to herself. *You remember perfectly well.* 'Oh, water under the bridge now, Mrs Gallagher. We're all family now, so we don't let silly things like that fester.' She tried to keep her voice light, biting her tongue not to say, 'Just like I've forgiven you for the names you called me when you found out Jamie and I were together, and the way you threw me out of his house in Dublin, and the way you got his creepy brother Brendan to try to talk Jamie out of the relationship.' Oh yes, she was very forgiving.

Elizabeth had counselled her to hold her tongue, to just endure Peggy once or twice a year for Jamie's sake. And she would do it, no matter what. Her husband was so good to her, he really was; she could do this for him. Though she was waiting for the day they announced they were going home to Kerry, once that happened she could breathe again.

'Well, exactly. Family. And this little pet is part of my family too, and so I... Well, I was hoping we could discuss – calmly this time of course – the christening.'

Liesl felt the vein throb in her temple. The nerve of the woman. Jamie had been crystal clear that Peter was Jewish by virtue of having a Jewish mother, and yet here Peggy was, sticking her halfpence worth in again. She took a deep breath. 'Mrs Gallagher, as Jamie has said already, Peter is Jewish, as I am, as my family is, so that is all there is to it.' She wanted to sound confident, assertive, but she feared it came out as petulant.

'Ah, but look at him, Liesl. He's such a little dote and only half a Jew. The other half is a Catholic, and surely that counts for something? Here's what I was thinking, and I'm sure you'll agree it's reasonable. Peter will be raised up here, surrounded by Jews, and so will have lots of time to see that...er...that religion. But if he were baptised a Catholic, then he could have the option to decide, once he is older? I mean…I think it's a fair compromise, isn't it? And Father Brendan – he is such a wonderful son and such a devout and pious priest – has even agreed to travel all the way up here to baptise him. So that's just marvellous, isn't it?'

Her smile never reached her small piggy eyes, and Liesl had to use every ounce of her willpower not to lose her temper. She turned and crossed the floor, taking Peter from her mother-in-law. He let out a squawk of protest at being removed from his grandmother's ample bosom.

'Mrs Gallagher' – she kept her voice even – 'my son is Jewish, one hundred percent. There is no such thing as half a Jew. Jamie is Peter's father, and he accepts that, willingly, and he is happy for our son to be raised as part of this community. It is something that means a lot to me, it is the reason Erich and I ended up here, and it is fundamental to who we are. And so joining my child in any other faith is not something I would ever do. I'm sorry if this disappoints you, but it is how it is. I hope you can accept it and not make a fuss because I can assure you that neither Jamie nor I will change our minds on this matter.' She held Peter close, lifting him onto her shoulder where he snuggled in contentedly. 'Now, if you'll excuse me, I need to go.'

Luckily Daniel had given her a car – he insisted on it now that they were out of town – so she wrapped Peter warmly and placed him in his Moses basket, secured it on the back seat of the car and drove furiously towards the village. Peggy had no time to react and Liesl just left her standing in the middle of her kitchen.

She needed to put some distance between herself and her mother-in-law before someone got hurt.

CHAPTER 32

Elizabeth was at school, Daniel and Willi were on a job near Bangor, and Ariella was having her hair done in Belfast, so Liesl thought about where she could go. The wind was biting, and in her haste to depart, she hadn't grabbed a coat. Sleet was carried on the wind, and the sea was a rough angry grey. She didn't want to take Peter out into the cold, but if she went to the pub now, Jamie would know something had happened and he'd get it out of her. Once he discovered his mother's plan, no doubt words would be said, which would mean yet another swift departure of the Gallaghers from Bally-creggan. Though Jamie would back her fully, it would hurt him to know another visit from his parents had ended awkwardly.

She decided to head to Miss McGovern's tea shop for something warm to drink. She'd forgotten her purse as well, but she could pay later; people in Ballycreggan were good like that.

She was sitting at the only junction in the village, outside the rabbi and Frau Braun's house, waiting for an enormous lorry to pass, when Frau Braun knocked on the car's window.

'Liesl, how are you?' She'd been putting her milk bottles out for collection.

Liesl leaned over and rolled down the window. 'Hello, Frau Braun

– I mean, Frau Frank.' She smiled. It was still hard to believe Frau Braun and the old rabbi had married. 'I haven't seen you since you were in England.'

'Oh, you've had enough to do with your little baby. But it's lovely to see you both now. Have you time for a cup of coffee?'

'I'd love it.' Liesl got out and Willi's mother helped her get Peter inside. Instinctively, Liesl touched the mezuzah nailed to the door-frame and then kissed her fingers.

It felt strange to see the rabbi sitting beside the fire, reading; she was used to him being at the farm. He looked so cosy and warm, and she was happy to be welcomed in. Frau Braun took Peter up, delighted with him.

'Ah, Liesl, shalom! Welcome, welcome. And little Peter, what a surprise. He's grown so much already.' The rabbi stood to greet her and she felt a pang of affection and a little guilt at not seeing them for a few weeks. She knew how much her family meant to them.

'Shalom, Rabbi.' She smiled and sat on the sofa at his gesture that she should. Frau Braun fussed around her, handed her the baby and then appeared with a cup of coffee and a huge slice of cinnamon cake.

'It is good to see you, child,' said the rabbi. 'How are you? And this little man, he's a precious little boy.'

Liesl noticed the signs of age on his face, but he looked so much better than he had of late. She'd been surprised when Elizabeth told her that he and Frau Braun had even taken a trip to London to meet up with some old friends of his, so he must really be on the mend. He had been at death's door by all accounts.

'Oh, he's fine, Rabbi. If only he would sleep.' She thanked Frau Braun for the drink and took a grateful sip.

'Ah, yes, I have heard they can be like that,' he chuckled, 'but I'm sure it will pass. And Jamie is well?'

'Yes, thank you, he's fine. Working hard, but he's so good, taking Peter at night so I get some sleep. He's trained Alfie – you know, who works at the creamery – to do the night shifts. Alfie's trying to save up enough for an engagement ring for Daisy Donnelly, who he's been courting for fourteen years apparently, so he's mad for work.' Liesl grinned.

The rabbi smiled and chuckled. 'Ah, *mein kleines Mädchen* has become an Irish woman. You sound just like them now.'

'I suppose I do.' She paused. Suddenly she knew he was the one she could confide in. She needed to get it off her chest, everything about Peggy and the whole mess, but she didn't want to tell her parents about Mrs Gallagher because it would embarrass Jamie.

'Rabbi, can I ask your advice about something?' She watched his face for a response. His beard was now completely white, and his hair was thinner than it was but by no means gone. He was always small and strong, and though the illness had diminished him to a certain extent, his natural vitality seemed undimmed.

'Of course, *sheifale*. What is on your mind?'

The whole story came pouring out, including Peggy's demands once again for a christening, and he waited without interrupting until she finally ran out of steam.

He nodded and sat back in his chair, his hands folded across his chest as he'd always done. 'Now, Liesl, the first issue of this baby's faith has already been dealt with, even if you don't think it has. You have explained gently but firmly to Mrs Gallagher the situation, and she will have to accept it. She knows she cannot now win because Jamie won't agree to her demand and she had hoped to strong-arm you but failed, so that is done, nothing more to be said. However, I would add, there was a time in my life when I would have been as appalled as you at such a request, but I am an old man now, at the end of a long and eventful life, and I have a different perspective. If you'll indulge me?' He smiled.

Liesl nodded, intrigued.

'Our faith is very important to us, Liesl. It is what we clung to when the worst happened, and it bound us together in ways Gentiles will never understand. I will soon die, and I will meet God and that is something I am happy to do. But I have two good friends, both Christians, one a Catholic and the other a Protestant, and their faith means the world to them as well. And I am sure that if I went to China or Russia or the North Pole –'

Liesl laughed.

'Then there I would find people, good people, who are sure their belief is right and good and the best way to be. And something made me realise, Liesl, that we can't all be right. Or maybe we can? Maybe our great heavenly Father comes to us in whatever culture or time or place we are, and makes Himself known to us in a way that is safe and familiar and in the same way as He comes to those we love.'

'Maybe you're right. I don't know...' She wondered where this was going.

'So Mrs Gallagher is saying what she says because she believes that is what would be best for this baby.' He nodded at Peter, who was gazing thoughtfully at the leaping flames in the grate. 'And we can be angry or frustrated, and I understand that, or we can take it as something good. She loves this child, she wants what is best for him, and to her a Catholic baptism is what is best. And you know better than most, things that are done from a place of love can never really be wrong.'

Liesl nodded, knowing he was right.

'And as I told your brother, the Talmud tells us that with each new baby, the world begins anew.' He reached over and took her hand. 'And so perhaps Jamie's mother needs reassurance that she will be part of this child's life. Perhaps she could have a special role, not just as *bubbe* but as the person who, for example, keeps Christmas for him, or Easter. We don't celebrate those in our faith, as you know, but we have Chanukah and Passover. Christmas and Easter are important to Christians, and we love them so then it becomes important to us.

Father O'Toole told me about how, back centuries ago, the Christians came to Ireland. They knew that the Pagans who lived here would not be happy about giving up their festivals, worshiping the sun and the moon, and the various phases of the year, so they didn't ask them to. Instead, they tied the Christian celebrations to the existing ones and so the people got to embrace both traditions, the new Christian way and the pagan way, without abandoning their old beliefs. They were sensible those early Christians and did you know, the Celtic Cross, the one you see in the graveyards, you know the cross with the circle in the top?'

Liesl nodded, the graveyard in Ballycreggan was full of carved gravestones with a circle around the cross .

'That is unique to Ireland, because the circle represents the sun and the moon, the pagan way, and the cross represents Christianity. The two traditions blended peacefully together. So perhaps Lieslelah, you could suggest that they could come to visit every Christmas, or Easter and you could have a tree and Father Christmas and chocolate eggs and all of that? I think you yourself grew up with those traditions?'

'I did,' Liesl agreed. 'Elizabeth always celebrated Christmas, and we hung up our stockings for Father Christmas to fill. And at Easter she would hide chocolate eggs in the garden for us to find. Even during the war she managed to have a little bit for us, so we had the best of both worlds.'

Perhaps he was right, though she was still furious. Maybe her mother-in-law just wanted to be involved and felt excluded by the Jewish lifestyle.

'Thanks, Rabbi. I'll suggest it, and maybe it will smooth things over a little.'

He chuckled. 'Father O'Toole also tells me that in an emergency, anyone can baptise a child, so do not be too surprised if you find your son's head inexplicably wet someday.'

'She wouldn't dare, surely.' Liesl was horrified.

He shrugged. 'Oy veh! It would be so bad, eh?'

She didn't understand.

'What harm will it do? To her it has meaning, to you it doesn't, to Peter it is just a wet head for a moment, no harm done.'

'Well, if she does, I hope she dries him afterwards. I'd rather not deal with that.'

'You will find in life, Liesl, that sometimes you have a choice to be happy or to be right.'

Liesl drained her coffee, feeling much better. 'Thanks, Rabbi. Oh, and by the way, Erich telephoned and said you told him it was safe to come back?'

The old rabbi just nodded.

'I don't mean to pry, but how can you be so sure? I only ask because I'm worried. Róisín's brothers are…'

He stood and put his hand on her shoulder. 'On this one, I'm afraid you just have to trust me, but it will be fine.'

Liesl knew he would say no more, but she did trust him, completely. 'All right.' She smiled. 'If you say so. Now, we'd better go over to Jamie, but I really appreciate your advice. I think things will be better now. I hope so anyway.'

She tucked Peter back into his basket and wrapped him in his blankets for the dash across the street to the pub.

'Good. I am always here for you, Lieslelah, for as long as I can be anyway. My wife' – she heard the pride in his voice as he said the words – 'is trying to kill me with cake, oy, oy, oy.' He flapped his hands as Frau Braun appeared with more coffee and cake.

'You don't have to eat it, you know.' She arched her eyebrow admonishingly. 'Always with the complaining, but always he clears his plate. You see, Liesl, men get more stubborn and cranky as they get older. Be prepared.'

The rabbi put his arm around his wife and pecked her on the cheek, causing her to push him off affectionately. 'Stop embarrassing the girl, foolish old man.'

The elderly couple followed her to the door.

'Here, take my coat,' Frau Frank insisted. 'I won't need it until tomorrow, so you can bring it back to me or Jamie can drop it off on his way to the bar.'

Liesl put it on gratefully, it was freezing outside.

'Thank you, I'll get Jamie to return it in the morning. See you both soon.' Liesl smiled and then did something she'd never done before – she kissed the rabbi's cheek. 'Thank you, Rabbi. You are so important to all of us. We all really love you.'

He blushed bright red and chuckled as his wife brought him in and closed the door against the winter wind.

CHAPTER 33

*D*aniel looked up from the door he was sanding as the rabbi entered the workshop. Willi and the two new apprentices were going to need the door later for the house extension they were working on out at Ballyhalbert.

'Ah, Daniel, shalom. I know you are busy, so I won't keep you.'

The rabbi walked with a cane all the time now, but it was wonderful to see him up and about.

'Shalom, Rabbi. I was going to stop for a break anyway,' Daniel lied. He'd had no intention of resting as there was too much to be done, but he didn't want to make the old man feel unwelcome.

'No, no, please. I am meeting Father O'Toole and Reverend Parkes anyway – Miss McGovern is expecting us.' He chuckled. 'I'm just coming by to tell you some news. Remember a while back you asked me if I could find an Irish woman called Rachel Abrahams?'

Daniel nodded. It had been a long shot, but Erich had written and told him all about Christy Costello and how he helped Erich and Róisín and he'd had an idea.

The rabbi really did have a huge network of connections. Before the war, he was on good terms with other rabbis in Germany, and subsequently, with his connections with the Kindertransport, he had

234

met either by correspondence or in person so many others. He had links in Israel and America and so was the only person Daniel thought might be able to help.

'Yes. Don't say you've found her?' Daniel asked incredulously.

'Yes, I believe so. She would be in her late fifties now?'

Daniel nodded. 'I would think so, yes.'

'Well, I asked around, and yes, there is an Abrahams family in Rochester, New York State, who have links to Cork, and there is a woman called Rachel who arrived there as a young woman in her twenties from Ireland.'

'Really?' Daniel felt absurdly pleased. 'This is wonderful.'

They'd sent a hamper of food and drinks to Christy to say thank you for all he'd done and got a lovely letter in return, saying how happy he was to be able to help. The nuns had dismissed him as their photographer, he said. They suspected him but couldn't prove he'd helped Róisín escape. He was delighted about losing the job. He'd hated going up there anyway, and felt complicit in the whole sordid business. Christy also told them about a woman who'd been in there for forty years and how he'd managed, with the help of her brothers, to get her moved to a nice nursing home where she was being cared for instead of living in drudgery. Apparently the nun who had also helped Róisín escape had left the order and gone to America. Christy had shown such kindness and bravery, Daniel really hoped finding Rachel would make him happy.

'Here is her telephone number and address. Her rabbi is a cousin of a friend of mine. He went to visit her – she's a widow – and told her about the man who helped Erich, and that he regretted how he was never able to see her again. She was very happy to learn he was alive and well and is looking forward to hearing from him.'

'You really are a marvel, Rabbi, you know that?' Daniel said, taking the piece of paper.

The rabbi shrugged. 'We Jews are such a small world now, it is not so hard as once it might have been. Hitler saw to that.'

The weight of sadness and resignation in that sentence settled on

Daniel. 'Yes, but if we can reunite two people, at least that might be something? I'll telephone him later. I'm sure he'll be thrilled.'

'Indeed. Now, I must go, let you to your work.'

'Thank you, Rabbi.' Daniel put his hand on his old friend's shoulder. 'Enjoy the tea and scones.'

The rabbi walked up the street, greeting this one and that as he went. Life in Ballycreggan had a lovely predictability to it.

Jamie was rolling last night's empty barrels out onto the side of the street for collection by the brewery later that morning. Elizabeth was standing in the schoolyard, wrapped up in a coat and hat, watching over the children as they took their mid-morning break. He smiled at the boys and girls playing in their shirtsleeves, though the temperature was only four or five degrees. Hetty Devlin was putting up a notice in the post office window that had to do with someone looking to rehome kittens, and the welcoming aroma of molten sugar wafted from Bridie's sweetshop as she made her famous toffee apples.

He pushed the glass door of Miss McGovern's to find three women of the WI enjoying their morning cup of tea while they discussed that week's project for the Institute. Fundraising for new windows for the church, he believed, was the latest cause.

Father O'Toole was hidden behind the morning paper, and of Reverend Parkes there was no sign.

'Good morning, Father,' the rabbi said, sitting opposite his friend.

'Shalom, Rabbi.' The priest smiled as he lowered and then folded the paper. 'I'm afraid the third member of this religious council is busy choosing curtains this morning.' The priest gave a chortle; the reverend's wife was not one to be trifled with. 'You know, Rabbi,' he whispered, 'it's at times like these that I think maybe celibacy isn't the worst thing in the world.' He winked.

'Well, as a newly married man myself, I can't be heard to say such a thing.' The rabbi grinned. 'But thankfully my wife feels no need whatsoever for my opinion on such matters as curtains.'

'I'm sure Reverend Parkes wishes the same,' Father O'Toole replied.

The Rabbi settled himself and prepared, he had a great one today.

'Now, today's joke, are you ready?'

Fr O'Toole sat back and nodded. The three clergymen knew it caused such bemusement in the village when they were seen laughing uproariously together in the tea-shop each Wednesday, as the weekly joke had become part of their ritual. It was the rabbi's turn this week.

'Go ahead, I could do with a laugh.' Fr O'Toole folded his arms across his chest.

'A priest, a vicar and a rabbi have a bet on, who would be the first to covert a bear to their faith.' The rabbi began.

The priest smiled and a few heads of fellow diners turned.

'So' the rabbi went on, 'they set out to complete the task, and reconvened in their favourite cafe a week later. The vicar had his arm in a sling, and said, "well at first the bear wanted nothing to do with me or the word of God, and in fact he attacked me and we wrestled and rolled into a stream, but there in the water I acted quickly, baptised him, and now he's gentle as a lamb, we spent the rest of the day praying together."

Then the priest, who was in a wheelchair spoke, "I had a similar experience, the bear was furious at first, and he really slapped me around, but I managed to pull out my bottle of holy water, sprinkled him with it and now he's as gentle as a lamb, he's getting First Holy Communion next week."

The rabbi knew he had the attention of the whole cafe by now and he grinned.

'Then the rabbi spoke up, he was in a full body cast, neck to ankles, his head bandaged, all of his fingers in splints. "I suppose looking back on it, circumcision wasn't the best way to start.'

The entire gathering guffawed loudly as Fr O'Toole wiped his eyes.

'Very good rabbi, very good.' He said.

Just then, Miss McGovern arrived to take their order. 'The usual, gentlemen?' she asked with a smile.

'Do you know, Miss McGovern,' the rabbi said, 'I think I'll have a scone with jam and butter and a pot of coffee.'

'For a change.' She giggled; this was his identical order three times a week.

'And I will have...' the priest paused.

'A rasher sandwich with a pot of tea?' she asked.

'How did you guess?' He chuckled.

'Oh, I must be psychic, Father.' She laughed as she walked away.

'I can give up women, but I must say I feel for you, a life without a rasher,' Father O'Toole said.

'What I never had, I never miss,' the rabbi said with a smile.

The business with Róisín had been resolved, and the priest and the rabbi had had a long chat one day, both agreeing that there were elements of their respective faiths that were not as they should be, but that it was a job for younger, fitter men than them to change things.

'Speaking of missing things, what do you miss most about life before coming here?' the priest asked.

The rabbi considered the question. 'It might sound strange to say, but nothing. My life before, it was so different. I would never have had friends, certainly not ones who eat pigs.' He grinned. 'And of course I wish things had been different – such pain, such loss. But for me personally, my life now is full in a way I never thought possible.'

'I must say, you look remarkably well these days.'

'Yes, I feel good. The doctors say the new drugs are doing a good job. The cancer is still there but not growing so much, I think. It will kill me, but not today.' He shrugged. 'I am an old man. I've lived a long time and seen much. Every day now is a bonus.'

That wasn't true. The doctor's prognosis was nothing as optimistic as he made it out to be, but what was the point of making people feel bad? He had only a short time left, and he was fine with it. The drugs took the edge off the pain and he slept a lot, but he could feel the welcoming breath of God on his cheek. It would not be long now.

Miss McGovern delivered their food, and they both thanked her appreciatively. As the priest tucked into his doorstep sandwich, he looked up at his old friend. 'So are you going to tell me, or am I going to have to drag it out of you?' He raised a cryptic eyebrow.

'Tell you what?' the rabbi asked, generously lathering the raisin scone with butter.

'Oh, I was just wondering how somehow my cousin's criminal son has decided that Erich Bannon is no longer the enemy and all is forgiven?' The priest locked eyes with the rabbi.

The rabbi allowed himself a small smile. 'I have no idea, but it is good news, no?' He took a bite.

'Oh, it is, it truly is. My cousin Maggie is delighted to have her daughter come home, but the boys in that family are not to be challenged. In truth, she's scared to death of her own sons. Fiach especially, but Colm and now even Neil are getting just as bad it seems. They've gone over to England and already are mixed up with the same people Fiach was, so it's just a matter of time before they wind up in jail. But the thing that puzzles me... I've known people like them all my life, and if there's one thing they excel at, it's grudges, so you can see the reason for my astonishment.' He wasn't letting it go.

The rabbi shrugged. 'Well, it is a good turnaround, but perhaps they just want their sister to be happy. And now she and Erich are married, and he's a good man, and the child will be loved and cared for, so what is the point of a grudge?'

The priest shook his head. 'That's not how it works, though. Never has, never will.'

'Well, let us try to see the good side then, eh?' The rabbi poured his coffee.

'And you're not worried at all that them coming back might be some kind of a trap?'

'No, not at all worried.' The rabbi sipped the coffee and tried not to grimace at its bitterness. Miss McGovern had not the faintest clue how to brew it, but he would never tell her that.

The priest sat back and shook his head. 'There's something you're not telling me. I don't know what, but something happened and I feel you had something to do with it.'

'I don't know what you're talking about. Now, how is the fund for fixing the leaky windows coming along?'

CHAPTER 34

*L*ater that evening, Katerin let herself in, calling as she went upstairs, 'Rabbi, I'm home.'

He laughed when she called him Rabbi and not David, but she was so used to it and it was easier. Just like people called her Frau Braun. She should probably resent it, given that it was Hubert's name, but she didn't care. Hubert and Berlin and all of that were like things from another lifetime, things that had happened to someone else.

She would bake her famous *flammkuchen* for supper, with cream and caramelised onions. Perhaps next week she and the rabbi could invite everyone to their house. She'd never in her life hosted a gathering. The tiny house in Berlin would have been too small, and besides, she'd had no friends or family to invite anyway. But would they think her foolish? Their houses were so much grander. She dismissed her fears. They were family and they would like it, and more to the point, the rabbi would love it. He enjoyed all the gatherings, though his appetite wasn't what it once was.

He would be having a nap now; he slept a lot more these days.

Elizabeth had just told her the wonderful news that Erich and Róisín were coming home in early February. Róisín's baby was due in

March, so he or she would be born in Ballycreggan surrounded by the family.

Elizabeth and Ariella had invited Róisín's mother to lunch on Monday, just the women, and they hoped that Frau Braun could be there too. They wanted her to feel included.

She caught a glimpse of herself in the hall mirror at the top of the stairs and went to the bathroom to fix her hair, which had been tossed about in the wind. She carefully removed the pins and went to pin it back again but stopped. She took the brush and brushed her hair over her shoulders. Nobody but the rabbi had ever seen her hair down, and the first time she'd been embarrassed, but he told her he loved it. It was mostly silver now, though some streaks of brown remained. She washed her face and on a whim applied a little cologne. She was sure nobody would call on such a cold night, so she would leave her hair down for him.

It was too early to go to bed, so she would wake him and they would have supper together and sit by the fire. They might listen to the wireless or read. She was going to start knitting a matinée jacket and booties for Erich's baby.

She crossed the small landing, not wanting to wake him suddenly. Sometimes he woke with a start, so she liked just to shake him gently. Usually just her opening the door was enough; he was a light sleeper.

'David, are you awake?' she said quietly.

The words died on her lips as she saw him, relaxed on their bed, fully dressed, his prayer book in his hands, resting on his chest. His eyes were closed, and there was a serenity to his features that he lacked even in sleep. The fire in their bedroom smouldered in the grate.

'David.' She rushed to him, knowing as she did that it was too late. He was gone.

Slowly, she took his siddur, open to his favourite passage, Yigdal, a poetic adaptation of Maimonides's principles of faith, and closed it, replacing it on the shelf where he always kept it.

The air in the room was warm. She went to the window. A flurry of snow banked in the corner of the sill as she drew the curtains. The small bedside light cast a yellow glow, and she threw another log on the fire, seeing it first smoulder and then crackle as the fire caught on the splintered edge of the timber. Then she turned and looked at the body of the only man she'd ever loved.

The whole village, as well as countless people all over the world, would be so saddened to hear of the death of Rabbi David Frank; he was much loved and respected. But for tonight, he was just her husband.

She lifted the patchwork quilt from the blanket box at the end of their bed. She'd made it as she sat by his bedside in the hospital day after day, wondering if he would pull through. He did, and they'd only had a short time together, but it was worth living her long life to have known a love like this.

She lay beside him, pulling the quilt over them both, and lay her head on his shoulder. She allowed the tears to fall.

'Goodbye, *schatzi*,' she whispered. 'Sleep well. Thank you for everything, for your love, for this second chance.

EPILOGUE

*L*iesl handed a struggling Peter to his father – at nine months he was just too heavy and wriggly for her to carry for long – while Róisín held the sleeping David in her arms.

'Enjoy that phase,' Liesl said with a rueful smile. 'Before long he'll be wriggling and determined to escape, enough to give you a permanent backache.'

'Aye, he's a wee dote now, but you should have heard him at three o'clock this morning, yelling the house down. And this one says he never heard a thing.' Róisín playfully punched Erich on the shoulder.

They gazed up at the gleaming white cruise ship. They could make out the passengers waving goodbye from the upper deck, but it was impossible to tell who was who. The warm autumn sunshine gave the entire port of Belfast a carnival atmosphere. The cruise liner dominated the skyline and could be seen from miles around.

'I thought Frau Frank was going to baulk at the end there,' Jamie said as he threw his son in the air, much to the baby's excited delight.

'Jamie!' Liesl admonished. 'Be careful! You could drop him.'

She rolled her eyes at Róisín. It was a running theme how Jamie loved playing with Peter, and although sometimes it was a bit too rough according to Liesl, the baby loved it.

Jamie threw his arm around his wife's shoulder. 'Have I ever dropped him yet?' he asked, kissing the top of her head.

'No, but there's always a first time,' Liesl said with a warning smile. She turned to her sister-in-law. 'Would you like to be going with them?'

They'd come to wave Daniel, Elizabeth, Willi, Ariella and Frau Frank off on their trip to Israel. They would be gone for two months. Erich was managing the business with the help of the two apprentices and some freelance contractors. He and Róisín were living with Elizabeth and Daniel, for the moment and would have the house to themselves.

They waved, hoping their parents could see them even if they couldn't make any one of the five of them out so high up.

'Och, no.' She was adamant. 'I loved the kibbutz and everything, and after the convent, they were so kind to me and all of that. But no, I can't stick the heat, so I can't.' Róisín shifted her son onto her shoulder. 'Nice Irish rain is just grand for me.'

None of Liesl's fears were realised, as she and Róisín hit it off from the day she and Erich arrived. She was open and honest and, as Erich had told her, very funny.

True to his word, there had been a gift of a silver spoon with his name engraved on it for the baby delivered from Fiach McAreavey and no further contact. Róisín's mother visited often and was a great help with the new baby. Liesl was so happy their sons would grow up together.

'Did you hear?' Erich asked. 'I got a letter from Christy Costello two days ago, the photographer I told you about who smuggled Ró out of the convent. Well, the rabbi managed to find his old girlfriend and she's alive and well and living in New York. She's planning a trip to Ireland later this summer with her son and they are going to meet up.'

'Oh, that's wonderful news!' Liesl exclaimed. 'I knew Daniel had passed on her information, but I'd often wondered how it all worked out.'

'It really is.' Erich agreed. 'The rabbi was an incredible man. It's hard to believe he's gone, isn't it?'

Liesl nodded sadly. The whole village had turned out for his memorial service, as well as visitors from all over the world. In keeping with the Jewish tradition, he'd been buried quickly, but because his life had touched so many the family had arranged a ceremony to remember him and invited his many friends and contacts. It had been the biggest gathering Ballycreggan had ever seen. Several of the children from the farm had returned from Israel, some from America, more from England. Karl Kolitz was inconsolable, tears rolling down his handsome face. Though the occasion had been sad, it was so lovely to be reunited with everyone again.

Liesl knew that Erich wished he'd made it home in time to thank the rabbi for all he'd done. But everyone assured him that the rabbi was in no doubt as to how Erich felt about him. His and Róisín's decision to call the baby after Rabbi David Frank was one that was welcomed by everyone in Ballycreggan.

'He told me once,' Erich said, 'that with each new baby, the world begins anew. And here we are, all beginning new lives, so I don't think he is very far away.'

'He told me the same thing.' Liesl blinked back a tear. The last time she ever saw him, she'd kissed him and told him that he was loved. She thanked God that He had prompted her to do that.

Erich smiled, his eyes shining brightly too. 'Remember when he and Elizabeth told us about the death camps when we were at school?'

Liesl nodded. It was a day nobody who was there would ever forget. Jamie and Róisín moved slightly closer to the man and woman they loved. They knew they could never truly know what they experienced, but they were united in their protection and loyalty to Liesl and Erich.

'Remember how the rabbi explained that a leaf grows from the tree and then falls into the soil and nourishes it, and more plants and trees spring up? That's how life is. Those who live and are kind and righteous, they nurture the lives of others. He said that we nourish the future through the influence we have on those that come after us.'

'Well, he certainly influenced lots of people for the better,' Jamie added. 'Poor Father O'Toole and Reverend Parkes miss him so much.'

'We all do,' Liesl said. 'He was a very special man, and we were so lucky to have him.'

The horn sounded, and the brass band engaged for the send-off struck up a lively tune. Children dressed in their Sunday best played chase on the quayside, and those staying at home waved enthusiastically at the passengers high above, who were leaning over the railings. There were several stops along the way on the cruise, and the Liebers and the Brauns were very much looking forward to the trip, which would finish for them in Haifa. They would spend a month there and then would fly home in early September. They had plans to meet up with several of the children who had once called Ballycreggan home. And a ceremony honouring Rabbi Frank had been arranged in Jerusalem for those that couldn't get to Ireland, at which his wife would be the guest of honour.

As the ropes were released and the ship slowly pulled away, sounding its horn amid cheering and tears, the four new parents waved and cuddled their children while their parents embarked on the trip of a lifetime to see the Promised Land.

The End

I SINCERELY HOPE you enjoyed this series. I always find it hard to say goodbye to the characters.

If you would like to try another series of mine, set in Ireland during WW2 you might enjoy The Robinswood Story.

The first book is called What Once Was True and it follows the lives of two families who live at a crumbling old mansion, Robinswood. Think *Downton Abbey* with an *Upstairs Downstairs* element but all set in Ireland.

You can get the first book here:

https://geni.us/WhatOnceWasTrueAL

. . .

HERE'S a sneak preview to give you an idea:

What Once Was True

Robinswood, Co Waterford, 1940

'Well, if you want to be the big man, going off to fly planes for the British, don't let me stop you.' Kate knew she probably sounded petulant, but Sam was being so annoying.

He grinned at her, the sun dazzling behind him. He looked so much older than twenty-one in his RAF uniform, and Kate hated the way he made her feel like a stupid kid.

'Kate, I *am* British,' he replied, delighted to annoy her. It was always like this—him teasing her, and her quick temper rising to it every time.

'And what about Robinswood? And all your responsibilities as the new Lord Kenefick? None of that matters anymore, I suppose? I know you are all caught up in the war and going off to be a pilot, but what about us? What about your home? Now that your father is gone, God rest him, you can't just up and leave this whole estate, the house, all the people who work here, who rely on Robinswood for their livelihoods.' She had to try to get through to him.

They walked through the orchard as they had done since they were children. The big old house up on the hill to the east of them might have looked imposing or intimidating to others, but to Kate and Sam, it was just home. And, indeed, it was a beautiful house. Four floors and a basement, built in 1770 of cut limestone with red sandstone edging, with a huge front door accessed by fifteen granite steps. Verdant green lawns stretched to the ha-ha, the sunken fence used to keep the deer and cattle off the perfect grass, and beneath the bank was rich farmland, acres of it, dotted here and there with belts of trees. The winding avenue up from the village was two miles long.

Kate often admired the paintings in the long gallery of hunt balls and parties at Robinswood years ago. It was where the landed gentry had come to play, in and around the house and estate. Of course, that sort of thing no longer happened, but in its heyday, the house was one of the finest in Munster.

Kate automatically pulled weeds from the strawberry beds as she had been taught to do since she was small. Her father was the estate manager and her mother the housekeeper, so she and her sisters had scampered all over every inch of that house, just as Sam and his older sister, Lillian, did.

Sam opened the orchard door, resting his hand for a moment on the warm stone wall facing west - it absorbed the evening sun. When Kate was a child, and several gardeners worked on the estate, glass houses were built against the wall, full of grapes and lemons and pears. But no more. Old Danny O'Leary did all the gardening now, and it was all he could do to keep the grass down. Only the hardiest of fruit grew now. Sam led her down the path to the old stone bridge over the river that ran through Robinswood. On one side of the bridge was an ornamental pond with a huge marble statue of a king-fisher in the middle, and the water's surface was covered with lily pads. Kate loved it there. It was where they'd had all their serious chats over the years.

He said nothing until they were both sitting on the bridge, feet dangling over the edge, the water slowly flowing from the pond into the stream below them.

'Look, Kate, I know.' Sam's tone was no longer teasing. 'I don't want to go - well, that's not true. I do, I want to fly, be a pilot, and of course we have to defeat Hitler. It simply must be done, and we are the generation to do it. My father's generation saw them off the last time, but now it's our turn.'

Kate could hear the excitement in his voice, no matter how hard he tried to sound regretful.

'But you're Irish, for God's sake, in every way that matters. I know you were born there and went to school, and you're Protestant, and the title and all of that, but you grew up here. This is your home. I just can't believe you're going to walk away from...well, from everything.' She coloured. What she could never say was how she hated the thought of him leaving her.

'No more Kenefricks at Robinswood? Your family have lived in Robinswood for centuries. It's just...well, it's just wrong.'

His voice softened, and he turned to face her.

'If there was any other option, some way of keeping things going here, I'd take it, I swear I would. But there isn't. The debts my father left are beyond even what Mummy knew, and she knew a lot. He gambled almost everything. Patches of land, the artwork, antiques, horses… He never really let on how bad things were. You know what he was like—all parties and whiskey and off to the races. He didn't want to face the truth.

'And now that it's all mine, well, I've been over it with my mother, and there's no other way. We'll rent the land to Charlie Warren and close up the house. We'll sell the rest of the furniture, china, silver— everything that we can, and that will have to be used to pay the debts. Nobody in their right mind would buy Robinswood. The house is too big, and it needs a fortune spent on it to even make it waterproof. You know yourself all about the damp and everything. I hate to do it, Kate, I really do, but there's no other way. I'm going to talk to Warren, though, to make sure you girls and Dermot and Isabella are looked after. He'll probably keep your father on; he can't manage four hundred extra acres on his own, and nobody knows Robinswood like Dermot Murphy, my father always said that.'

Kate swallowed. 'When Daddy hears about—'

Sam interrupted her. 'Kate, please,' Sam interrupted her. 'Let me try to sort everything out first. Don't say anything to your family until I can make sure they are provided for. Please, there's no point in worrying everyone unnecessarily. Promise me?' He lifted her face with his finger to look straight into her eyes.

She sighed.

'Please, Kate, just let me deal with it.' He gazed at her, and she melted inside.

'Fine,' she said gruffly to hide her embarrassment.

'Thanks. I'll sort this out for your family.' He looked around, taking in the beautiful vista of the trees, the babbling brook, and the glimpses of the azure Atlantic in the distance. 'I'm heartbroken, but we'll have to ship out. It's the only way.'

'There's always another way,' Kate muttered, though she was only parroting something she'd heard in a film. She'd had no idea things were so bad. Daddy and Mammy were appalled at how much land Austin, Sam's father, had given up, and while her father was excellent at his job, she knew he was being expected to do more and more with less and less money. She and her sisters, and her mother too, were taking on so much more work. Half of the household staff had been let go, and many of the farmhands were no longer full-time. No matter what Dermot did, he couldn't work with nothing.

'Look, Kate, my mother is so fed up at this stage,' Sam went on. 'Lillian is swanning around in London, not a care in the world except where her next bottle of champagne is coming from, while Mother is trying to keep my father's creditors at bay. And now that I'm going back to England as well... Well, she's had enough. But I'm going to make sure you and your family are taken care of, I promise.

'To be totally honest, she'd been trying to tell me for ages, but I didn't want to hear it. My father always said to ignore her, she was always fussing or worrying about something, and that seemed by far the easiest option. But now that he's gone and all of this falls to me, I've come to realise I should have listened to her a long time ago. Maybe if I had, I could have averted this mess before it went beyond saving. But I didn't, and here we are.'

Kate turned to look at his profile as he stared despondently into the river below. She knew he loved Robinswood and this wasn't easy for him, but surely there was something less drastic that could be done? She couldn't bear the idea of him leaving—maybe even forever.

He'd always been handsome, even as a boy, but in his RAF blues, and his curls Brylcreemed back under his hat, he was just irresistible. Of course, she would die if he ever realised how she felt about him. He saw her as a tomboy, the servants' child. Sure, she was a girl who could beat him at arm-wrestling and was not afraid of anything, but that was all he saw. Her love of Sam, and that's what it was, pure love, took her by surprise.

She was seventeen, and while she knew she wasn't very worldly, she knew how she felt about Sam Kenefick. Growing up in the dullest village on earth - Kilthomand, County Waterford - so far, her life experience went from Robinswood, to their farmhouse on the estate, to the school in the village. Someone like him, who had been to boarding school in England and regularly went to Dublin or Galway or even over to London, and now was joining the RAF... No wonder he saw her as a provincial nobody.

'You can't promise that, Sam. Nobody can. If Charlie Warren takes over Robinswood it will be up to him who he hires. He won't take instructions from you or your mother. And what about Mammy? She's a housekeeper, but Charlie Warren's wife runs their house. So she's going to be out of a job as well, all because you want to play war games with the Germans, defending a country you're not even from. No, we Murphys will have to take care of ourselves.'

She'd hoped to see a spark of something in his eyes. At night, she dreamed that he realised she wasn't some ragamuffin servant child but the great love of his life. But so far, there had been no indication of that.

'Well, I hear Aisling is going to be alright anyway. Isn't she doing a line with Sean Lacey? She'll do well there, getting her feet under the table of the draper's only son?' He nudged her to show he was joking, but Kate was suddenly angry and defensive.

'You don't know what you're talking about! My sister is not trying to get her feet under anyone's table. Aisling isn't like that. She would never go out with someone just because he had money. It shows how little you know about real life here in Kilthomand. Maybe it is better if you take off for your precious England.' Kate jumped up and stalked off the bridge. 'So go on off, Sam, and to be honest, I couldn't care less if I never see you again!'

She stormed off, seething all the way home. She was so upset at Sam leaving tomorrow for God knew how long—maybe he would never come back—and then how dare he say that about Aisling? She was by far the nicest of the three Murphy sisters, two years older than Kate and two years younger than Eve, and she was in love with Sean Lacey. Even if nobody in the Murphy family thought Sean was good enough for Aisling—he was a bit of a Mammy's boy and really boring with it—Aisling really liked him.

When she let herself in to their house, everyone was out. The clock ticked loudly on the dresser as it had done for as long as she could remember. She loved their home, though technically it belonged to the Keneficks. It was as part of Dermot's package that they got to live there, but they saw it as theirs. In fact, Kate didn't think any of the Keneficks had ever stepped inside the door.

In lots of ways, it was so much nicer than the big house. It was cosy and warm and always smelled of baking or fresh laundry. It had a large kitchen where everything happened, with a huge AGA stove for keeping the whole house warm. There was a parlour as well, but it was north facing and always felt cold so they hardly ever used it. There were three bedrooms and a bathroom upstairs, but the three girls shared a room, and the spare room was full of stuff. Mammy was a meticulous housekeeper, and the place was always neat and tidy, but that one room was full of clothes that didn't fit, old coats, toys, and all manner of other rubbish she should really have thrown out but had yet to get around to. The girls were happy sharing anyway. They had three single beds in a huge sunny bedroom that overlooked the river on one side, and on the other, you could see as far as the ocean. Her parents had the back bedroom.

Kate checked the cake tin, and sure enough, there was an apple tart inside. Kate could eat anything she wanted and never gain an ounce of weight. It drove her sister Eve mad because she had to watch her figure, though Kate thought she was imagining the fat. She went to the larder, spooned the cream off the top of the milk, and poured it on her apple tart. She always ate when she was upset. She never understood those ones in the films fading away to nothing when the hero goes off with someone else. She was the total opposite.

Mammy would be still up at Robinswood, cooking and cleaning, and Daddy would be out milking for another hour at least. Eve was helping him, because yet another farmhand had been let go, and Aisling was gone into the village for some groceries, hoping to bump into dreary Sean, no doubt.

So Kate went up to their bedroom and threw herself on the bed. Only then did she allow herself to cry. She really didn't want

Robinswood to change. It was all she knew; her whole family relied on it for everything. But that wasn't the main cause of her tears.

What if some German shot Sam's plane down? What if he got killed and the last thing she ever said to him was that she didn't care? Maybe she should go back and apologise. He was leaving tomorrow morning.

But she couldn't. She'd have to go up to the house, and though it wasn't ever said outright, she knew Lady Kenefick would not be in favour of their friendship, so they'd always kept it under her radar. She was such a snob, Kate couldn't stand her, but neither her father nor her mother allowed any talk like that in the house.

She cried into her pillow. Even Eve and Ais wouldn't understand. They'd think she was off her head to be setting her cap at Samuel Kenefick. She probably was, too.

Chapter 2

'Mammy will murder you if she sees you with that,' Eve warned Kate, who was busy pulling all sorts of faces in the mirror to spread the tiny amount of scarlet lipstick on her generous lips. She was testing it out in the hope of being allowed to go to the dance.

'Where'd you get it, anyway?' Eve flopped down on the middle bed.

'It's Aisling's, but don't breathe a word or she'll go mad. Old Lady Kenefick gave it to her, said it was almost gone anyway. But sure that old bat is half blind—there's loads left.'

'Kate, don't say that about the mistress, you know full well she's only in her fifties and she is remarkably well preserved at that. I do wish she'd employ some more young lads for the milking, though. I'm exhausted from it.' Eve sighed and examined her cracked and broken nails.

'Well, she's like a briar since her precious Sam is gone off to single-handedly finish off Hitler,' Kate muttered. 'Not that he ever did much farming anyway, but still. The workforce situation is getting ridiculous. Daddy is shattered; he nearly bit the head off me earlier when I mentioned about the dance in the hall on Friday night.'

Eve smiled at her sister's indignation.

'Not that there's going to be any point anyway. There'll probably be nobody even half decent left to dance with anyway. All the good-looking fellas are gone over to England—Sam Kenefick, Douglas Radcliffe, Daniel Burgoyne...'

'All the Protestants, you mean.' Eve grinned. 'There's plenty of local lads who are still here. Sure, can't you dance with them?'

'Ah, Eve, you're as bad as Aisling, in love with that clown, Sean Lacey. She is so much better than him, I just don't see what she sees in him. I met him in the village earlier, and he hardly was able to string a sentence together.'

'You probably scare him.' Eve winked. 'There's some nice lads still left. What about the O'Learys? Or Damien Keane, he's always smiling at you at Mass?'

'Damien Keane is a child; sure, he was a class below me in the national school. And as for the O'Learys, all they care about is heifers and silage, and they'd bore you to tears. The only hope would be a gang would come out from Dungarvan; otherwise, we're stuck with the local eejits here with their dung-encrusted boots trampling the toes off you and thinking if they buy you a bottle of lemonade they'll get a grope in the bushes on the way home. Sam is so lucky to be away from this place. Imagine what it's like in England compared to here? I was reading that there's going to be Americans over there soon, and dances every night, and everyone in uniforms. It sounds fabulous, doesn't it?'

Eve threw her eyes heavenward. Kate was full of the romance of the war. It was all over the newspapers, every single day, and Mr deValera was full of how it is nothing to do with us and we're a neutral country and all of that. Eve was sick of it already, and it was only just started. She hoped it was going to be over quicker than the Great War. They said the last time that it was all going to be finished by Christmas, but it dragged on for four years. Chamberlain had done his best to avoid a war coming so soon after the last one, but Hitler wasn't going to be stopped, it would seem.

Most of the local Protestants were gone, but then, they felt more

English than Irish. Kate had expressed a wish to join them as the family walked home last Friday night after Mass. Mammy and Daddy had nearly gone cracked when she said it.

'Would you have a hair of sense, you foolish girl?' Daddy said unusually sharply. He usually indulged Kate's mad notions. 'The British have sent more than enough young Irish men to their deaths that last time out. At least this time, deValera is keeping us out of it, and out of it we'll stay. Now, I'll have no more talk of such rubbish. Join up indeed, and go over there and fight their war for them? No chance. Churchill and Hitler can be scrapping away to suit themselves —'tis one of them, two of them, as far as I'm concerned. But I'll tell you this: no child of mine will have anything to do with it. Do I make myself clear?'

'Yes, Daddy.' Kate had been despondent, and Eve squeezed her arm. She was the youngest, and she was a divil for a bit of adventure. Eve could hardly blame her; life these days wasn't exactly exciting. The same dull routine of housework and farmwork, day after day. They were expected to pitch in even more now as staff were let go.

'Come on, let's go down and have a cup of cocoa to warm us up.' Eve dragged her weary body off the bed with a sigh. 'I'm fit to collapse, but I'm freezing. Let's get a heat up downstairs and then get into bed.'

Kate looked down ruefully at her chapped hands as she got up to follow Eve downstairs.

'I'm wrecked, too. I swear Mammy was finding smears on purpose,' Kate grumbled. 'I polished the fire irons about fifty times, but still, it wasn't good enough. And anyway, it's all going to be sold and the house closed up, so why on earth is she on a cleaning frenzy? She had Sheila Hanratty and Jenny Glavin helping poor Ais to clean the flipping windows. Four floors and only three of them to do it, and all of this before Aisling went to visit drippy Sean and his scald of a mother. And Lady Muck then swanning around as if she's loaded when the whole parish knows she hasn't one shilling to rub off the other.'

'If Mammy or Daddy hears you talking like that, you'll be for it,'

Eve warned. Since they were small girls, their parents had drilled into them the need to keep a respectful distance from the family of the house and estate they served.

'I know, I know, but I'm only telling you, Eve. Sure, I can tell you anything; you're like the grave, Mammy says.'

Eve gave a hoot of laughter.

'Oh yes, Kate, I'm like a grave all right.' She winked and pushed the door open into the big warm kitchen. 'Aisling should be back soon.'

'And we'll have to hear all the fascinating details of Mrs Lacey's latest hymn for the choir.' Kate sighed dramatically.

'Ah, Kate, don't be mean. You know Aisling was all excited to be invited to Laceys for her tea. I know he's a bit of an eejit, but she's mad about him, so try to be nice, all right?' Eve shivered and pulled the old brown flannel dressing gown around her. It had been left behind by one of the guests after the Robinswood New Year's Eve Ball two years ago, and even though it was a man's dressing gown, Eve loved how cosy it was.

Their parents were still out, so Eve set some milk to heat on the stove and Kate went to the larder for the cocoa.

'I'll be absolutely gushing, I promise. Though why our Aisling, who is gorgeous and could have anyone she wants, is considering shackling herself to the monosyllabic Sean Lacey and his warbling screecher of a mother, I will never know.' Kate shook her head theatrically, and Eve giggled. 'He's not even good-looking. Not like Sam!'

Eve swiped at her and rolled her eyes.

'You better not let anyone hear you going on like that about Samuel Kenefick, miss.'

Despite the years between Kate and Eve, they were very close. And even though the little sister was incorrigible, she had a way of making everyone see the funny side of things. For example, Mrs Lacey ran the choir with an iron fist, and even poor old Father Hartigan was afraid of her, so nobody challenged her. That's why the devout of Kilthomand had to endure her ear-splitting version of 'How Great Thou Art' every Sunday, trying not to wince as she almost reached the high notes. Her only child, Sean, was her pride and joy, so the invitation extended to Aisling was a very significant event.

Eve went on to admonish her youngest sister,

'And anyway, Sean is nice.' Eve poured the hot milk into two mugs and stirred in the cocoa. 'He's just a bit shy. But Aisling says he's very chatty with her, so that's all that matters.'

'I'll never understand it.' Kate shook her head and took her cup to the old armchair beside the stove. 'There's a whole world out there beyond this place, and yet she's hitching her wagon to Kilthomand's bachelor boy. I'll tell you something for nothing—I definitely don't want to go with any of the fellas from around here. Sure, where would that lead? Only to a life that never ventures beyond the parish of Kilthomand for your whole life? Not for me, Eve, no way. I'm going to travel the world and have adventures and give scandal wherever I go by keeping bad company and drinking gin.'

Eve laughed out loud at her little sister. She really was a character.

Kate drew attention wherever she went with her unruly black curls. She looked like a painting Eve had seen one time of a gypsy girl, all dark hair and flashing eyes. She was tiny, barely five feet, with a handspan waist that Eve could only dream of. And Kate knew full well the effect she had. Men found her delightful, and women thought she was flighty. Both were right.

There was no mistaking her and Aisling as sisters. Aisling was taller, and her hair was straight but the same jet-black. And she had the same voluptuous curves and dark-blue eyes—almost navy blue. They both took after their mother, who always told them they got their looks from their grandfather, who had been a Spanish sailor who fell in love with an Irish woman in the west of Ireland when he was delivering wine. The story went that he couldn't bear to leave her, so he settled in County Galway and they raised a huge family, Isabella being the youngest. When people questioned her exotic name, their mother explained she was named after her father's mother, who pined away in Granada for her only boy, who would never leave Ireland.

Eve caught a glimpse of herself in the mirror over the dresser and sighed. To be fair, the brown dressing gown and beige bedsocks probably didn't do much to improve the situation, but she definitely was more like her father's side. Tall and well built, strong from all the manual labour, with copper-coloured hair that was neither curly like Kate's nor shiny and straight like Aisling's but just kind of wavy with a mind of its own. Her hazel eyes were set wide apart, and a sprinkling of freckles dusted her nose. She didn't take the sun, unlike her sisters and mother, who in the summer were the colour of conkers. She felt so dowdy beside them and was sure that where looks were concerned, she'd really drawn the short straw.

Aisling burst in the door. It was unusual for the three girls to be at home alone, but their mother had gone to settle Mrs Kenefick in for the night and Daddy was out looking for poachers. Someone was helping themselves to rabbits and pheasants off the estate, and he was determined to find out who it was.

'Well, how was the big occasion?' Kate delivered the last word in a high-pitched warble that had her sisters giggling.

'Stop!' Aisling took off her coat and hung it up behind the door. 'She was grand. Not exactly welcome-to-the-family, but fine. Poor Sean was mortified, though, with her going on and on about how he was top of his class in school, and all the hurling medals he won, and how he was basically the best person for four counties. Poor fella nearly died. He kept trying to change the subject, but she's determined, you'd have to give her that. I had to see his certificates and medals and everything. That house is like a shrine to him. He was disgraced.'

'So did he walk you home?' Kate asked slyly, nudging Eve.

'He did, and that's as much as I'm telling you because you are obsessed with sins of the flesh, and 'tis down on your knees you should be, praying for your own black soul instead of worrying about what two respectable young people get up to on a perfectly innocent walk home. Now, is there any more cocoa going? I'm perished.' Aisling winked at Eve behind Kate's back.

'A chance to be obsessed with sins of the flesh with someone would be a fine thing,' Kate responded, not realising her father had entered the kitchen behind her. Eve smiled as she made her sister a drink.

Dermot Murphy looked suitably horrified at the conversation going on between his daughters.

He opened his mouth to say something but closed it again. He once tried to be an authoritarian, but with three opinionated daughters and a spirited wife, he had long since accepted his fate.

'Don't worry, Daddy, we're only messing,' Kate said when she spotted him. 'Sure, nobody around here is up to anything, only working and sleeping.' She smiled sweetly and kissed her father on the cheek.

To read on, click here

https://geni.us/WhatOnceWasTrueAL

ABOUT THE AUTHOR

Jean Grainger is a *USA Today* bestselling Irish novelist living in a stone cottage in rural County Cork, Ireland. She writes a combination of contemporary and historical Irish fiction. She lives with her very nice and patient husband, and the youngest two of their four children. The older two come home occasionally to raid the fridge and moan about the cost of living now that they are paying for the toothpaste themselves. She also has two very cute but utterly clueless dogs called Scrappy and Scoobi.

The World Starts Anew is her 21st book.

f

ALSO BY JEAN GRAINGER

To get a free novel and to join my readers club (100% free and always will be)

Go to www.jeangrainger.com

The Tour Series

The Tour

Safe at the Edge of the World

The Story of Grenville King

The Homecoming of Bubbles O'Leary

Finding Billie Romano

Kayla's Trick

The Carmel Sheehan Story

Letters of Freedom

The Future's Not Ours To See

What Will Be

The Robinswood Story

What Once Was True

Return To Robinswood

Trials and Tribulations

The Star and the Shamrock Series

The Star and the Shamrock

The Emerald Horizon

The Hard Way Home

The World Starts Anew

Made in United States
North Haven, CT
26 February 2022